JERSEY TOMATOES ARE THE BEST

JERSEY TOMATOES ARE THE BEST

Maria Padian

Alfred A. Knopf
New York

THIS IS A BORZOI BOOK PUBLISHED BY ALFRED A. KNOPF

All rights reserved. Published in the United States by Alfred A. Knopf, an imprint of Random House Children's Books, a division of Random House, Inc., New York.

Visit us on the Web! www.randomhouse.com/teens

Educators and librarians, for a variety of teaching tools, visit us at www.randomhouse.com/teachers

Library of Congress Cataloging-in-Publication Data
Padian, Maria.
Jersey tomatoes are the best / Maria Padian. — 1st ed.
p. cm.
Summary: When fifteen-year-old best friends Henry and Eva leave New Jersey, one for tennis camp in Florida and one for ballet camp in New York, each faces challenges that put her long-cherished dreams of the future to the test.
ISBN 978-0-375-86579-4 (trade) — ISBN 978-0-375-96579-1 (lib. bdg.) — ISBN 978-0-375-89609-5 (ebook)
[1. Best friends—Fiction. 2. Friendship—Fiction. 3. Ballet dancing—Fiction. 4. Tennis—Fiction. 5. Anorexia nervosa—Fiction. 6. Camps—Fiction.] I. Title.
PZ7.P1325Jer 2011
[Fic]—dc22
2010011827

The text of this book is set in 11.5-point Goudy.

Printed in the United States of America
March 2011
10 9 8 7 6 5 4 3 2
First Edition

For Conrad, who is our rock,
and always for Madsy

Chapter One

HENRY

I know I've won when she starts talking to herself.

"Stupid, Emily!" I hear her say. "Stupid! Stupid! Stupid! Watch the ball! Not the target!"

She paces and mutters, and as I wait on my side of the net, I calmly bounce the ball on the baseline.

That's right, Emily. Eye on the ball. You wouldn't have just hit it into the net if you'd kept your eye on the ball. Watch it closely. So closely that you can read the manufacturer's name as it connects with the strings on your racket. Say it as you smack it: Penn. Wilson. Dunlop.

Emily stops pacing, places her racket carefully on the ground and bends over to tie her laces. Pretends to tie her laces, that is. Classic. No line judge or opponent would dare accuse her of stalling. Of catching her breath and settling her nerves. But that's what she's doing. I've used that strategy myself when I want to interrupt the pace and play with my opponent's head.

Or when I'm losing.

She straightens up and slowly walks to the left corner of the ad box, preparing to receive my serve. She practically straddles the alley, that's how far left she stands. Protecting her backhand. Assuming that I'm going to serve into her backhand.

If you can't read the name on the ball, then you're not looking hard enough. How many times have I heard that? And still, in a match, especially a big one like this, you could forget. Forget the most basic, Tennis 101 lesson in the book: watch the ball hit the racket. Although, quite frankly, Emily my dear, even that won't save you now. You're down four games in the second set, it's 40–love, and I'm about to serve you into five games down. You're not stupid, Emily. You're toast.

"Forty–love," I call out, as if she doesn't know. I twist my hand counterclockwise on the grip, lean over and bounce the ball one, two, three times in front of me. A little compression in the knees, then spring! Both arms up in a perfect V. My left hand releases the ball, palm open to the sky, like I'm catching raindrops, while my right arm bends at the elbow as if the racket were a giant back scratcher. The ball floats up and over me, hovers in the air briefly at two o'clock, and as my arm snaps forward, hurling the racket face as if I were pitching a baseball, I see the word imprinted on the fuzzy yellow surface: "Wilson." The ball makes a solid popping sound as it connects with the strings.

It arcs high over the net, down the center of the court. A loopy, twisting floater right down the T, a big fat second serve

2

to Emily's forehand. Never mind that she expects a hard first serve to her backhand. The ball bounces an inch inside the line, then kicks high and away from her. She doesn't move. Doesn't even whiff at it. Ace. My game.

Applause, chatter, the usual eruption of spectator sound as we switch sides. We've parked our bags at opposite ends of the net, eliminating the need to make eye contact as we swallow water, towel off and take a quick bite of a half-eaten PowerBar. We're allowed ninety seconds to make this journey from one side to the other, refueling as we cross the line. We aren't supposed to talk to anyone, especially not a coach. Just drink, gulp and go.

As I rescrew the top of my water bottle, I glance down the length of the net toward Emily. She has her head down, breathing hard. The red Nike top she wears has darkened during the course of the game, drenched with sweat. She has both hands on her knees, and a man wearing a blue polo shirt crouches beside her and speaks urgently into her ear.

"Hey! None of that!" a deep male voice bellows to my right.

The chatter stops and every head turns in the direction of the voice. Seated on the aluminum bleachers not a dozen feet from where I stand, another man, markedly tan, glares at Emily and her companion. He has a slim notebook opened across his knees and a pencil tucked behind one ear. Anyone who doesn't know him might wonder: is he a reporter taking notes? Of course, I know that he's been carefully recording

3

every stroke of the game in that book, every point won or lost. A methodical, unblinking diary of the afternoon's event, to be analyzed in minute detail before the sun sets.

Tan Notebook Man is my father.

Blue Polo Man straightens, and raises one reassuring hand.

"It's okay," he says. Emily picks up her racket and begins walking to her side of the court.

"No coaching allowed!" my father shouts. "You want to get her disqualified?" Gasps of surprise. The whisper of hushed, urgent conversation from the spectators.

Here we go again.

Emily halts, midstride, and looks hesitantly at Blue Polo Man.

"It's okay," he repeats, firmly, to her. Then he turns to my dad.

"I'm not her coach," he calls back, then returns to the bleachers on his side.

"Oh yeah?" my dad retorts. "How do we know that?" He stands up, clutching his notebook so it doesn't fall.

"Hey, buddy, chill," I hear someone call out. "Just let the kids play," chimes in another voice. "Delay of game!" calls a third. My father doesn't sit.

"Daddy!" I hiss. Heads swivel in my direction.

"Pipe down and let me finish beating her, okay?" A moment's shocked pause, then laughter, rippling through the crowd. At first my father frowns, then his mouth twists into a knowing smile. Even if Blue Polo Man were Emily's coach, it doesn't matter. I need one more game, just four points, to wrap

4

this up and become Henriette Lloyd, Northern New Jersey 16-and-Under Junior Tennis Champion. Emily could be on a cell phone life-lining Venus and Serena, for all I care. Read her body language, folks. This one is mine.

My father sits.

Emily prepares to serve. She has a good serve. Not much spin, but fast, and she can place it. I've been having a hard time predicting where it will land.

She bounces it, tosses it high over her head, then fires it at me. It shoots straight down the middle of the court, a rocket into my backhand. She follows it in, racing to the net. This girl's still got some life in her.

I barely manage to get my racket on it. My return pops high and short, a big fat sucker ball to her forehand. A silver-platter shot. Just handing her a point on a silver platter. Damn.

She winds up and smacks it, aims it down the line and behind me, to the far corner of my backhand side. A dead winner. Except . . . it hits the tape on the top of the net. It hits with a sickening smack, and drops on her side. My point.

"Ohhh." Big sigh of disappointment from the fans. The poor kid. Getting trounced out here in the hot sun. The soon-to-be-runner-up who had a chance to salvage her pride with a winner and remind us why she's here, in the 16-and-Under state final. They feel sorry for her.

I hate that. I hate the way fans side with my opponents, as if they're helpless victims and I'm some creep for beating them. I mean, am I supposed to feel guilty for being the better player? This is a game, people. We play to win.

Emily stares in disbelief as the yellow ball rolls gently toward her. She lets out a deep, long breath.

"Tough luck," I call out, shaking my head in sympathy. "And your serve was so awesome."

She looks stricken. It is probably the worst thing I could have said to her. Not only to point out how great the serve was, how the point should have been hers and she blew it. But to sympathize with her? You never want other players' sympathy. You want their fear, their respect. If they offer kind words, you know they think you are the most pathetic little bug ever to swing a racket.

I can't help it. I hate myself for it, actually, but I glance at my father. He's heard my comment, and barely, almost imperceptibly, he winks. Then he looks down, busying himself with his notebook. He and I both know it's pretty much over now.

Next serve: Emily double-faults. Then puts up a puff ball which I put away. At love–40, championship point, she tries to lob me, but it falls short. I finish with an overhead slam into her forehand corner. She watches it go by.

To the velvety sound of outdoor applause, we trot to the net, hands extended for the courtesy shake.

"You play very well," she says. "You deserve the title."

"Thank you," I reply, pumping her hand, and wondering how it can be so sweaty and so cold at the same time. "You have a great serve. I had to work hard to return it." I smile. The game is over. We can be friendly.

Emily shrugs.

"Not hard enough," she comments. "Listen, I want to tell

you something." I gaze at her, puzzled. People from the bleachers are spilling onto the court and walking toward us.

"That wasn't a coach talking to me. That was my dad. He was asking me how I felt. See, I'm diabetic. Exercise really affects my blood-sugar levels, and if I'm not careful I could go into a seizure. My dad wanted to know if I needed to test my blood." Emily stares steadily into my eyes.

"I don't know who that loudmouth in the bleachers was, but I want you to know that I would never cheat," she says. "I know we're not allowed coaching."

I swallow hard. She obviously hadn't heard me talking to the loudmouth.

"So, are you okay? I mean, the rules allow us to stop to pee. I'm sure you could have stopped to test your blood, or something."

"I'm fine." Emily smiles, thinly. "No insulin shock. Just tired. You beat me fair and square."

At that moment, Blue Polo Man appears. He wraps one arm tightly around Emily's shoulders and gives her an affectionate squeeze.

"I'm very proud of you," he says firmly. "You played great." He looks across the net at me. "Congratulations," he says politely.

"Thank you," I reply. Then Emily's dad shifts his gaze over my shoulder, and a frown appears on his forehead. I don't need eyes in the back of my head to know who he sees.

My father, aka Loudmouth.

"Way to go, Henry!" he booms. He raises one hand, palm

facing me, to slap five. "Way to go, *champ!*" I slap him a quick five, then move immediately toward my tennis bag near the exit. Hoping against hope that he will simply follow me.

No such luck. He turns to Emily and her father.

"Kid," he says, "I'm sorry that you lost. But this should be a lesson to you. It never pays to cheat."

"Dad!" I say sharply. "Let's just go. Okay?"

Emily's father removes his arm from her shoulder and takes one step toward my dad. His face twitches with controlled rage.

"I don't know who you are, or what rock you crawled out from under, but I would advise you in the future to not speak to my daughter, or to me. Is that understood?" he seethes. "Otherwise, I'll see that you're barred from the circuit. You won't be allowed within a ten-mile radius of a junior tournament for the next fifty years."

My father laughs.

"No worries, bro. Especially since I don't think we'll be seeing much more of her at match finals anyway, *comprendo?*" He gives another short laugh, turns his back on them and walks, with me following, off the court.

In the parking lot about an hour later, as we load my bag and trophy into the back of the Navigator, Dad still crows about the win.

"You did good today, Hen. Granted, she isn't as talented as you. But that serve could have messed you up. She's got a nice serve. But you stayed tough, hung in there. That's your ace in the hole, kid: mental toughness. Gets 'em every time."

"You know, Dad, she's diabetic. Her father was just asking—" His short bark of laughter cuts me off.

"Yeah, and I believe the moon is made of Swiss cheese," he sneers. "Don't be fooled, Hen. She's saying that so you won't report her. Ah, what the hell. You won. We'll let it go."

He pulls out of the parking lot, and I see tournament officials folding up tables, striking the registration tent, dumping ice from coolers. The state championships are in two weeks, in Princeton. It's the first time I've made it to the state finals, and Dad is pretty excited. You can always tell he's pumped when he goes on about mental toughness. Which, in Dadspeak, is code for "trash talk."

I sigh. Mental cruelty, more like.

Chapter Two

EVA

The woman in the black warm-up suit tells us I have thirty minutes to get ready. Perfect.

Well, perfect for me. Rhonda's freaked. Freaked, flipped, hyped to the max. Just another day in the life of my over-the-top New-Jersey-housewife mother, although this afternoon she's got more than the usual amount of adrenaline flowing. It's the day of my solo audition for the New York School of Dance, and she's just finished attempting to drag-race her SUV through traffic on the George Washington Bridge.

Usually it takes us fifty-five minutes to cross the Hudson River between New Jersey and the city. Today Mom made the trip in forty-two minutes flat.

"Arrive alive, Rhonda," I told her after she cut off a tractor trailer that laid on the horn like the entire brass section of the Philharmonic.

"And I've gotten you safely to the city how many times?" she replied sweetly. We both grinned, but I gripped the armrests for the whole trip. I hate weaving in and out of traffic. It's not a fear factor, although driving with Mom is legitimate grounds for terror. It's the lines.

Linear. I like things linear. Straight, uninterrupted lines, cars moving predictably forward. No breaking the pattern. It's one reason why I love ballet. The straight, clean lines. The patterns.

Mom parks like she drives, and when she spied a vacant metered space a few hundred feet from the entrance to the ballet school, she slammed on the brakes. Empty metered spaces just don't happen in New York. She nosed into it, didn't even try to back up and parallel-park, for fear that someone else would steal it from behind her. We ended up at a forty-five-degree angle from the curb.

"Whoops," I said brightly. "Try again."

"This is fine," she said, turning off the ignition. "C'mon, grab your stuff." I didn't budge.

"Eva," she said, "we don't have time for this."

"We have three minutes for you to park the car straight," I replied. I stared out the windshield. I breathed deeply, from my diaphragm, and focused on stillness.

There is no way you can enter that building and concentrate on your audition dance with the car left outside in this position. Rhonda knows this.

She swore as she fired up the engine again. The car lurched as she rapidly backed out, as she hit the brakes, then raced forward, lurched again when she stopped, then glided smoothly

 11

backward, cutting the wheels sharply so we slipped in eight inches from the curb and parallel to it. Perfect.

"I tell you, Rhonda, Danica Patrick has *nothing* on you," I said, reaching behind my seat for the bag containing my ballet clothes. She didn't laugh, just sighed impatiently and got out of the car. Okay, so maybe it's too much to expect that Mom would know the most famous female IndyCar racer. But Henry would've laughed. Henry, whose bedroom walls are plastered with pictures of her favorite female sports icons: Danica, Mia, Venus, Misty.

The New York School of Dance is housed in a former elementary school, and there's something stern and unsmiling about its brick face. Its lobby is empty, except for a big ficus plant, and as we ride the elevator to the fourth floor I hear the tinkle of a piano as music seeps through the walls. Before I can identify the melody, the box grinds to a stop and the doors slide open.

A young woman in a black warm-up suit waits, holding a clipboard.

"Eva Smith?" she says pleasantly. "Right on time. Please follow me." She walks quickly down the corridor.

This is such a contrast from the afternoon when we arrived for the group audition. There was a line out the front door as dancers waited to squeeze into the elevator. Inside, it was this frenzied cattle call as they checked off our names from a big list and handed out paper numbers, which we affixed to our leotards with safety pins.

In groups of thirty, nameless and numbered, we positioned ourselves along the *barres* in the big practice room, where an instructor worked us through a class. You could hear hips and knees crack as we started with *pliés* from first position, then deep breaths from around the room as we advanced to *grand battement:* the knees straight, the body quiet, the working leg raised from the hip, and those pretty satin *pointe* shoes elevated above our heads. Then stretch, remove the *barres,* and in smaller groups move to center for *adagio* (slow, sustained movement), *pirouettes* (spins) and *allegro* (brisk, lively steps).

We were all dressed in identical black leotards and tights. We all wore our hair in smooth buns. We all wore the same expressions, radiating ease and joyfulness as our ligaments screamed or our sore-toe-with-the-nail-about-to-fall-off threatened to derail the tryout completely. Or our concentration flagged as our eyes inevitably moved around the room to the other girls, the other members of the Clone Ballerina Army, vying against each other for the handful of spots at the school. Somehow, miraculously, you were expected to move so elegantly, with such precision and such clear capacity for strength and grace, that one of the three wandering, observing instructors might actually notice and jot down your number.

Somehow, my number had made it into someone's book. So I get to audition again—this time, alone.

The piano grows louder as we proceed along the hall. It is accompanied by a woman's commanding voice: "And *plié!* And *relevé! Plié! Relevé!* And jump and jump and jump and jump! Little jumps, little jumps, toes all the way off the ground!"

Halfway down the corridor, the walls become glass on one side, and we can see into an enormous studio. The ceiling rises at least two stories high, and is bordered by windows that reveal the tops of distant skyscrapers. A full-length mirror panels one entire wall of the studio, and the wooden floors, beaten smooth by years of soft satin shoes, are dusted with traces of rosin powder. At least twenty dancers, a few men but mostly women, are positioned at the *barres* set up throughout the room.

"Now *tendu* front, side, back! And *tendu* front, side, back!"

I stand stock-still, mesmerized. These are the company dancers. I have never peeked into a company dance class, never seen so many who have crossed over to "the promised land" in a professional company all in the same room, rehearsing the same basic moves. Not only that: rehearsing them in perfect time, with textbook precision. They are in the early stage of class: many of them are layered with leg warmers, sweatpants, a sweatshirt tied around the waist, as they try to coax tired, hard muscles to become as flexible as rubber bands. Despite their motley assortment of clothing, they share a seemingly effortless execution of each move.

Oh my god, are you kidding? Are you kidding me? These people are awesome. They are so much better than you. You and your big fat butt have no chance.

"Please, this way," the woman urges. I pull myself reluctantly away from the studio windows, and she smiles at me.

"We do many, many *tendus* here," she says. "We think it is probably the most important exercise a ballet dancer can do."

I smile back at her, trying hard not to look surprised. *Tendu?* A simple toe drag from first position, the most important exercise? I wonder if this is a test. To see how I'll react. I glance at my mother, but she's looking at her watch.

The woman pushes open a door at the end of the hall, and we enter a smaller version of the earlier studio. Mirrors, a *barre*, an upright piano. But the floors here gleam, immaculate.

"Now, there is a dressing room next door on your right. Madame will be here in thirty minutes, so you have that much time to change and warm up." She places the clipboard on top of the piano, smiles once more and leaves us alone.

By the time Madame arrives, I have stretched, *pliéd*, *tendued* and *dégagéd* just beyond warm and just before sweat. My favorite, most recently broken-in *pointe* shoes are securely wrapped at the ankles; I wear my good-luck lavender leotard. Madame, slim and silver-haired, strides into the room without knocking, surprising us both. Another woman accompanies her: roundish, dressed in street clothes.

"Hello," Madame says, hand extended. "I am Gloria DuPres."

"Rhonda Smith," Mom replies, returning the shake. "And this is Eva."

Gloria DuPres's eyes dart to the top of my head and the tightly gathered knot of long hair, then flit down the length of me to the feet, registering height, weight, build and potential for strength and elegance in about two seconds. I search her

15

face for a sign of either disapproval or pleasure, but other than a slight twitch at one corner of her mouth, Madame reveals nothing.

Fat. She thinks you're fat, Eva. And what the hell were you thinking, wearing a purple leotard today?

She holds a pencil and studies the clipboard left atop the piano; the roundish woman sits before the keyboard.

"Eva, you are . . . how old?" she asks, eyes locked on her sheet.

"She'll be sixteen in September," Mom says. Madame looks up at me and waits.

"I'm fifteen," I reply. She nods, returns to her clipboard.

"And you have been on *pointe* how long?" she asks.

"About six years," I say.

Madame looks up. A line creases her smooth forehead.

"Define 'about.' Does it mean more than six, or less than six?"

"Eva went on *pointe* when she was nine," Mom says.

"That's young," says Madame, redirecting her gaze to Mom.

"When it comes to ballet, Eva's done everything early." Mom smiles. She can barely contain the gush in her voice.

Madame's lip curls. Slightly. But I notice.

"I do not have a single girl here who wore *pointe* shoes before eleven," she says to Mom. "The feet, the bones, were not developed enough. The muscles in the legs were not strong enough. In some schools, they do bone scans on their students to make sure their growth plates have closed before

 16

putting them on *pointe*. Otherwise, you can cause irreparable harm."

Rhonda doesn't even blush. Amazing. My stomach is doing 360s, but right now my mother is smiling at Madame Gloria DuPres like we've just won the lottery.

"I know exactly what you mean! Our Eva hit all those milestones so early. It was really something."

Madame returns to her clipboard, the furrow in her brow smoothed over again. She writes, and I suddenly have an overpowering urge to vomit.

You're ruined, career over, at the ripe old age of fifteen. What do they do with horses who've gone bad in the knees? Oh, right: glue factory. They grind their hooves into glue. So, let's just melt the girl down and pour her into a bottle of Elmer's school glue. Only we can call it Eva's loser glue.

"Eva, did you bring your music today?" Madame's voice cuts through the silence in the studio, pulling me from my thoughts.

"Yes," I tell her, and reach into my ballet bag for the sheet music. I've chosen *Swan Lake*, the section where Odile, the black swan, performs before the assembled court.

Madame takes my music and hands it to the accompanist seated at the piano.

"Mrs. Smith," she says, "in our sitting room down the hall you'll find coffee, tea, other refreshments. I will send Eva out to you when we're finished."

I think it takes Rhonda several full seconds to realize she's been dismissed. Her eyes go all big and round. She doesn't argue, just turns and walks compliantly out the door. But not before flashing me a big, exaggerated wink and whispering, "Good luck!"

As the accompanist arranges the sheets of music on the stand, Madame looks over her shoulders. Her eyebrows arch when she sees my music. I'm doing final stretches, trying to shake out the jitters.

"Tell me, Eva. Have you ever seen this ballet performed?"

"Oh. Gosh. Maybe a dozen times?" I reply. *Swan Lake* is my absolute favorite. With my favorite composer: Tchaikovsky. I can never decide which is his best all-time tearjerker—the finale to *Swan Lake*, or the part in *The Nutcracker* where Clara leaves in the magical sleigh.

"When I was a young dancer it was without a doubt my favorite to perform," Madame informs me. She settles gracefully in the aluminum chair.

"What part did you dance?" I ask. She smiles smoothly.

"Odile. Just like you."

It's over, kiddo. Can we skip this part and just go home now?

"Please, Eva. Begin."

I take my position in the middle of the room and breathe deeply. Slowly, deeply, from the diaphragm. I close my eyes. I imagine the diamonds.

This is how it always is for me: the space I inhabit when I dance becomes a three-dimensional grid of perfectly stacked diamonds, my movement within their confines precise, predictable, controlled. I love the music. My heart soars with the music, and I don't imitate but actually *become* the character from the ballet. And my body obeys in strictly timed, rehearsed motion.

I begin in B-plus position: *attitude à terre*. One arm curves gracefully above my head; the other is extended to the side. One more deep breath, and the pianist begins.

It's a slow, lovely, deliberate dance. No breakneck runs; no vaulting leaps. Instead, graceful, swanlike arms, delicate *piqué* steps that appear light, effortless. I begin with *soutenus* . . . a sustained chain of turns in fifth position, then *pirouettes*. Spins. Then, from *attitude*, a poised moment of stillness, one leg balances while the other is drawn up, tracing the knee, then extending outward in a holding position: *développé en l'air*.

At some point, muscle memory takes over, and the music washes over my nerves. I forget to think of these as steps. I forget Madame. I forget my purple leotard and the battalion of impossibly perfect dancers down the hall, and I am a girl, a swanlike girl, dancing before a prince. He looks at me and something breaks in him: he wants nothing, nothing more than me. He could die for loving me, and it's all because I dance. . . .

I don't hate Odile. I don't think Tchaikovsky did, either. He wouldn't have written anything this beautiful for something we're supposed to hate. But that's how the story supposedly goes: Odile is the evil black swan who tricks the prince into thinking she's the perfect Odette, the white swan he has fallen in love with. But when she dances, this Odile, isn't she asking, with every graceful sweep of her arms, every breathless, airy step: "Love me. I deserve love, too."

I end in fourth position, my feet parallel, one behind the other, after a run of *piqué* turns. The pianist has stopped and I am breathing hard. It's odd, to end in silence. A performance is supposed to end in applause, not the pounding of my heart in my ears. I look at Madame, her expression unreadable, her legs crossed and her hands folded neatly in her lap. After what feels like forever, she speaks.

"Well, Eva, I think that piece was very ambitious for you. A very ambitious choice." She stands. She nods to the accompanist, who neatly gathers the pages of my music. Madame crosses the room to me and puts out her hand, which I take.

"After you change, you go down the hall, turn right, and you'll find your mother in the reception room. Thank you for coming in. We'll be in touch."

Not until the two women leave and the door clicks behind them do I allow myself to flop on the floor. I go all oozy. Like spilled glue. And I can't decide whether I feel like crying, or like standing up and wheeling that piano across the smooth studio floor, and crashing it through the windows so that it drops to the street below and smashes into a zillion little pieces.

Chapter Three

HENRY

You've got to have attitude if you're from New Jersey. At least, that's what Eva says.

Face it: Jersey jokes probably outnumber Polish jokes and lawyer jokes combined. Even our cars, with "The Garden State" license plate logo, get laughs. "Don't you mean 'The Chemical State'?" people sneer, referring to the stretch of the New Jersey Turnpike just south of New York City, where the refinery fumes are so bad they set off the smoke alarms in passing RVs. "What exit?" they cackle, when you tell them you're from Jersey. "Do you glow in the dark?" they laugh, referring to the countless gallons of toxic waste produced by and deposited in New Jersey, aka the Armpit of New York. After a while it gets to be a drag.

When I was little I wished we were from Montana (their license plate says "Big Sky Country") or Maine ("Vacationland"). But Eva keeps telling me there's no point wishing for things you can't change. So put a smile on your face and just keep saying to yourself: "Jersey Tomatoes Are the Best."

That's Eva Smith, Best Friend Forever and fellow Jersey Girl.

"If we can survive New Jersey, we can survive anything," she likes to say. As if she's some sort of survivor, which I don't quite get. She says it now, the day following my tournament. We sit in her kitchen, blending strawberry smoothies and discussing the dubious honor of being a New Jersey State Champion of Anything, let alone tennis. Eva is convinced that I am bound for glory, especially because some recruiter from a tennis academy in Florida called our house after the match. He's planning to be at states in a couple of weeks.

I'm wondering whether reading my name above the fold in the sports section of the *Bergen Record* qualifies as glory. I'm *so* suffering from an attitude deficit today.

Usually Eva and I spend postmatch days hanging out. If I win, that is. On the rare occasions when I lose, I spend the afternoons calling the dogs.

As in Penn, Wilson and Dunlop. It was a game I made up, pretending the balls my father fired at me from our ball machine were dogs. Starting when I was . . . I don't know . . . eight? I'd stand on the baseline of our backyard clay court, waiting for a fresh feed, and he'd fill the machine with all the different brands. I had to see the seams, he said. Call out the manufacturer's name just before I hit.

"Here, Wilson! Here, Penn!" I'd shout as I slammed forehands. "Roll over, Dunlop!" I'd exclaim, nailing a topspin backhand. Dad loved it, and whenever he wanted me to practice with the ball machine, he'd say, "Time to call a few dogs."

Of course, as many hours as I've logged on a tennis court, Eva's logged more in a dance studio.

She was wearing a leotard, tights and rubbery ballet slippers the day we met: in the grocery store. We were six. I was shopping with my mom, tagging along as she wheeled our metal cart along the aisles. Ahead of us I spied this girl acting weird.

She had one hand on her mother's cart and one arm curved over her head. She had her eyes closed, her nose tilted toward the ceiling, and she kept rising up and down on tiptoe. As her mother pushed their cart forward, rapidly tossing boxes of frozen pizza and icy bags of peas and corn into the cart, the girl minced slowly along, oblivious to the groceries flying past her head.

"Eva, we don't have time for this," her mother said impatiently. "Lessons start in fifteen minutes."

My mom and I had just pulled parallel with them. The girl opened her eyes, and her gaze fell immediately on me.

"Oh. Hello," she said without hesitation. "I'm Eva." I just stood there, slack-jawed with surprise. I'm good at that. "What's your name?" she persisted.

"This is Henry," my mother filled in for me kindly. "That's a very pretty leotard you're wearing. Are you a dancer?"

Eva nodded solemnly. Her brow wrinkled as she processed this information.

"Henry is a boy's name," she finally announced. A little accusingly.

I'm also pretty good at stating the obvious, so "I'm not a

boy" sprang to my lips. As if my waist-length blond hair and pink baseball cap weren't enough evidence. Eva smiled widely, clearly pleased and amused by me. Meanwhile, our moms spoke over our heads. They recognized each other from around town, in that Jersey-mothers-who-shop-at-the-same-grocery-store sort of way.

"Would you like to come over to play?" Eva asked. I shrugged. I had no interest in this odd kid and her food-chucking mother. But Eva had made up her mind, so before Rhonda hustled her out of the store, the mothers exchanged phone numbers and a playdate was planned.

It was like hanging out with a pint-sized dictator. She bossed me around for hours as we played make-believe games of her invention. We weren't just Henry and Eva: we were lost mermaids in a haunted lake; princesses who had been turned into white mice by a jealous queen; children who sprouted wings at night and flew over the rooftops of their parents' homes. She staged a ballet, creating sets by draping gauzy material over the backs of kitchen chairs and playing tapes from Disney movies. She danced the lead, and for a while tried to get me to dance. It didn't take her long, even at age six, to realize I was incapable of moving my feet to music, so she made me something stationary—a tree—while she cavorted around me.

I laughed so much that day my cheeks hurt. As we played, I lost all track of real time and space, and when my mother arrived to pick me up, Eva and I both begged for another playdate. They couldn't refuse us.

 24

Here's what we never did: keep score. Eva doesn't play competitive games. Nothing with points, nothing with balls, nothing with sticks, bats or rackets. That's because she hates those games. Says losing makes her sad, and winning makes her feel sad for the other person. I've never minded. Playing Eva's way was a nice break from . . . well, the dogs, for one thing.

One hot summer day Dad wanted me to call dogs before lunch. It was, like, ninety degrees. I argued, but he turned the machine on anyway. Then he told me I didn't have to just call the names: I had to call the numbers, too. Which is impossible because they're too small.

I was so pissed that I just started calling out any old number. "Wilson Three! Penn Two!" Smacking away and lying my head off. Finally, he turned off the damn thing. Said he'd filled the machine with Dunlops. Said he knew I cheated on our drills. Said I didn't work hard enough, and it showed. He punished me for lying by taking away my TV privileges for a month and making me do dogs for an extra hour a day.

I was nine years old.

Around that same time, Eva traded in her rubbery ballet slippers for *pointe* shoes. Ballet started getting serious for her around then, and hours spent just hanging out . . . or playing pretend . . . became rare. By now I'll bet she's accumulated enough frequent driver miles crossing over or under the Hudson River into the city for ballet stuff to travel to the moon and back. She tells me I'm wrong.

She says she's earned enough miles to make it to Pluto.

25

Today is a rare Sunday afternoon we *both* have off, and . . . predictably . . . Eva has dictated that we *must* spend it together drinking her famous Pink Decadence smoothies. Once upon a time this was a regular event. Now I can't remember the last time we had smoothies.

"For example," Eva says, continuing to make her case for surviving New Jersey. "Take . . . cancer."

"Pass," I groan. But Eva's on a roll.

"I once saw a map of the U.S. that had a tiny red dot wherever there was a cancer cluster. I don't know how many cases per thousand the dots represented, but the state of New Jersey? Completely red. That's how many dots we've got."

"And this is supposed to make us feel good?" I say.

"Yes!" she exclaims. "*We* don't have cancer! What are the odds of that, living in New Jersey? If we haven't gotten cancer by now, we probably never will."

"Eva, we're sixteen. Well, at least I am. We've got, like, another seventy years to get cancer," I say. Eva shakes her head as she presses the plastic lid onto the top of the blender. She's loaded it with fresh strawberries, vanilla yogurt, lemonade and chopped ice. She pushes a button and the whole thing spins and shakes. When it all turns a uniform shade of pink, she shuts it off.

"My point is that if you can emerge from the heap in Jersey, you can make it anywhere."

"Uh, no offense, but I think that comes from the song about New *York*."

Eva smiles and fills two tall glasses with the creamy liquid, then pushes one across the counter to me. She raises hers in a toast.

"Today New Jersey, tomorrow . . . the world!" she declares. "Congratulations, Hen." We clink, then drink. Yum. Total Pink Decadence, but Eva insists it only has 180 calories per serving. Not that it makes much difference to me. I'm a pretty mindless eater, devouring whatever is on my plate until the growling stops. Ballerina Eva, on the other hand, never seems to eat a morsel without whipping out her calculator.

When she lowers her glass, she's wearing a pink mustache.

"Your dad must be happy," Eva says. I reach over and wipe her upper lip with my napkin.

Eva knows Dad.

"Something did happen," I say.

"Of course," she says matter-of-factly. "Spill, girlfriend. You'll feel better."

Ages ago, Eva and I figured out that we're good friends because we never compete with each other. Except about one thing: who has the most obnoxious parent. She insists her mother takes the prize. Once, when Eva didn't get the lead in a local production of the ballet *Coppelia*, her mother let all the air out of the casting director's tires. Eva claims my dad's outbursts are nothing compared to her mom's terrorist attacks.

"This girl I beat, in the final? Dad accused her, right in front of everyone, of talking to her coach between games." Eva's never so much as even picked up a tennis racket, but years of hanging out with me have made her a tennis rules expert. She knows: no coaching during tournament play.

 27

"And . . . was she?" Eva asks.

"I don't think so. She told me she's diabetic and *her* dad was just asking how she felt."

Eva rolls her eyes.

"Let me guess: Mark learned the truth and apologized to the diabetic girl?"

"Guess again," I say.

"Hmm. He continued to press his point? Even after his little darling triumphed?"

"Try: he rubbed it in her face that she'd lost, accused her of cheating and pissed off her dad so much that I thought the guy was going to deck him." Eva lets out a long, low whistle of admiration.

"Ten points, Mark!" she exclaims. "Watch out, Rhonda. If he keeps this up, we'll have to transfer the Obnoxious Parent of the Year trophy from the Smiths' house to the Lloyds'."

The Obnoxious Parent of the Year trophy was Eva's idea. She bought it a couple of years ago from this online trophy and plaque place and got them to engrave OPY on the brass plate at the base. Depending on Mark's and Rhonda's latest escapades, we swap the trophy between us.

I know I should be laughing, but the Attitude Deficit has a real hold on me today. The bubbles at the top of my smoothie are suddenly fascinating.

Eva puts her hand over mine.

"You know I'm kidding," she says. "Honestly, Henry, was it really that bad?"

My throat closes at this point. Even to Eva, this is hard to say. Because it's not just Dad's behavior that has left me feeling bad about this match. I'm used to Dad. The whole Jersey junior circuit is used to Dad.

"I don't know," I finally say. "It's like . . . the crowd is never with me. They're always pulling for my opponent. And I know, you think that's because I've got the bigmouth father. And probably that's partially true. But it's something else, and I don't get it."

"Well, you're pretty dominant," she suggests. "Maybe they're pulling for the underdog because they want to see a big upset?"

"No," I say firmly. "Look at Mike Adams, that guy from Port Chester. He's the uncontested New Jersey boys junior champ every year, and fans, like, follow him from court to court. His opponents almost seem *happy* to play him. Like it's an honor to get bageled by Mike Adams." I don't need to explain "bageled" to Eva. She knows it means losing a match 6–0, 6–0.

"They probably feel sorry for your opponents," Eva suggests. "I mean, you crush them."

"What's more crushing than a bagel?" I counter.

"Not the score, Hen. The whole thing. I've seen you do it. You . . . well, it's what I said. You crush them. You make it so that they dread ever having to play you again."

"Yeah, but this is competition tennis. You *want* them to fear you," I explain.

"But it won't win you the Miss Congeniality award, will it?" Eva laughs, coaxing a smile out of me, as well. The idea of

Henriette Lloyd winning a Nice Kid prize at a tennis match is . . . pretty unlikely.

"You can't have it both ways, Hen," Eva concludes. "You can't humiliate them on the court, then expect them to friend you on Facebook afterward. Put on your big-girl panties and handle it: you are a badass, kick-ass tennis player."

"Hmm," I reply, a little skeptically. Eva smiles and dumps some of her smoothie into my now-empty glass. She moves lightly on to the next subject, this topic dealt with and checked off in some imaginary box in her head. She's good like that, compartmentalizing messy emotional junk into neat boxes that you can label, then seal tight with packing tape. I wish I could do that, but my junk spills out and runs around, and even if I could stuff it in a box it'd squeal to get out.

There's more to say, and I worry that Eva's too nice to say it. To say that maybe when it comes to me and my dad, keeping an eye on the ball isn't the only thing I've learned.

Chapter Four

EVA

Paybacks are hell. Which is why I find myself in Henry's kitchen the morning of the state tournament.

The Lloyds are jumpy. Even Henry's mom, the sane parent. She's nuking oatmeal in the microwave, grabs the hot dish without mitts and drops it. The oatmeal hits the floor and spatters spectacularly, soft gray blobs daubing the cabinets, the dishwasher. Her shorts.

"Damn!" she exclaims. Mrs. Lloyd never swears. At least, not when I'm around.

"What?" Henry's dad walks in, freshly showered, his hair slicked back like the fur of a wet seal. His white-collared golf shirt makes his tan neck look practically maroon.

"I dropped the oatmeal," Mrs. Lloyd says, ripping off a paper towel. "It's everywhere." I grab a napkin and go after blobs on the floor as Mrs. Lloyd starts on the cabinets.

"Eva, you don't have to do that," she says. I smile at her. Of course I do. Oatmeal streaks the straight lines of the tiled floor.

 31

"Where's Henry? She needs to eat," Mark says. "Did *all* the oatmeal spill?"

"More like, flew," I comment. I look up at him and my eyes glance over his head.

"Oh no," I groan. They follow my gaze. A line of oatmeal blobs stretches across the ceiling. It reminds me of the girls' bathroom at school, where kids take handfuls of toilet paper, soak them in the sink, then fling them up, so they stick. The custodian has to climb a stepladder in order to scrape them off.

"What the hell did you do, Marian?" Mark demands. Mrs. Lloyd's eyes narrow.

"I was doing the oatmeal dance, Mark," she says. "You whirl around in a circle yelling 'dammit' and fling hot oatmeal everywhere. Then the tennis gods guarantee you a victory that day. I'm surprised you had to ask."

I suck in my breath and wait for the onslaught. I haven't witnessed Lloyd-on-Lloyd battles, but from what Henry tells me they aren't pretty. I'm wishing I hadn't shown up so early today. Wishing Henry weren't my best friend and I didn't have to be here.

But I do, because that's the thing about a best friend: for all the big stuff, she is *there*.

It's the sort of thing a lesser mortal, like my Family Frenemy, Paige, doesn't get. (Henry uses that word for her: a cross between friend and enemy. *So* much love between those two.) Paige's mom and my mom went to college together. She's in our class at Ridgefield High and usually doesn't like anyone who has better hair. Not only does Henry have movie-star

32

long blond hair and a Victoria's Secret body, but she's got Olympic gold athletic ability and rocket-scientist intelligence.

"Honestly, Eva. Isn't it *depressing* to be around that much perfection?" Paige once said. How could I explain to a person like Paige why I love Henry? Who has no clue how gorgeous she is. Who lives in jeans and sweatshirts. Who doesn't own a microgram of makeup, doesn't know her own weight. And when I do my *South Park* imitations? She laughs until she cries. Unlike Paige, who says, "Could you, like, *not* talk in that funny voice for a change?"

Of course, sometimes, like this morning, I wish I didn't love Henry. Then I wouldn't have agreed to spend the day with her warring parents, watching her play tennis. But she's put up with equally boring afternoons, and with Rhonda, too. Like the day I got my first *pointe* shoes, a red-letter day in a dancer's life.

My mother had scheduled a fitting at the Gaynor Minden showroom in New York, an old Victorian brownstone in Chelsea. Gaynor Mindens are like no other shoes, and their showroom is like no other ballet store. An imposing iron gate greets you at their front door, and you have to buzz to be admitted. Once inside, you sit in an elegant living room, before a fireplace, as a salesperson spends unlimited time making sure the length, width, box, shank, vamp and heel of your little satin shoe is perfect.

Other ballet shoes have to be broken in. I know girls who press new shoes under the tires of an SUV a few times before dancing in them. Gaynor Mindens, however, start out perfect

 33

and stay that way; when they stretch, you replace them. At eighty dollars a pop. I can usually get six weeks out of a pair of *pointe* shoes. Principal dancers in big companies might replace theirs every three days. So not only are *pointe* shoes a huge investment; they are also a sign that, as a dancer, you've "arrived." Finally strong enough and committed enough to go on *pointe*.

Henry had asked to come along. Nine years old, a non-dancer, and she wanted to be there. She watched with interest. She clapped when we finally found the right pair. And as we skipped down Gaynor Minden's front steps—our next destination Ruby Foo's, where my mother had made a reservation for lunch—Henry slipped her hand into mine, and squeezed.

You can forgive a girl for looking like a supermodel if, at age nine, she was already such a good friend.

Miraculously, she appears that moment at the kitchen entrance.

"Hey, Eva," she says in a cheery voice. She sees her mother and me, paper towels in hand, wiping. She frowns. "Smells like breakfast but looks like a food fight."

"Right on both counts," I reply. I tip my head toward Mark, who steps over some blobs.

"Henry needs to eat," he repeats, opening the fridge. "And we need to walk out this door in twenty minutes."

"Cold cereal, Dad," Henry says briskly. "Breakfast of champions." She grabs the Raisin Bran, a bowl and the milk, and I follow her out to the patio table. As she eats we pretend not to hear her parents' muted angry voices from the kitchen. The

34

scrape of chair legs across the floor as someone climbs up to wipe the ceiling.

Henry looks across the table, her eyes strafing me from head to toe.

"Let me guess: Lawrence of Arabia?"

"Very funny," I reply. I'm wearing a long-sleeved white cotton shirt and baggy white parachute pants. My white cap has a flap down the back to protect my neck, and my nose is coated with zinc oxide. I smell like a Coppertone factory.

"I may be dressed for an afternoon in the desert, but when you sun worshippers are all wrinkled and leathery by age forty, my face will still be as smooth as a baby's behind," I say.

"You look great," she says, laughing. "Thanks for coming today."

* * *

When the four of us drive up to the Lenz Tennis Center in Princeton, we see scores of other competitors dressed in their snazzy outfits. It's only May, but the day burns hot and humid. Henry has been seriously thriving on Poland Spring water during the trip and needs a bathroom break, fast.

She's gotten quiet during the last fifteen minutes of the drive, and she stares intently out the window, at the crowds of players. She jounces one leg rapidly, up and down, and anyone who didn't know her might mistake it for nerves. I know it's pure, pent-up energy.

Here's the thing about Henry: she's a ruthless competitor. Not Michael Jordan ruthless, mind you. He's the type who freaks out if you beat him in tiddlywinks, while Henry only cares about tennis. But when it comes to tennis . . . she's a little scary.

It's a part of her I don't *get*. I mean, this winning and losing stuff? Why? Who cares how many points you earn or how many times you throw the orange ball through the metal hoop? Can't we just enjoy the beauty of Michael Jordan flying through the air without keeping score? Why do we always have to measure, assess, tally up the count or register the applause meter? Why does somebody always have to *lose*?

I tried to explain this to her once. She had attended one of my performances as Clara in *The Nutcracker*. It was this totally crazy season where I'd committed to dancing Clara with three separate groups, and the schedule was brutal. The toll on my body was terrible; every tendon ached, and I went through a whole bottle of ibuprofen. We even started calling it Vitamin I. I moved as if in a bad dream, through the shows, the lights, the music, the endless driving in bad weather as my mother raced me from one stage to another.

Henry had come to the show at our high school and the next day told me I'd done a great job.

"You know," I said to her carefully, not sure she would understand. "That wasn't my all-time favorite performance."

"Yeah, you didn't have much of a partner," she said, laughing a little. "I mean, where did you dig up the prince? Eva, the guy was useless, he—" I cut her off.

"I'm not talking about 'best.' I'm talking 'favorite.' As in most joyful, 'dancing in my happy place' performance. Can you guess?" Henry frowned.

 36

"You played the Mouse King," I prompted. The lines of her face relaxed when she remembered a once-upon-a-time afternoon at my house. She and I staged *The Nutcracker* in the basement, with the help of my dress-up box of costumes, sheets from Rhonda's linen closet and a fake, plastic sword. The Nutcracker was a big stuffed panda.

"I kicked the Nutcracker's ass," Henry said.

"You skewered him with the sword and his stuffing poured out," I corrected her. "Rhonda was predictably pissed off, but Henry, we *were* Clara and the Mouse King. I felt more alive in the story that day than I ever have in a staged performance. Does that make sense?"

"Sure," she said easily. "I think when we're little kids our imaginations take us places that we just can't go when we get older. Reality is never as much fun as make-believe. I mean, no amount of imagination could get around that Nutcracker Prince last night!" She laughed.

I didn't push it further with her. Henry's a competitor. A scorekeeper. It's coded in her DNA, like her flawless facial bone structure. And even though this killer competitive thing bothers her, she couldn't change it any more than she could rearrange her own skeletal system.

Mark drops us off at the registration building and goes to park.

Inside the tennis center the line for the women's room snakes out the door and into the hallway. We get behind some gaggle of little girls in matching Fila dresses. They share a three-pack of Reese's peanut butter cups, breaking them into bits, licking melted chocolate off their fingers. They do this while reading a sheet of paper taped to the wall.

I move in close to see what's so interesting.

It's the day's lineup: who's playing whom, and where. I try to read over their shoulders, to find Henry's name in the 16-and-Unders. One of the gagglers lets out a little scream.

"Oh my god! The bitch is here!"

It's weird to hear a girl who might be all of ten years old say "bitch."

"Who? What are you talking about?" the others ask.

"This really mean girl," she replies, pressing her finger to a name on the paper. "She's not in our division. She's older. My sister knows who she is."

"What's she do that's so mean?" one asks.

"Mind games," the girl explains. "Like, she calls people for footfaulting even though you *know* she can't see that far. She questions calls. She bounces the ball, like, twenty times before serving; then, on the next serve, she'll do it real fast. Junk like that."

"My coach says you have to ignore that sort of stuff," says one.

"Yeah, but this girl won't let you ignore her," the other replies. "She *talks* to you. My sister said if you make a mistake, like hit it out? She pretends to feel all sorry, ask if you feel all right . . . you know, make out like you're some loser. It makes you really angry, and next thing you know, you're making all these mistakes."

"God, I hate that," sighs one.

 38

"She's not even that good, you know?" The gaggle has rounded the corner passing from the hallway into the restroom proper. "My sister says her strokes are okay, but she wins all these matches by making her opponents mess up."

The restroom door closes on their conversation. I can finally get a good look at the paper. My eyes scan rapidly down the list.

I find Henry halfway down the sheet. Court three, eleven o'clock. It's not easy to read 'cause there's a chocolate fingerprint smudge right on Henry's name.

Our eyes meet, and she doesn't have to say a single word. She's been listening to the whole thing, bladder distress and all. Her blue eyes are cloudy with some emotion I don't recognize, and I don't know what to say, or how to reassure her.

Except to simply be here.

Chapter Five
HENRY

Halfway through my first set of the day, it's clear: I'm unbeatable today.

I know it when I toss the ball overhead for the serve and it looms as big as the moon, each thread of fuzzy yellow sharp, distinct. The racket head lasers through the air, and the ball explodes. I don't have to look: I imagine the target, and Wilson, Dunlop and Penn obey. I am in the zone of tennis dreams, and my opponent has lost ten consecutive points.

The audience, which started out politely clapping, grows silent. They came to watch a game, not a massacre. "Go, Brenda!" a voice calls when we switch sides. My opponent turns to the voice and miserably shakes her head. People begin to leave, to pack up and search for a real match on a different court.

Meanwhile, I concede nothing. Not a single shot. Unsmiling, silent, I claim what belongs to me. This game is mine. And I dare anyone to say I'm just "okay."

Even Dad looks subdued when it's over. He, Mom and Eva

join me courtside as I'm zipping my racket into its case. I have bageled Brenda in just under one hour.

"Geez, could you at least have tossed her a *point*?" Eva says, throwing her arms around me and giving my shoulders a tight squeeze. "I mean, hit it out once or twice just to make her grandma in the stands happy?" I stare at her.

"No, actually," I say, abruptly. "Not today."

"I think that's the best I've ever seen you play," Dad says, picking up my bag. As we turn to walk off the court, we almost knock over some guy who stands right behind us. He's dressed like Dad, got the golf-shirt thing going, but there's a lanyard around his neck with a laminated ID card. He sticks his hand out.

"I'm Jerry Goss," he says. "Chadwick Tennis Academy. We spoke on the phone a couple weeks ago."

"Mark Lloyd," Dad replies curtly, shaking the hand.

"Congratulations on an impressive first round," Jerry says to me. "I think that was one for the record books. You didn't lose a single point."

"Thanks—" I begin, before Dad cuts me off.

"We're going to find some shade for Henry and get a little lunch into her," he says abruptly. "You'll have to excuse us." Dad shoulders past Jerry.

"Sure thing," Jerry Goss replies, his face reddening. "Why don't I catch up with you folks when the tournament is over?" Mom, trailing Dad, smiles apologetically.

"Yes, please look for us later," she says. Eva and I follow quickly behind them.

41

"What was *that* about?" she says under her breath to me.

"He's that recruiter from the tennis school in Boca Raton, Florida," I explain. "Basically, a control-freak parent's nightmare." Eva bursts out laughing.

"Hope Jerry likes getting chewed alive by a lion," she says.

"Wouldn't be the first time," I sigh.

He'd called our house after I won the northern final. Wanted to come over and talk about this residential tennis academy. Dad was beyond rude to him over the phone.

"Mark, why can't we simply hear him out?" Mom argued afterward. "This could be a marvelous opportunity for Henry."

"Marian, these are the sorts of people who ruin kids like Henry!" Dad insisted. "They make 'em pros when they should still be junior amateurs. The tennis world is littered with their disaster stories. Remember that kid with the pigtails, when we were growing up? Andrea Jaeger. Whatever happened to her? And that other prodigy. Tracy Austin. They ruined that kid's back. And what is she today?"

"A very wealthy TV sports commentator," I called out from the other room. They didn't know I was listening in.

"A has-been!" Dad barked back. "A talented kid who never reached her potential because people were trying to make money off her!"

"I wouldn't mind people making money off me," I replied, "as long as I get to keep some." It's a strange thing about my dad: he's sort of anti-money. Running down people in our town with big houses . . . McMansions, he calls them . . . or assuming rich people got there by cheating somehow. The good news is he's not materialistic. Suspicious, controlling, bad-tempered, ill-mannered, but not materialistic.

Jerry Goss pushes all his buttons. But I'm interested in hearing him out. I get the feeling Mom is, too.

As it turns out, my bionic powers don't extend to winning every single point for the rest of the day. I do manage, however, to win every game. Every set. The whole enchilada. By five o'clock that afternoon I am the newly crowned 16-and-Under New Jersey State Champion.

When the last point is played out, I walk toward my opponent to shake hands. She stands at the net, still panting. She's short and muscular and she hit the ball like a man. Rockets, one after another, most of them fired into my backhand. A bit too predictably into my backhand. She'd revealed her strategy only a couple of points into our first game: she was going to blast me off the court, slam me all the way to Pennsylvania on the sheer power of her strokes.

So I made her run. I took the pace off every shot, moonballed them deep to her corners, followed by short drops over the net. Two games into it, she'd probably run a mile, and her balls were firing a hell of a lot slower.

I never spoke a word to her; I let my shots do all the talking. "You're out of shape!" they screamed every time she raced for the ball but didn't quite make it. "Power is no substitute for placement!" they laughed, as she exhausted herself with her slams.

"Henry Lloyd owns this tournament!" they crowed, finally, when it was all over. No mind games. No distracting comments. Just tennis, pure and simple. It felt great.

When I reach her, hand extended, I notice she's got a little fan club walking across the court toward us.

It's the Reese's gang. The ones who think "the bitch" is just "okay."

They watch me, slyly, as we shake. One whispers into the other's ear, stifles a giggle. Something inside me turns, and the great, floaty feeling I just had evaporates into something more familiar.

"Nice game," I say, grasping her hand.

"You, too," she says. "Congratulations." That's usually it, so she tries to pull away from me. But I don't let go.

"You hit that ball *so* hard!" I say, smiling. "Almost like a man."

"Thanks," she says. She actually tugs at this point, but I hold her in a death grip.

"Do you lift?" I ask her. She looks puzzled.

"You know, weight-room stuff. Because it shows. You look like you could bench-press . . . what? . . . a hundred fifty?" I flash her my most brilliant smile and release her hand. I don't wait for a reply. Her mouth has opened into a perfect little O. I glance behind her and give a short, perky wave to the gaggle.

"See you around, girls," I say, before turning on my heel and striding to the umpire's chair for the obligatory hand-

44

shake. Eva and my parents are off to one side of the court. A few paces from them, I see Jerry Goss.

When our eyes meet, he smiles calmly, and nods. Once.

* * *

He tracks us down at the hospitality tent, where we've gone to find cool drinks. I've located an icy lemonade for myself and am considering a very chewy-looking chocolate-chip cookie, when I feel a hand on my elbow.

"Henry, do you think we could talk?" Jerry asks. I glance at Mom, who nods assent; Dad has taken a trip to the Porta Potties. Jerry Goss and I find a quiet table and chairs outside the tent. We sit, and he gets right down to it.

"I enjoyed watching you play today," he begins. "You have a good game."

"Thank you," I reply. But it's not lost on me that he says "good." Not "great." It occurs to me he's seen a lot of players win state tournaments.

"So let me ask you," he continues. "What are your goals?"

"My goals?" I repeat.

"For your tennis," he says. "What sort of player do you imagine becoming?"

"The best I can be," I say automatically. What does he expect I'd say?

"And that means . . . what?" he asks.

"Well"—I smile at him—"how about winning the Jersey 16-and-Under?" He shrugs.

"Seriously," he says. Then waits. Which surprises me.

 45

"You don't think this is serious?" I reply, my voice rising a bit. "Those girls crying into their lemonade over there?" I gesture toward the hospitality tent. "They thought I was serious."

"If you think beating the stuffing out of a bunch of prepstrokers is serious tennis, then I've been misinformed," he deadpans back at me. His eyes glitter like hard, blue marbles.

"Let me fill you in on a little secret, Henry. Your opponents today? They suck. They're high school athletes whose parents have paid for a lot of expensive lessons. They'll collect a few plastic trophies, fill scrapbooks with clippings. One might even play in college. Which is fine. But I don't think that's what Henriette Lloyd has in mind for herself. Or am I wrong?"

The player in me says not to respond right away. Not to reveal how insulting it is that this dude thinks the girls I beat are a bunch of losers.

I take a long pull on my lemonade before answering him.

"What if I told you I *like* cheap plastic trophies?"

Jerry Goss throws back his head and laughs.

"I'd say, 'Sayonara, sweetheart.'" He grins. I smile, too. In spite of myself.

"So, if everyone in this tournament sucks, why are you here?"

"To see you," he replies. "People like me are in the business of checking out kids like you."

Whoa. There's no disguising my total shock. A scout from a tennis school in Florida . . . a school I've never heard of . . . has come all this way just to see *me*? I assumed he was watching lots of people.

 46

"So, back to my question," he continues. "What are your goals?"

Goals. Sure, I've got a few. I want to get my permanent driver's license. Date a really hot guy. I want my own television for my bedroom. I want to *finally* get my ears pierced. Maybe I can use this championship as leverage with Dad, get him to say yes, at last.

Of course, Jerry doesn't want to hear all that. He's talkin' game, and beyond winning the match I'm playing on a given day and massacring whoever is across the net from me at the moment, I haven't thought much about it. I love to hit balls; I love to win. But lately the only "goal" has been to do whatever Dad says so he'll get off my case.

Then, for some reason, I remember the Reese's girls. And I think of something I want.

"I want to be different."

I am different. Always have been. Always have felt. Thing is, Jerry Goss, I don't want to be hated for it. I want a trophy for it.

"Chadwick players are different. They're the best," he says. "I think Chadwick can help you reach your goal. I think you should consider coming to Chadwick."

I stifle the impulse to laugh out loud.

"Mr. Goss, that's really nice of you, but my parents don't have that kind of money." He waves his hand dismissively.

"Money is no object for a talented student," he says. The blue marbles are trained hard at me. "There are people out there who care about you and want to see you reach your potential."

"Okay, now you're creeping me out. Who are we talking about?"

"I'm not at liberty to say."

"Well, I'm not at liberty to sit here talking to you anymore if you're going to get all CIA with me. All covert, you know?"

Jerry chews on this for a little while. Then he sighs.

"Fine. But I think when I tell you, you'll understand why this has to go no further."

"We'll see."

"Ray Giordano is a friend of mine. He told me, 'Jerry, you don't want to miss this kid.' Told me you could really benefit from Chadwick."

I breathe in sharp, and deep. It all makes sense now. And he's right. Even whispering the name of my former tennis coach, Ray Giordano, in front of Dad would be disastrous.

This has to go no further.

Chapter Six

EVA

Madame DuPres was far too evil to end the torture immediately, and just tell me on the spot that I wasn't qualified to mop the floors at her school, let alone study there.

No, she promised to "be in touch," which means that for the past two weeks, every time the phone rings in our house, Rhonda responds like she's been tasered. She jumps up and races to it, answering in this unnatural, high-pitched voice that also has a trace of sickly sweet in it, "Helloooo?"

I just feel like I'm gonna hurl.

It's not like I've never been rejected. Take the time I tried out for *Coppelia*, an epic disaster, not because I danced poorly or even deserved the part (it went to a girl three years older than me, who entered the Joffrey Ballet School that year) but because my mother went psycho. When the casting director gave the lead to another girl, Rhonda drove to the theater parking lot during rehearsal one night and carefully deflated all four tires on his BMW.

She told me this herself, a little triumph in her voice.

"No one crosses my daughter," she said, smiling and putting her hand over mine.

It felt like I was living with Michael Corleone's female alter ego, capable of unspeakable acts of retribution behind a cool facade. I didn't know how to tell her the part hadn't meant all that much to me.

Unlike this audition with the New York School of Dance. For the first time in a long time, I'm hungry. Not for fame or attention or bragging rights; that's Rhonda's territory. For . . . perfection. For achieving the highest level of artistic perfection possible, whether that happens on a stage or in a rehearsal studio.

I want it. And that's scary. Because what do I do if I don't get it?

The ride home from the audition for Madame DuPres was a total Rhonda stress fest. The usual speeding and weaving in and out of traffic, plus the interrogation.

"Did she say *anything* about how you danced?" Rhonda pressed.

"Ambitious, Mom. She said it was ambitious."

"Well, I would think she wants her dancers to be ambitious. To challenge themselves. So that might be a very positive thing. Did she seem positive?"

"She was completely unreadable."

"Was she friendly? Did you chat?"

"Nope."

"Did she ask you about yourself? Try to get a sense of who you are?"

"Nope."

"So she didn't ask you any questions?"

"She asked me if I'd ever seen *Swan Lake*."

"And what did you tell her?"

"I said yes, probably a dozen times." Rhonda paused.

"And?"

"And what?"

"What did she say next?"

"She said nothing next. She smiled, I danced, she said she'd be in touch. That's it."

"She smiled?"

"Yes, she smiled."

"Well, that's good, isn't it? She was probably impressed that you're so familiar with the ballet." Pause.

"Did she say whether she thought you pulled it off? The interpretation?"

"Ambitious, Mom. She said it was ambitious."

Weirdly enough, I haven't mentioned the audition to Henry. Partly because I don't want to jinx things. But partly because . . . well, she wouldn't understand. Henry thinks I'm great, and she'd say something like, "Eva, you're amazing. Of course you'll get in." She never appreciates that I'm completely average and rejection is a real possibility. Sometimes her confidence in me is hard to take.

But I decide to tell her today: cake day. I haven't done one of my cakes in ages, and this baby's long overdue. Not that I'll be able to eat it. I've barely been able to manage much besides Pink Decadence since the audition. It's not intentional. I just can't swallow when I'm nervous or upset. My throat sort of closes up, a little door shuts and this voice says, *"No! Don't eat that!"*

But Henry, who eats everything and anything, always adores my cakes. When I tell her I'm whipping one up in honor of her state championship triumph, she arrives half an hour early.

"Hungry?" I say when she bangs through the kitchen screen door. I'm putting the final touches on my masterpiece: a lemon cake shaped like a tennis racket, with cream-cheese frosting. I've borrowed Henry's racket to use as a model, and every detail is perfect, down to the tiny letters that read "Wilson" on the grip tape. When Henry bursts in, I'm piping the last of the strings.

"Oh. My. *Gawd!*" she exclaims. *"Yer da bomb, goil!"* Joisey-speak. Henry loves talkin' Jersey. She leans over and sniffs. "Lemon!"

"Of course, your favorite," I tell her. I step back to take a look. The strings are a little wiggly. But the Wilson logo looks good.

"Eva, I'm serious, this might be one of your all-time best cakes. It's amazing!"

"I don't know. I still like the 'Hello, Kitty' I did for your sweet sixteen."

"This is better."

"And don't forget Elmo. Elmo was wonderful."

"Elmo was toxic, Eva. You had to use so much red dye to get his fur right that our teeth and tongues were stained for days and Frenemy Paige barfed. Come to think of it, maybe Elmo *was* the best cake ever. . . ." I elbow Henry, and she laughs. Her perfect teeth look brilliantly white in her tan face. Her eyes are bright blue. I want jewels that color. The purest blue of a spring sky.

"Let's just admire it for a while," Henry suggests, pulling a stool up to the granite countertop. The two of us sit, gazing at my confectionary wonder and breathing in the rich scent of lemon extract and cream cheese. It's one of my favorite flavors, too, and I'm wondering if I could manage a slice. I can't remember the last time I ate cake. Elmo might have been the last, and that was when we were . . . what? Twelve?

Maybe a piece of the grip, where the cake is narrow and the frosting is thick. . . .

Yeah, right, eating cake after sitting on your duff all day? That'll get you into the New York School of Dance for sure.

I suddenly have this uncontrollable urge to wrap my legs around my neck. Instead, I jump off the stool, take a deep breath and go up on *pointe*. In my sneakers. Henry grimaces.

"I don't know *how* you can make yourself do that," she says.

"Well, I don't know how you can make yourself chase little yellow balls in the hot sun all day," I say serenely. I return my heels to the floor, first position, then rise again, this time circling my right arm in a sweeping, grand gesture. It feels good to move. Henry smiles at me and shakes her head.

"So . . . I auditioned for a summer camp," I say. Henry is edging one finger toward the cake. I slap it away.

 53

"Auditioned . . . so it's ballet camp?" she asks.

"Of course. It's in New York."

"Wow. Does that mean you'll have to go into the city every day?"

"They have dorms, but that costs more money. I don't know . . . I mean, I probably won't even get in. It's really competitive." Now she's picked up a fork. She's going to dive right into the cake without first cutting a slice.

"Don't go there, girlfriend," I say threateningly. "We're still admiring." She puts the fork down and sighs. I return to my toes, then lower myself to my heels.

"All summer?" Henry asks. I nod, and she makes this little pouty face.

"Hey, I need something to do while you're in Florida! Otherwise I'll get stuck hanging out with Paige and Company. Eating bags of Skittles and getting mani-pedis at the mall." Henry snorts. She has this great, unladylike habit of snorting when she laughs. Another reason I love her.

"First of all, you don't eat Skittles," she says. "Second, your toes are too ruined for pedis; third, I know your families are friends but you *don't* have to spend time with that witch; and fourth, I am *so* not going to Florida. You should've heard my father last night. . . ."

The sound of the kitchen door opening interrupts us.

"Eva, *what* are you doing?"

The return of Rhonda. Perfect.

"Oh, possibly the only thing Henry Lloyd *can't* do," I say

breezily. I *piqué* step over to my mother, *en pointe*, arms over my head, and plant a kiss on her cheek.

"*Not* without *pointe* shoes, please. Especially on a tile floor," she says. "That's a good way to injure yourself." I return to earth, arms at my sides. "I have a few grocery bags in the car, if you girls don't mind."

As Henry and I start for the kitchen door, Rhonda can't resist asking.

"Eva, did anyone call? Have you heard from Madame?"

"No," I reply, walking fast.

"Madame?" Henry repeats. "What, are you taking French lessons now?"

I shoulder past Henry, out to the car and the groceries, muttering, "She's making me crazy," but before we escape the phone rings. Rhonda practically leaps in its direction, and even though I wish—god, how I wish—that I didn't care, my stomach lurches and this morning's Pink Decadence threatens to become Pink Reappearance.

Over the sound of our feet crunching along the driveway gravel, I hear, "Helloooo?"

55

Chapter Seven

HENRY

I'm off the dogs the following Saturday. Given I just won states, I think I should get a whole month off dogs, but Dad laughs at this suggestion, like I've made a good joke.

Anyway, dog reprieve means Mom and I are free to attend Eva's dance recital. This is something she does twice a year, a fairly low-key event put on by the Sonia Fleisch Ballet School, where she takes lessons. Mrs. Fleisch's student recitals include everyone from Eva, the future prima ballerina, to chubby, pink-leotard-clad six-year-olds demonstrating first position for wildly applauding parents.

These recitals are low-key, as opposed to the high-key, superstress stuff Eva usually does, like dancing as one of the kid angels in the New York City Ballet's *Nutcracker* last year. I haven't seen Eva dance in ages, a fact I mention to Mom as we settle into our aluminum chairs and open our paper programs.

"You know, you're right," she muses. "I can't remember the last thing we saw her in."

My mind scrolls back through the long list of Eva's

appearances. Two winters ago, she was Clara in *The Nutcracker*, for a children's repertory company in Bergenfield. And for the New Jersey Youth Ballet in Hillsborough. And for our high school. She signed on for three Claras during the month of December, a scheduling nightmare that required the Bergenfield folks to double-cast the role for two shows. But they did it. Anything to snag Eva. She's a hot property in the kid ballet world.

"We saw one of the Claras," I tell Mom.

"Yes!" she exclaims. "At your school. How could I forget?"

"How could you forget the Nutcracker Prince?" I smile slyly. Mom gives me a playful slap on the knee.

"Be nice," she says, but she's grinning. Boy dancers are in short supply at my high school, and the guy they dredged up to play the Nutcracker Prince was not . . . good. Eva, however, never said one bad thing about him. When I brought it up, she cut me short.

"I think he did a very convincing job slaying the Mouse King," she said. Eva is probably the nicest person in the world.

Which makes you wonder: where the hell did she get a mother like Rhonda?

That question crosses my mind almost every time I see Rhonda. Like now. As Mom and I quietly look over our programs, she lands in the empty seat next to us, a highlighted burst of tousled hyperactivity. Preoccupied, abrupt and ever-stressed. People who know her expect this behavior. First timers to Rhonda World think she's unbelievably rude.

She throws her arms around Mom's shoulders and gives her a quick peck on the cheek.

"You are so sweet for coming! I saw you across the room and had to say hello. I haven't seen you in ages!"

"How are you, Rhonda?" Mom smiles.

"Oh . . . it's crazed. But good. Things are good. I guess Henry's told you: Eva's been accepted to study at the New York School of Dance. We *finally* found out this week. We'd been wondering *what* is the holdup? But they came through, and with a nice scholarship. So it's great. Really. This will be her last performance with Sonia. You're here for her swan song!"

The lights begin to dim, and Rhonda jumps up.

"There's a little reception after the recital. We'll catch up then!"

Rhonda darts across the room, then settles into a chair next to Eva's dad, who looks as if he was about to nod off. I really like her dad. The guy is so calm you wonder if he's got a pulse. Wonder how he and Rhonda ever hooked up . . .

The curtains part, revealing a line of six little girls in tutus and tights. From the audience comes a long, low parental "oooooh," flashbulbs, and the blue glow of video cameras from every corner of the room. The program promises Eva at the very end, so Mom and I have to politely clap through a lot of tutus.

Eva got her call from New York a couple of days after I played the state tournament. Apparently the big "Madame" herself called the Smiths to offer Eva a spot at the school, and Rhonda practically had an aneurysm, she was that excited. Eva called me late that night, after Rhonda dialed everyone in the greater metropolitan area with the news.

 58

"Are you sitting?" Eva said when I picked up the phone. "I got accepted to the New York School of Dance."

"Shut *up!*" I exclaimed. "Eva . . . congratulations!"

"I'm still pinching myself. I can't believe it."

"Well, I can. Maybe now you'll finally start believing everyone who tells you how incredible you are. How's Rhonda taking the news?"

"Let's just say she may spontaneously combust."

I laughed. "*That* I gotta see!"

"No, you don't," Eva replied. "This much parental enthusiasm is way scary."

Eva went on to give me the details. She'd start this summer, five days a week, going into the city for a sort of ballet "camp." Really intense, full days of dance. Then, toward the end of August, a few of the very best girls would be invited to stay on for the full-year program. They'd take classes at the High School of Performing Arts in the morning, then head over to the School of Ballet in the afternoons. After that, she told me, they could begin auditioning for spots in professional ballet companies.

"But I am getting *way* ahead of myself," she exclaimed. "The chances of getting invited to the full-year program are one in a million."

"Oh, so there are a million other dancers going to your summer camp?" I told her. "Eva, it's a good thing you're so much better at ballet than you are at math."

As the tutu torture draws to a close, I elbow Mom, who has her eyes closed. Eva is next. As the young dancers leave the stage, the curtains open. I see my friend on the floor, one leg extended, arms draped gracefully over her head and hands brushing her toes. The music begins and instantly I recognize it. The grand finale to *Swan Lake*. Rhonda wasn't kidding.

Years ago, for one of Eva's birthdays, her parents took us to Lincoln Center to see a performance of *Swan Lake*. It was my first professional ballet, and probably the third time that Eva had seen this one. But it was her favorite, and she had begged her parents to bring me along. She wanted me to see the snowflake lights.

New York's Lincoln Center is built to impress. Tier upon tier of crushed-velvet seats, gold boxes ascending the walls, an enormous orchestra pit containing a full contingent of black-clad musicians. And giant crystal lights, suspended from the three-story ceiling by long cables. They're round, with crystal-studded arms sticking out at different lengths. When a performance begins, the house dims, the immense stage curtains part and the great lights float upward, like snowflakes blown to heaven. Eva was determined that I would see them.

I thought they were cheesy. Fake. Plastic. Had to be, no way those were real crystals. I couldn't believe Eva thought they looked like snowflakes, and as I watched them rise on their cables I turned to her, a sarcastic comment at the ready. But the look on her face cut me short.

She was smiling, her eyes brimming with tears, gazing at the lights as though she beheld an angelic vision. She believed, she completely believed, the magic. The lights, the music, the whole crushed-velvet gilded thing. She reached out one hand and grasped mine.

"Isn't it just like I told you?" she breathed.

Every once in a while I get lucky, and something happens to prevent me from making a complete jerk out of myself. Eva's hand, on my wrist, was one of those lucky things. I swallowed, took a deep breath and smiled back at her. Somehow, I kept my mouth shut and managed not to wreck her birthday.

As the music from the CD player throbs, Eva rises in one smooth motion as if lifted by invisible strings. She does not dance like a swan. She is not "like" anything. She *is* the swan. Despite the tinny accompaniment and the audience full of squirming children, Eva convinces us that she is the most beautiful creature in the world, that she is dying, and that we are sadder than we have ever been before. Even musically challenged me appreciates that I'm seeing something special up there on the stage, and for a moment I forget that this is my best friend, Jersey Girl Eva, who came to my tennis match looking like Lawrence of Arabia.

We stand, clapping madly, when she's done.

"Was she amazing, or what?" I shout into Mom's ear as the applause goes on and on. Mom nods but her lips form a thin, tight line.

"What?" I ask. Mrs. Fleisch returns to the stage and announces that everyone is welcome to gather for some light refreshment. Families begin filing toward the exit doors. Mom still doesn't answer.

"What?" I repeat. "Didn't you think that was awesome?"

"It was incredible," she replies.

"So why the look?" We're moving slowly with the jostling, chatty crowd. When Mom does speak, she leans close to me.

"Is Eva dieting, do you know?" she asks quietly.

I sigh impatiently. It's bad enough Dad is always going on about Eva's eating habits, but now Mom? I mean, when is Eva *not* dieting? She's been drinking Diet Coke and counting calories for as long as I can remember.

"Mom, she's a dancer. Her whole life is a diet."

"She's an athlete," Mom corrects. "She works her body as hard as you do, and she needs to feed it."

"Fine, point taken. So why are you bringing this up right now?" I ask.

"She's too thin, Henry," Mom replies.

"Oh, give me a break! She's always been thin."

"Not like this," Mom insists. "Not so thin that you can count her vertebrae and see her ribs through her back."

"Your problem is that you think anyone who isn't built like Venus or Serena is undernourished," I joke. "You're beginning to sound like Dad." Mom smiles ruefully.

"Your father is not always wrong," she says.

As we move with the crowd toward the reception room, my mind scrolls back to the last meal I saw Eva eat. We'd all gone to Ruby Tuesday following the state tournament. As we stood on line at the salad bar, I noticed she was shivering.

"Are you cold?" I asked her.

"Freezing," she replied. "Is this a restaurant or a walk-in refrigerator?" I slipped off my Windbreaker and put it over her shoulders. I was still burning up from playing six-plus hours of tennis in the sun.

As we moved down the line, I shoveled mesclun mix and chopped carrots onto my plate. A heap of garbanzo beans, shredded cheddar, tomatoes. They had potato salad, which I adore. I noticed Eva primly arranging a little fan of colorful vegetables on her plate. One beet slice. Two cucumbers. A strip of green pepper, two cherry tomatoes. Lettuce sprinkled in the middle.

"This is a gross salad bar," she muttered to me. "The macaroni salad looks like worms squirming in shiny glue. The potato salad is like chunks of plaster of Paris."

"Yum," I said to her as I slapped a big scoop of it onto my plate. But she didn't smile. She turned to head back to our table.

"Is that all you're going to take?" I couldn't help asking. She shrugged, then plucked two packets of saltines from the basket.

"Oh yeah, *now* we're pigging out," I said, laughing.

"I'm not that hungry," she replied, and walked away.

At the entrance to the crowded reception room, Eva stands just inside, with her parents and Mrs. Fleisch. She still wears her ballet costume, and her skin glistens with perspiration. She reminds me of a china doll: porcelain pale, freckles sprinkled across her nose and shoulders. Her long, red-gold

 63

hair is gathered into a tight, smooth bun. Other families gather around them, and it reminds me of the receiving line at a wedding I attended. Mom and I move toward the dessert table, but not before I manage to catch Eva's eye and flash her a big thumbs-up.

I polish off two of the biggest and best brownies known to mankind, and wash them down with sweet red punch before Eva appears at my elbow.

"Thank goodness that's over," she breathes into my ear. "My cheeks hurt from smiling."

"Get used to it, girl," I tell her. *"Yer a stah."* I put my arms around her shoulders and squeeze.

"Oh my *gawd!*" she exclaims. "A *stah?* Really? Me?"

"A dancin' *stah.* From *Joisey."* Eva giggles. She loves talkin' Jersey.

I glance down at the desserts and notice that I'm not the only one who has discovered the to-die-for brownies. There are three left. I scoop one up in a white paper napkin.

"This is a life-changing brownie," I say seriously. "You must have one." I lift the brownie to Eva's mouth, holding it for her to take a bite.

She backs away as if I were holding a snake. Her eyes actually widen in horror.

"No!" she exclaims. "I mean . . . I'm really full. We ate breakfast late, and I never feel like eating right after I dance. But I'm so thirsty! Is there anything to drink?"

She pivots and walks quickly down the length of the table toward a bowl filled with ice and bottles of sparkling water. I stare at her retreating back before she disappears in the crush of people. Her shoulder blades stick out like stunted wings. Beginning at her neck, you can see lumps along her spine, knobby vertebrae that disappear into her waist. The bones that frame her back fan out from the spine like long fingers just beneath her skin.

As if some creature had her in its clutches.

Chapter Eight

EVA

"I can't wait to show you this. You are going to be *so* psyched."

"So why do I feel *so* nervous?"

Henry and I sit in my bedroom, eyes glued to the laptop, where, amazingly enough, I am introducing her to Facebook. My latest obsession in particular: a page I've created for her. And a group I've joined for her: the Chadwick Tennis Academy Summer Camp group. It's a crucial step in her education.

Because Henry's leaving for Chadwick. In a week.

To her credit, she has at least *heard* of Facebook, but up until this point she hasn't joined. I realize it's not her fault that she is cyberculturally inept: Mark polices her computer access with secret police–like zeal. It's not that he suspects she might post lewd pictures of herself, or knowingly join chat rooms with pedophiles. He just thinks everyone's out to stalk his daughter, and the computer is one hole he is bound and determined to plug.

Anyway, several days ago the gods of tennis and ballet got together . . . just like our parents, downstairs at this very

66

moment, sipping gin and tonics and discussing their daughters' brilliant careers over a smoking grill . . . and good fortune rained down on Henry and me. Within days of my hearing from Madame DuPres, Chadwick offered Hen a summer scholarship. Depending on how things go, that could become a full-year scholarship.

How Mark agreed to this is beyond me. Henry says the price was right. Plus he thinks it's just for the summer. Plus her mom went to the mat for her. Voices were raised to epic volumes, she says.

I think they slipped something into his nightly cocktail to make him less controlling.

I've opened Henry's page, and a photo of her appears on the screen. It's a picture I took in May, at our school's spring formal. She's wearing makeup and clip-on, gold hoop earrings.

"Hey! That's me!" she exclaims.

"Glam, don't you think?" I say.

"Yeah, but I'm not glam, Eva," Henry says. "This is false advertising."

"This is a smokescreen," I explain. "Think: everyone is checking out everyone else. All the Chadwick girls are looking at your picture and thinking, 'No comp! We'll take pretty girl in straight sets.' Meanwhile, the guys are thinking, 'Hot babe!'" Henry looks confused.

"Why would anyone at Chadwick read this?" she asks.

"Because you've joined the Chadwick Tennis Academy Summer Camp group, and I've already garnered forty-eight friends for you," I tell her. I glance at the screen. "Correction!

Fifty-one friends. Three more requests were answered overnight. Oh, and look! You have a message."

"Message?" Henry asks, blankly.

"People who have friended you, or whom you have friended, can leave messages," I explain.

"Cool," Henry says. "Who messaged me?" I don't bother to explain that while "friend" is a verb, "message" is not, so I just read it:

"Hola, Henriette! My name is Yolanda Cruz, and I'm going to be your roommate! I'm 15, cubanita, from Miami. Write to me!
Your roommate, Yoly
P.S. Quinceaneras Rule!"

"*What* rules?" Henry says.

"We need to email her *immediately* and set her straight about this Henriette thing," I say. "Didn't she read your profile? I wrote very clearly, 'Nickname: Henry.' I will murder anyone who calls you anything else."

"Hold it. You wrote a profile of me?"

"Of course," I say.

"Eva!" Henry shrieks.

"What?" I reply, innocently. "This is how you make friends! 'I love you, you love me . . .'" I sing the theme song of *Barney & Friends*. We loved Barney when we were little. She grabs me around the shoulders.

 68

"Show me," she says, faux-menacingly.

I point to the profile box on the screen and read aloud:

"Henriette Lloyd. Age: 16. Home: Ridgefield, New Jersey. Nickname: Henry. Status: Single. I love chocolate, great-looking guys who don't know they're great-looking, music, my backyard ball machine and tennis . . . but not necessarily in that order. I hate liverwurst, stuck-up guys who don't know they're stuck-up, my backyard ball machine and losing . . . not necessarily in that order. Jersey Tomatoes Are the Best!"

Henry looks completely confused.

"I've never eaten liverwurst in my life," she says.

"Trust me, you would hate it."

"Eva!" she shrieks again. This is becoming a pattern.

"What?" I counter. "It's cute. It's funny. And it's not controversial; everyone agrees about liverwurst, and there is not a single stuck-up guy on the planet who *knows* he is stuck-up."

She puts her head in her hands.

"Let's check out the other happy campers," I say brightly.

The Chadwick group appears on the screen as an array of thumbnail photos. Most are pretty traditional head shots. A few are these teeny action pictures you can barely make out of someone swinging a tennis racket. Everyone, in every picture, however, looks tan.

"Promise me you will use sunblock," I say, scrolling through the photos. "These kids are going to look like alligators before they're thirty."

"Click on him," Henry says, ignoring my upbeat observation. She points to a cute blond. She's getting into the spirit of Facebook.

I click and his photo enlarges. He is seriously hot, and he has great teeth. I'm a little OCD about teeth. I mean, they are the gateway to the French kiss, a phenomenon I've yet to experience but whose success I imagine is wholly dependent on fresh breath and sound oral care. Blond dude has awesome ones: very straight, highly polished white perfection gleaming from a broad smile in an unfortunately overly tan face. Hair is good, though. Kind of long, with these light streaks.

"'Jonathan Dundas,'" I read aloud from his profile. "'Home: Salinas, California. Age: 17. Nickname: Jon.' Hmm. That's original. Okay, here's what he has to say about himself: 'I love the high you get after groovin' on backhands for an hour in 80-degree heat, then jumpin' into an icy pool. I love workin' out, anything that gets my heart rate up, especially if I can do it outside. I like chillin' with friends, playin' guitar, especially around a fire, at night. Life is Good then.'" Henry snorts, and we look at each other.

"Eeeeew!" we both squeal simultaneously, then dissolve into laughter. This is our signature reaction to guys who are totally full of themselves.

"He has completely negated the allure of his excellent teeth," I say.

"No way are those streaks natural," Henry adds.

"Next," I say.

We go on like this for a good half hour, rating the guys from Hot But Pretentious (Jon Dundas), to Super Jock With Kissing Potential (very buff fellow from Florida, more great teeth), to Foreign and Hopelessly Incomprehensible (some Czech kid with no vowels in his name). There are plenty of girls, too, but they all blend together for me, like one giant Megan or Amber, with tight ponytails, freckled turned-up noses and muscle definition in their arms. Henry, however, seems fascinated by them. She leans forward, head close to the screen, reading their tennis "pedigrees": what tournaments they've entered, and won; how long they've played; whether they work with private coaches or have attended other academies or camps.

I watch as she stalks her prey. To her, the Chadwick guys are an interesting diversion. But the girls? They are already on the other side of the net.

After we've read every friend profile, Henry sits back. She looks thoughtful.

"I doubt anyone will get the tomatoes thing," she says.

"Ah," I reply. "Funny you should mention that." I go over to my closet, where I've hidden a box. It's wrapped with this great paper I bought that has little tennis rackets all over it. *That* was a find.

"What's this?" she asks.

"A very appropriate going-away gift. Let me ask you, although I'm sure I already know the answer. What are your plans for T-shirt night?"

"What's T-shirt night?" Henry's brow furrows.

"Hen, *what* are you going to do without me?" I sigh. "It's on the Chadwick website, and I'll bet it came in that orientation packet you got. Every camper is supposed to wear a T-shirt that describes where they're from. As a fellow Jersey Girl, I thought it was appropriate that I gift you with the perfect T-shirt representing the Garden State."

Henry looks touched.

"Eva, that's so thoughtful. It almost makes up for the liverwurst."

"Open it," I prompt.

Henry rips the amazing paper. (I have to hold my breath. I always carefully pull off the tape and unfold the paper in a single, intact sheet.) From the gift box within, she pulls out a short-sleeved white T-shirt.

"'Jersey Tomatoes Are the Best,'" she reads aloud, then gasps. The words are emblazoned across the chest of the shirt, just beneath the neck. Beneath the words are two strategically positioned plump, ripe red tomatoes.

"You will be the rage of the opening-night ceremonies," I tell her.

"I will be the slut of the opening-night ceremonies!" she exclaims. "No way can I wear this. It'd be like *asking* guys to stare at my . . . tomatoes!"

"Only the perverted guys will stare, and *that's* how you'll sort them out from the nice guys," I say.

"Any guy over the age of ten with a pulse will stare!" Henry insists.

"Put it on," I suggest. Henry yanks the T-shirt over her

head, and we move to my full-length mirror for a look. The tomatoes fall precisely where they should.

"Let's go downstairs and see what Mark thinks," I suggest.

"You are so nuts!" Henry is yelling and laughing at the same time. She begins prancing around in front of the mirror, sticking her tomatoes out as far as possible.

"Look out," she says to her reflection in a deep, sexy voice. "I'm going to kick your ass in straight sets."

Henry cavorts like this for a few minutes, and I stand back from the mirror. No girl wants to get a look at herself side by side with Henriette Lloyd. It's like agreeing to pose for photographs with a Russian supermodel. Makes your own thighs expand.

Henry finally flops on my bed. I flop beside her.

"I'm gonna miss you," she says quietly.

"I know. You'll be completely lost without me." She reaches behind her, grabs a pillow and bats me over the head with it.

"You're welcome," I say.

"You do understand that I can't possibly wear it?" I roll over and look Henry in the eyes.

"No. Explain to me why you can't do something wacky and funny *for once*."

"Gimme a break, Eva. Would *you*?"

"Henry Lloyd, I have just one thing to say: Tinky Winky." Her eyes widen.

"Oh god. That's right," she says.

Freshman year, October, Henry and I gathered our courage

and went to our school's Halloween dance. We both loathe and despise school dances: Henry, because despite her looks she is shy around guys, and me, because it kills me to watch my peers grinding and sweating to bad music and calling it dance. Anyway, dress code for the night was "costumes optional," so most people wore jeans and a dumb hat, or some lame pirate thing. Paige came as a hula girl and wore a top that was nothing more than two coconut shells and some bungee cords.

I got hold of a totally authentic Teletubbies suit and came as Tinky Winky.

At first no one knew who I was, which is a remarkably liberating thing. I could go up to the cutest guys in our school and body-slam them with my enormous, plush purple bottom, and they'd start to dance with me. They thought it was way fun to grind with Tinky Winky, and they'd laugh. With me, for a change. Not at me.

The fact is I've been getting laughed at since I started going to school with my hair in a ballet bun. Since I started getting excused from gym because my mother felt it might lead to a dance-career-ending injury. Started carrying umbrellas on sunny days, or wearing Capezio leggings and short, flowing dresses instead of jeans and T-shirts to school. I've been the object of other kids' jokes from the moment they figured out I wasn't like the rest of the pack.

What Henry doesn't *get* is that if you want to survive that sort of thing, you have to make it work for you. Play up the things they mock, like sliding into leg splits at inappropriate moments, or wearing eccentric styles of dress. Then they start to think you're in on the joke. They think you like them, and they like you, and they never realize they're mean little bastards who lacerate your feelings every day.

Here's the thing: Henry's a competitor who never lets her game face slip. I'm a performer. A master performer.

At some point that Halloween night I started to actually dance: a run of *soutenus*, a split. Kids went wild, applauded, and I heard, "Oh my god, that's Eva!" The cute girls reclaimed their cute boyfriends at that point, but the dance was nearly over, so it was fine.

Footsteps creak on the wooden stairs outside my bedroom. Henry sits up and pulls off the tomatoes T-shirt.

"Girls? Burgers are ready," I hear my dad say through the closed door.

"Coming," I answer. Henry is staring at the T-shirt in her lap.

"I wish I were more like you," she finally says. "But I'm only brave when I'm holding a racket and firing balls at someone." I place my hand over hers.

"Just bring it," I say. "Deal?"

"Deal," she agrees.

We head downstairs, and happy party sounds drift up to us. The sliding screen door opening and closing. The clink of ice in glasses. Smell of meat sizzling on the grill. My mother's sharp, high-pitched laugh. I stifle the urge to turn tail and run back to Facebook. All lined up properly on my computer screen.

If I'm so brave, why do I always feel like I might just . . . scream?

Chapter Nine

HENRY

Boca is *so* not New Jersey.

For one thing: palm trees. I've never seen one in real life, and now I see them everywhere. Lining the highway, dotting the gazillion golf courses we drive past and shading the entrances to these walled, gated developments that look like private clubs from the outside and have names like Bella Terra, or Golden Grand Harbor.

Another thing: the birds. I've already fallen in love with this funny white bird that has a long, curved beak. Mom calls it an ibis and tells me it's practically the symbol of South Florida. For a girl whose entire bird experience is limited to sparrows, blue jays, crows, robins and an occasional cardinal, watching an ibis step with its long, pencil-thin legs through marsh grass, and poke that unlikely nose in the water, is completely fascinating.

Finally: the light. It's so different from the light up north that you've got to wonder whether a whole other, way more intense sun hangs over Florida. It makes the colors different. Red in Jersey doesn't burn the way red burns in Florida. Yellow, orange, green . . . they seem brighter and weightless down here. Plus everyone wears these colorful clothes that just *go* with the sun. You see all these grandmas in teal, lime and magenta. Dressed in fruit-yogurt-colored golf shorts, with leathery faces bronzed burnt umber.

Eva would be horrified. I imagine her strolling the streets of Boca Raton dressed in a snow-white burka, carrying a parasol. *And* slathered with sunblock.

I'm determined to get a picture of a really tan person and email it to her. I've got my camera out now, as Mom and Dad and I sit at this little outdoor café, looking over lunch menus. We're a few miles away from Chadwick, near the ocean, and our table is shaded by a big awning. We've been on the road for three days, driving straight on through from Bergen County to Palm Beach County, stopping only for bathroom breaks, meals or sleeping in a motel off the highway. Check-in is one p.m.

I'm trying to calm my nerves by looking through the viewfinder of my camera. I am absolutely surprised by myself. Henriette Lloyd, Tennis Terminator, is officially freaked out. My hands, attempting to hold the camera steady as I survey the other patrons through the tiny peephole, shake noticeably.

"You know," I say, scanning the patio, "I feel like L. L. Bean at Paris Hilton's birthday party."

"Excuse me?" Mom asks.

I gesture to our clothes. We each wear some shade of tan shorts, and primary-colored, short-sleeved shirts. My parents wear sneakers with ankle-high socks; I've got my favorite Teva flip-flops. The other diners are dressed like tropical parrots. Men wear shirts with dizzying patterns. Women wear bright sundresses and glittery jewelry. Their sandals are studded with colorful beads. Every female toenail and fingernail is painted.

Dad chuckles. Nice to see *some* semblance of a smile on his face.

Mom looks at her watch. She swivels in her chair and her eyes dart impatiently.

"I'm going to find out whether anyone plans to take our order," she announces, and walks briskly from the table. Mom's usually pretty patient in restaurants, so this surprises me. Dad doesn't seem to notice anything odd. He looks like he has something else on his mind.

"Henry," he begins. I recognize the tone. "You know I haven't been too keen on sending you to this school."

Oh god, not this again. Can we please not have a scene in a restaurant right now?

"Uh, yeah, you weren't shy about how you felt," I reply dryly.

"I'm still not sure this is the right thing for you," he says firmly. "But as I've said, and as I've promised your mother, I'm willing to give it a try. At least for the summer."

"Dad, it's just camp," I said. Repeated, for the millionth time. "How many kids go to summer camp?"

He puts up his hand. Stops me, right there.

"No, Henry, it's not just summer camp. I don't want you to be naïve about this." I shift in my chair.

"This is the big leagues, Henry. Kids here are getting groomed."

Poodles get groomed. Horses get groomed. But kids?

"You're not used to this heat. You're not used to this level of physical pressure."

"We've been through this, Dad . . . ," I try.

"If something hurts, stop. Go to the trainer right away. Never play through pain."

"Dad?"

"Hydrate. Lots of water before, during and after workouts."

"I'll be the Poland Spring Queen, Mr. Lloyd."

"Most of all: trust your instincts. You're a good kid. You have good instincts. If something doesn't feel right, say it. Never be afraid to say no."

I say no all the time. You just never listen.

Mom returns, ending the lecture. She flashes Dad this knowing look.

"The waitress is coming," she says to me. Then she reaches into her bag and pulls out a small, gift-wrapped box. She hands it to Dad.

"Henry, we thought that since you're going to be so far away, you might like to have something to help you stay in touch." He hands me the box.

"Oooh," I say. Medium light. Nothing rattles when I shake

it. I know what I *hope* is in here, but I'm afraid to let myself in for disappointment, so I just rip it open fast and . . .

˙ "Yes! Oh, awesome! Thank you *so* much!" A cell phone. Not just a cell phone: an iPhone. This is a complete and total great surprise. Then, as I remove the phone from its box, it rings. It blares Krystal Harris's song "Supergirl."

And a photo pops up. A girl in a ballet leotard.

"Hmm," Mom says. A very exaggerated "hmm." "I wonder who could possibly be calling you?"

"Better answer it," Dad says, grinning.

"How?" I exclaim, laughing. He leans over and taps the photo with his finger. I lift the phone to my ear.

"Hello?" I say, hesitantly.

"Assure me you are wearing sunblock," says a familiar voice.

"Oh my god!" I laugh. "Were you in on this with them?"

"Are you kidding? I advised them all the way," Eva says. "They went all out; I think they're going to miss you. So, tell me: how's Florida?"

"Flat. Sunny. Hot. Very cool birds, very colorful clothing. The natives are stylin'.'"

"Would I hate it?"

"You'd like being warm."

"Where are you now?"

"We're at this lunch place near the ocean, sitting outside, and it's around ninety. How did you know to call me?"

"Your mother just phoned. How does it feel to be completely set up?"

"I'm getting used to it. Especially after the Facebook thing."

 80

"That phone takes pictures. Send me some. Tonight. Promise."

"How 'bout now? I'll show you this restaurant."

"Excellent, but I want the dorm room, too."

"You're amazing, Eva."

"I know. So go back to your French fries. I miss you." I press "end."

"That was very cool," I say, smiling at my parents. "Thank you."

*   *   *

The thing I can't get over is their bags. I've seen some of these bags before: advertised in *Tennis* magazine. Enormous, with capacity for five rackets, not to mention all the water, food, towels, extra clothes, extra shoes and who knows what else you could possibly want during a match. Naturally, each has a logo in big, splashy letters: Wilson. Fila. Head. These are the sorts of bags I assumed six-figure professionals carried, not kids at a summer camp.

We're standing several campers deep in the registration line, beyond the shade of the awning set up over the long table where smiling Chadwick people are handing out room keys and directing players to the dorms. It's hot in the sun, and I'm dying to move forward, but some mother is holding up the line, asking a million questions about the vegetarian options in the dining hall.

I don't know anyone who has five rackets. I think Mike Adams has two. Only last week Dad bought me a second, and that's because the camp requires it.

Stop it, Henry. Deep breath, girl. Just because they accessorize like pros doesn't mean they play like pros.

"Excuse me. Are you Henriette Lloyd?" A girl's voice speaks behind us.

I recognize Yolanda Cruz instantly from her Facebook photo. But even without the photo I would have identified her and her family in this lineup of disproportionately trim, blond people.

Yolanda's little brothers and sisters all look like mini versions of her. Black hair, complexions like creamy coffee, brown eyes so dark you can't see the pupils. They cluster close to their parents, and in addition to being remarkably well-behaved for a bunch of children forced to wait on a line in the hot sun, they are impeccably dressed. Even the next-to-littlest, a guy who might be all of four, wears pressed shorts, a belt and a shirt neatly tucked in.

"Umm, yeah. But it's *Henry*," I reply, surprised at how awkward I feel. "Yolanda, right?" She's short, this Yolanda Cruz, and . . . stocky. Not fat, although when she smiles her cheeks look like these two round apples. I can't imagine she moves very well on the court.

She puts out her hand, which seems a little formal, but her face melts into this expression of relief. I notice that she stands beside *two* rackets, each zipped into individual covers, and leaning against a square, brown suitcase.

"Excuse me, can we move forward, please?" Some mom standing behind the Cruz clan sounds impatient, and I realize we've advanced in line. As we shuffle toward the table, nudging our luggage ahead with our feet, my mom introduces herself to Yolanda's mom.

"You look just like your Facebook picture," Yolanda begins. "I recognized you right off."

Hmm. I don't think that looks anything like me, but okay. . . .

"Did you fly into Fort Lauderdale?" she continues.

"Actually, we drove."

"¡Ay, Dios mío!" she exclaims. The family standing in front of us turns and looks. "Straight through?"

"Oh, no, we stopped at night. Twice," I add. Yolanda turns to the little brother with the belt.

"How would you like that, Mr. I-Get-Carsick?" she says to him. "Three days in the car?" He looks at me shyly, shakes his head no, then buries his face in his sister's hip. I hear him whisper to her. "*Sí, es muy bonita,*" she replies quietly.

"He thinks you're very pretty," she tells me.

"Tell him he can be my boyfriend," I reply seriously. "I like younger men." Yolanda whispers to him again, and he squeals. He runs to hide behind his mother.

"He's really cute," I say to Yolanda. "I don't have any brothers and sisters."

"I have a few you can borrow," she says, and we both laugh.

"Uh, some of us would like to get out of the sun?" The impatient mother behind us again. It's our turn at the table.

The Chadwick people exude high-voltage helpfulness as they hand us our room keys and point us toward our dorm. Girls, we learn, are on the third floor; boys are on the second. There's a gathering at three o'clock, in the dining hall, for all

 83

campers and parents, then campus tours for new players. Dinner, to which families are invited, starts promptly at six. After dinner . . .

Well, then it begins, doesn't it? Mom and Dad drive away. Three days between here and New Jersey.

The Lloyds and Cruzes, weighed down by luggage, head toward the dorm rooms. Mom and Mrs. Cruz chat away like old friends, and I know it won't be long before Mom gets her hands on the baby Mrs. Cruz holds. The dads seem very preoccupied with carrying suitcases.

Just before we round the corner, Yolanda nudges me and gestures with her head toward the line.

"One, two, three . . . fifth guy back," she murmurs. "Recognize him from Facebook?"

Right about where I think the fifth camper might be, I see a blond-streaked head. He's a lot taller than I imagined he'd be.

"Jonathan Dundas!" This comes out a bit louder than intended. Heads on the line turn, luckily not Jonathan Dundas's. But another guy's. He's standing just beyond the awning, alone, not really part of the line. More like he's checking it out. He has long brown hair, sort of Roger Federer–ish. It swings when he whips his head around. I don't recognize him from Facebook.

He obviously heard me, and he stares. *Great, Hen. Haven't even dragged your duffel up to the room, and already made an idiot out of yourself. Ten points.*

As we walk on, Yolanda whispers in my ear.

"What did you think of his profile?" She looks at me carefully.

I smile and raise my eyebrows suggestively.

"What did *you* think?" I return the question.

She crosses her eyes, clutches her throat and makes mock gagging sounds. I burst out laughing.

"I mean, could you believe him?" she says, relief in her voice.

She chatters unrestrainedly now. As she walks ahead of me, the muscles in her calves bulge.

Bet she's one of those heavy hitters. She's carrying too much weight to be quick. Then again, you never know. Don't underestimate the big girls.

Chapter Ten

EVA

It begins with *plié*. It always begins with *plié*.

A simple bend of the knees from first position, where the heels touch and the feet swivel out in a parallel line. Do this while resting your hands on the *barre*, a long wooden railing that extends around the perimeter of the room. First, the *demi-plié*, a partial knee bend, heels remain on the floor. Again. Again. And again. Slowly the calves warm, the thighs stretch, the buttocks and stomach tuck in. Always the line straight and the center firm.

Next, the *grand plié*. Bend so the thighs are parallel to the floor. The heels can rise now, and one hand rests on the *barre* while the free arm sweeps a graceful, circular motion. As if you're embracing a big beach ball. The head tracks the arm: dreamlike, hypnotic. Give no hint of the rigid concentration and strength it takes to repeat these movements again and again, as the muscles move from warm to burn and sweat glistens on your neck.

And always, always in front of you: the unforgiving mirror.

I'm the biggest in the class. Tallest. Fattest. A giantess in a room full of pixies. You suck, and they stuck you in a class with girls two years younger.

Your head is held on a string that pulls you up to the ceiling. Even as you *plié* down, that string pulls, keeps you from folding in on yourself. Straight, long and tall on the way down, and slowly straight, long and tall on the way up. The legs grow warm but the strength comes from the abs. The focal point for every move.

Madame approaches. I see a suggestion of her quick step in the mirror. As her assistant calls out, "And *plié*! And up. And *plié*! And up," Madame visits each girl at the *barre*, murmuring comments, making corrections. I turn my eyes toward the mirror in fierce concentration. Now, Eva. One perfect *plié*.

She stands slightly behind me. Then I feel her hand between my knees, gently coaxing them open.

"More turnout, but from the hip. Open at the hip. If you cheat with your knees you'll injure yourself."

I imagine my thigh bone twisting in its socket ever so slightly. Ligaments scream, but I ignore them. I check the mirror. Better. Definitely more open. I begin the descent, this time for *grand plié*, and focus on the straight line of my back.

Madame has one hand on my butt and another on my stomach. She pushes my butt forward.

"Tuck the buttocks *in*, Eva!" she says firmly. Again, I check the mirror. I correct, instantly, but Madame has already moved on. My straight, clean line is lost on her.

Ballet booty. That's what you've got. Big fat butt sticking out of

your leotard. That butt alone weighs more than one of these other girls. You're the fat elephant in the kids' class, Eva.

It goes on. For ninety minutes. From *pliés* we move to *tendus*, from *tendus* to *frappés*, then on to *ronds de jambe*, first *en dedans*, then *en l'air*. I have never spent so much concentrated time at the *barre* in my life. The words of the woman in the black warm-up suit return to me: "We do many, many *tendus* here."

Somewhere between the umpteenth *tendu* and *ronds de jambe en l'air*, I lose track of time. I lose track of everything, actually, except the particular movement I'm called upon to perform. I'm in this place that Henry calls the zone, where all the background noise fades and the only thing that exists is what you're doing right at that moment, whether it be a forehand or a *plié*. The instructor's voice, my burning calf muscles, even Madame's striding presence among us, disappear, and I'm in a small space where the perfection of the simplest step commands me. It's a quiet, pure place, and as I work I feel the pace of my heart lessen and the nervous tension in my shoulders loosen.

Then, at *grand battement*, it happens. Leg lifts: one leg planted while the other is raised into the air from the hip, then brought down again, knees straight. The goal is to loosen the hips, turn the legs out from the hips. Over and over we lift *devant* (in front), *à la seconde* (from second position) and *derrière* (behind). Each time my foot goes a little higher, the joints relax a little more, and on the third *grand battement à la seconde* I feel completely loose, I see my foot soar above my head, the leg scissors down, straight, and I realize: it is the best, most perfect *grand battement* I have ever done. I feel this . . . rush . . . of elation.

This is when it happens for me. Never during a performance, or onstage, or in the mirror. But at these unexpected moments, when I'm too tired to look in the mirror, and just slip into *feeling:* one perfect execution. Something lovely, beautiful, created by me. Only for an instant, then it's gone.

But this is why I dance.

When the instructor calls for *révérence*, the stretch that marks the end of the exercise and is the traditional gesture of respect for the art, I feel a pang. I hate to stop. Hate to abandon this space.

As I reluctantly leave the *barre* and head with the rest of the class to the changing room, I see Madame. She is watching me. Probably has been, for I don't know how long. Our eyes lock, and reflexively I smile at her. God knows why. And in return she does . . . nothing. Her expressionless face is flat. Neither approval nor disgust registered there.

I'm a stranger blocking her view of the wall. I am molding clay. Anonymous, beige, to be twisted and retwisted into sylphlike shapes of ballet perfection.

I can't decide whether to lunge at her and seize her by the throat, or collapse on the floor in hysterical sobs. So since I can't decide, I quietly follow the line of girls out of the studio.

* * *

We have two hours before *pointe* class at one o'clock. Perfect. There's a lounge on the second floor with big couches and a drinks machine where I can get a bottle of water. Just the place to put my feet up and eat my bag lunch, but as I head for the elevators, one of the pixies invites me to join her and several others at the canteen.

"Thanks, but I brought," I say, displaying my bag as evidence.

"Oh, they'll let you take food in," she assures me.

Next thing I know I'm riding the elevator with three of them. The girl who invited me does the introductions.

"I'm Marguerite," she says. "This is Anna. Caitlin." Each nods and smiles. Each has her hair smoothly pulled back in a tight bun. No one wears jewelry, not even earrings. We've all changed into leggings and loose T-shirts. Soft wool clogs that could double as bedroom slippers. "Eva," I say, smiling back.

"Is this your first summer?" asks Marguerite.

"Yes," I reply, surprised. "Have you done this before?" All three nod.

"Third time," Marguerite says matter-of-factly. "Third," she adds, pointing to Anna. "Fourth," she says, pointing to Caitlin. I don't even bother to hide my astonishment.

"I didn't know people repeated," I say. Anna shrugs.

"Still trying to get an invitation to the full-year program," she explains. "They'll let you keep trying until you're, what? Seventeen?" she asks Caitlin, who nods. "So I've got one year left."

"You're sixteen?" I ask. No way is this flat-chested pipsqueak older than me.

"Yup. The old lady of the group. Everyone else is fifteen. You?" The elevator doors slide open.

"Same."

The canteen looks like a cross between a high school cafeteria and a hospital lunch café. Smells about that appetizing, too. We find an empty table with four metal and plastic chairs, and sit. All the pixies carry their lunches.

"Where are you from, Eva?" Marguerite rips the top off a yogurt and stirs vigorously.

"Ridgefield, New Jersey. It takes a little less than an hour to drive here."

"You drive into the city each day? That must suck," says Caitlin. She's unsheathed the largest spinach wrap I've ever seen. It's practically a torpedo. It leaks veggies, cheese and something resembling turkey.

"I'm used to it. Do you all live in New York?" I pull out my bag of carrots. Twelve organic Bunny-Luv brand baby carrots in a Ziploc bag.

"For the summer. We're all in the dorms," Caitlin says. She takes a wolfish bite of the wrap.

"I heard they got more requests for boarding students this year than ever before," Anna says quietly. "They turned the rooms in Marks Hall into triples." She's unwrapped a little square sandwich on brown bread. PB and J on whole wheat.

"Those were tight as doubles. I don't want to think about three beds in there," says Marguerite. "Caitlin, what *is* that?"

We have to wait for Caitlin to chew and swallow before

she can answer. She's dropping shredded lettuce into her lap, and dressing drips from one end of the wrap.

"It's called a Turkey Buster," she finally says. "I got it from the deli across the street." She takes another huge mouthful. We watch in fascination as she works her cheeks around the meat and vegetables. You can actually see a lump travel down her throat when she swallows. She holds the oozing mass out to Marguerite.

"Wanna bite?"

Marguerite doesn't hesitate. She leans forward and with both hands cradles the torpedo. She inspects every corner, carefully deciding where to attack this behemoth. She goes for the drippy dressing end and unleashes a torrent of something resembling ranch.

"Ah! Help!" she cries, mouth full, laughing. Anna reaches across the table, holding out a safety net of napkins. Marguerite passes the wrap off to her, and now Anna looks it over. After carefully considering her choice, she bites from the fat end.

"Umm," she says, nodding approvingly. She looks at me. I feel this tight constriction in my throat. No one warned me that membership in this club would involve exchanging saliva and eating deli meats.

Don't even think about it, you pig! Do you know how many pliés *are in one bite?*

"No thanks, I'm good," I say, holding up my carrots and willing myself to smile. *Breathe, Eva*, I think. Anna passes the wrap back to Caitlin.

"So where are you all from that you have to board?" I say,

nonchalantly. I am determined to *not* watch Caitlin demolish the rest of her lunch. I pluck carrot one from its bag. I nip one end, then the other. Chew. Swallow. Nip one end, then the other. Chew. Swallow. Repeat until the carrot is so small there *is* no end. Just this little bit I pop into my mouth. Perfect.

"Bedford," Marguerite says. She's back to the yogurt now, carefully scooping bites with a small plastic spoon. "You know, Westchester. Not much further than you, Eva."

"Caitlin's from Philly. I'm from Newton, Massachusetts," Anna continues.

"Why don't you board?" asks Marguerite.

"I signed up for the program too late," I reply easily. "The dorms were full." Nip. Nip. Chew. Swallow.

"Madame knows your name."

Anna. Her statement sounds flat, and somehow accusing.

"I met her at the audition," I reply. I don't know why I think this is a helpful thing to say.

Marguerite scrapes the last of her yogurt from its plastic container.

"I don't think she knows my name," she says. "At least, I've never heard her say it. What about you guys? Has Madame DuPres ever said your names?" The others shake their heads.

"Yeah, well, I guess that does it for me," I say, laughing nervously. "Tell me something: does that woman *ever* smile?"

"She smiles when the principals visit class," says Caitlin. "You know, the *famous* ballerinas." The Turkey Buster is gone, and she reaches into her brown paper bag again. She pulls out a giant, shrink-wrapped cookie.

 93

"She doesn't criticize you unless she thinks it's worth it."
Anna again. Sounding thoughtful. "I know it's perverse, but
the more she seems to hate you, the better she thinks you are."

"Oh, *puh-leeeeze!*" Caitlin exclaims. "How would anyone
know what Madame thinks? The woman's a . . . what's that big
Egyptian thing called?"

"Sphinx," says Marguerite.

"Yes, thank you," says Caitlin. "She's a mystery. Her only
expression is annoyance. You just have to get over it and not
care. It'll make you crazy otherwise."

Crazy. I'll tell you what's making me crazy. Watching
Caitlin devour that cookie. The thing is huge. Two thousand
calories, at least.

Marguerite has rolled her bag into a tight ball; Anna has
moved on to an apple and munches contentedly. I'm on carrot
seven.

"Well, it's too bad you're not in the dorms," Marguerite
concludes. "It's a lot of fun. We're all in a suite together. Two
bedrooms, with an adjoining lounge. Television."

Caitlin stands up. She's still chewing, and has scrunched
all her garbage together. Her eyes dart.

"Anybody see the trash can?" she says. Before we answer,
she's up. She strides to the exit. Still clutching her bag, she
leaves the canteen.

I can't hide my surprise. There's a trash can not three feet
from us.

"She went to the restroom," Anna says.

"Huh?" I reply. "I thought she said . . ."

"Don't worry about it, Eva," Marguerite says shortly. She winds up and tosses her bag ball into the trash. I look at Anna.

When our eyes meet she takes two fingers and pretends to stick them down her throat.

It doesn't take a genius to know where the Turkey Buster ended up.

Chapter Eleven

HENRY

It begins with forehands. It always begins with forehands.

I don't know why, since backhand is supposedly the more natural stroke. With a backhand you start with your arm across your body and open up, like a gate swinging out. With a forehand you start open, but cross your body. Block it, actually. Block the natural, forward movement toward the net. So, go figure.

A dozen of us girls have gathered at the hard courts with Missy Thompson, the Chadwick coach we met last night. She reminds me of an otter. She's sleek and brown, and moves with these efficient, fluid steps. I'm no good at figuring out how old adults are, but Missy has these little lines at the corners of her eyes. They could be from smiling. Or squinting at the sun. Or age.

I'm surprisingly energetic, given that I kept waking up in the middle of the night. It is so weird to share a bedroom with a complete stranger, and somewhere around two a.m. I became obsessed with the sound of Yolanda's breathing. Like she had her mouth open. I predict she's going to turn into one of those old ladies who snore.

The other thing that kept me up was the smell of the *empanadas* Mrs. Cruz left us. The closed air in the dorm room was heavy with the smell of seasoned meat. Earlier that day, when we were all sitting around, the Lloyds and the Cruzes, eating these deep-fried pastries stuffed with ground pork and mystery spices, I thought they were the best things I'd ever tasted. But at two a.m., in a strange place with a raspy girl I barely know, and Mom and Dad somewhere on the highway between the Alligator State and the Garden State, that pork was doing a dance in my intestines.

"Good morning, everyone!" Missy chirps brightly. "The forecast is for bright sun and mid-nineties by afternoon, so I'd like to make the most of the morning and the cooler temps.

"Let's start with drills. First forehands, then backhands: crosscourt, down the line, then inside out. One hundred consecutive of each shot, ball landing beyond the service line every time. If you hit it out, you start the count over."

Someone lets out a low whistle. Sounds like a falling rocket. Missy laughs. "I'm looking for consistency and placement. Power is not part of this drill. Grab a can of balls and head out." She reads from a clipboard: "On court one: Adams and Burke. Court two: Cruz and Delmonico. Court three: Lloyd and Maney. Court four . . ."

New balls. Dad and I beat balls until they're practically hairless. On my high school team we only break out the new balls for matches.

97

Allyson Maney introduces herself as we walk to court three. She wears this hot little red and white Fila outfit. I've got on my Ridgefield High cotton shorts and a gray tee.

"Henry Lloyd," I reply.

"Henny?" she asks.

"Henry. It's how I survive 'Henriette,'" I explain. Maney smiles.

"Where are you from?" she asks.

"Jersey. You?"

"My mom and I live in a condo off campus so I can train here year-round. But my dad and little brother still live in Philly. Dad's job is there. No way he could move to Florida." We've reached court three, and she drops the oversized tennis bag she's carrying. *She could carry a baby elephant in a bag that size.* As I pop the tab on the can . . . I love that *whoosh* and new-ball smell . . . she glances at the girls on the next court.

"See the tall, really tan girl in the blue shorts?" she murmurs. I follow her gaze. A lanky kid with a long braid down her back is opening a can of balls. Even from where we stand I can see the muscle definition in her arms.

"She's twelve," Maney says. I gape.

"No way," I declare. The girl is just too tall. Nobody can grow that much in twelve years. But Maney nods.

"She's a six-footer," she says, reading my mind. "Usually hits with the boys. The *older* boys." I stare as this miracle of athletic DNA walks to the baseline and begins smacking warm-up balls to her partner. Maney pivots, directing her gaze down the

 98

long length of courts. When she finds what she's looking for, she takes hold of my arm and turns me in the right direction.

"Last court. The blonde." I see a little girl hitting with a man in a Chadwick T-shirt. He's feeding her forehands and the kid wails on them. Her feet leave the ground with every shot.

"She's nine," Maney says. "Parents just moved here with her from California."

Okay. Thanks, Allyson Maney. I am officially freaked out and intimidated.

The two of us take up our positions on the baseline and begin. On the first ball we get to twelve before she hits one wide, into the alley. She looks at me accusingly.

"Hey, could you lighten up? Missy said no power."

"Uh, sorry," I say. But I'm surprised. I wasn't hitting hard. We start over and I add a little loft to the ball. Slow it down with topspin. Maney makes it to twenty-five before sending it out.

"Damn!" I hear her exclaim. She glances down the line of courts. Missy is working with the girls next to us. "Start over."

We make it to twenty-five. Fifty. Seventy-five. Then Maney hits it into the tape. Sounds like a whip cracking. She stands there, stupidly, for a second, then half tosses her racket on the ground and puts her hands on her hips.

"What the hell are you doing?" she demands.

"What?" I ask, mystified.

"How do you expect us to reach a hundred if you're gonna pound it?" she continues.

"I'm not pounding," I reply. I can't believe she is blaming me for her errors.

"Yeah, well, try a little less aggression and a little more consistency," she snaps. "This is a *drill*. Henriette."

I feel my face flush red. It occurs to me that I didn't drag my butt all the way to Florida to get attitude from some girl who can't complete a forehand drill. As she bends over to retrieve her racket, I pull a ball from my pocket. I smack a forehand at her. It whizzes past her head and bounces off the fence.

"One," I say, loudly.

"Nice shot," I hear.

Missy stands behind me. I don't know how much she's seen, but from the expression on her face I can tell: enough.

"Maney, take five," she calls out. "Lloyd, you'll hit with me."

This sick feeling settles into the pit of my stomach as I watch Missy walk over to the other side of the net. Maney stands to one side, sucking on a Powerade. Big grin on her face as she lowers it.

Ten points, Henry. Bet you'll think twice before you try to peg another camper. Less than an hour into your first lesson and you're already making friends.

"Let's start at half power," Missy says when she reaches the baseline. "Deep to the corners. One hundred forehands." I nod and hit one over. She returns it harder and closer to the line than anything Maney hit.

Missy's about to give me a public spanking.

Take your medicine, Henry. You deserve it.

 100

I return her shot. Her next. The next. So at twenty-five, she picks up the pace.

"Three-quarters power, Lloyd," she calls out. Her next ball zings over the net.

I shorten my backswing, train my eyes hard on the logo, the Wilson, and increase the racket-head speed as I connect. My balls *zing* back to her. They kick high as I exaggerate the topspin. At seventy-five, Missy calls out again.

"Give it everything you got, Lloyd!"

I explode. My feet leave the ground with each stroke. The strings connecting with the ball make a *pock!* like gunfire. At some point, other players lay off their drills to watch, and begin counting out loud as Missy and I approach one hundred. I try not to let it distract me. Try not to notice how hard I'm breathing.

At ninety-seven, Missy hits it wide. The counting stops. Players stare at her, stunned.

She wipes her forehead on the sleeves of her shirt. She walks toward the net and motions me to join her. As I approach, I see that sweat soaks the front of her shirt.

"The question is, Lloyd," she says, when I get close, "can you hit *soft?*" She grins. Relief washes over me when I realize she's not mad.

"To be honest with you, Missy, when I was hitting with Maney? I thought that *was* soft."

She looks at me quizzically, as if she's trying to decide whether I'm serious or not. When I don't say anything else, she nods. Like she's made up her mind about something.

"Let's do a little switch here. Yochenko!" she calls out to the next court. The twelve-year-old wonder child halts her drill. "Swap with Maney," Missy tells her. As the kid walks over, I head to my bag for some water. Maney is gathering her things. She moves in close to me.

"Forgot to mention: she's Russian." I look Maney right in the eye.

"Bring it on," I whisper.

My water is already warm, so before the six-foot Russian and I head out, I trot to the big coolers for a refill. They're set up one court over, shaded by green umbrellas, and the water within is icy. The staff has also stacked soft white towels on a bench, just in case any of us needs a fresh one.

As I fill up, someone presses against me.

"Ay, *Dios mío*, I am so hot!" It's Yoly. She holds an empty water bottle. She looks at me and grins. "But I think you might be hotter. Or burned. Henry, your face is so red!"

I release the tap and move out of her way. As she fills her bottle, I take a swig from mine and glance around.

Someone stands outside the fence, staring at us. A guy. Not much taller than me. Front of his shirt stained dark with sweat, long hair pulled back with a sweaty headband. Federer-like.

Right. The guy from the line.

When he realizes I've caught him staring, he turns and walks quickly away.

"I guess Little Andre's already wrapped it up for the morning." Maney has come up behind us.

 102

"Who?" I ask.

"Chadwick's brightest star. David Ross, but everyone calls him Little Andre. He's crazy good, but rebellious, you know? Refuses to wear tennis whites, even at the all-white clubs . . . keeps his hair long. Kind of like Andre Agassi before he started doin' bald, doin' meth and hating on tennis. Ross *lives* for tennis. The coaches work pretty much one on one with him because the other guys can't hang with his shots. We reckon he's gonna go pro soon."

Yoly joins us as we watch the guy's retreating back.

"He's not very big," she says. Maney shrugs. She steps toward the cooler.

"News flash, girls," she says. "Size *doesn't* matter."

I watch him with a bit more interest now. That's a pro stride, I think. Sweaty, pro hair curling at the base of his neck. I have to agree with Yoly: I wouldn't have picked him out of a crowd. David Ross is a wiry, average-sized guy who looks like he plays an average game. On appearances alone, Jonathan Dundas looks a lot more athletic. Still, he's cute. Okay, hot, in that not-jacked-but-fit way. I wonder why he was staring.

Wonder how much of my drill session he'd seen.

Chapter Twelve

EVA

Someone taps on my door. I think. Hard to tell, because I've got the covers pulled over my head, and through the walls of my insulating bed-cocoon, sounds seem muffled and distant.

"Eva? Honey, are you asleep already?"

It's Rhonda. The door swings into the bedroom with a familiar, faraway groan, and a pie-shaped wedge of light falls on the floor. My room is dark, the hallway bright. I've pulled the shades against the setting summer sun, and wrapped myself in flannel pajamas to ward off the air-conditioning. My parents live like Eskimos. It's late June in Jersey, but you'd think this house was an Inuit igloo in January.

I try faking sleep, but Rhonda's on a mission. I hear her place something on my desk, hear the clink of glasses. The slide of a tray. My bedside table lamp clicks on and illuminates the inside of my cocoon to daylight bright. The mattress yields to Rhonda's weight as she sits beside me; the covers rustle as she pulls them down. I blink in the lamplight.

"Hey, sleepyhead! How're you doing?" She smiles, but it's a real question.

"Great," I say, pretending to yawn. "What time is it?"

"Only seven. You slept right through dinner."

"Wow. I must've been pretty tired." I sit up. A smell fills my room. Grilled chicken. She's carried grilled chicken in here, on the tray.

I used to love grilled chicken. I imagine tasting it, and my stomach roars in response.

Are you kidding me?? Are you f-ing kidding me?!

She presses the back of her hand against my forehead, the way she used to when I was a little girl and she thought I had a fever.

"They must be working you pretty hard," she comments softly. "This is the third night in a row you've slept through dinner."

"Yeah," I say. "But it's okay." Rhonda sighs.

"It's not okay to miss dinner, Eva. You can't be your best if your body is depleted." I flash her my most reassuring smile.

"Mom. Give me *some* credit for not being a total idiot."
Tell her to go. And take that crap out of here.

She gets up and carries the tray to my bed. An entire chicken breast, with its crosshatched grill lines across the flesh, rests on a nest of salad greens, which are flecked with white cheese. Goat. Rhonda puts goat cheese in practically everything. There's a tall glass of milk, and a bud vase with a single flower from her garden. Nice touch.

 105

"Would Your Highness like to eat sitting up in bed, or at the desk? Or, better yet, we could carry it downstairs so you could actually visit with your father."

I've barely seen Dad these past couple of days. Maybe we could sit outside on the deck where it's warm. I could eat the chicken; that'd be all right. . . .

Get rid of that dead animal. Take that decaying bird out of here.

"I always spill stuff when I eat in bed. Just put it on the desk." Rhonda replaces the tray but remains standing. She folds her arms tightly across her chest.

"Eva, is everything okay?"

"Why wouldn't everything be okay?" I answer quickly.

"Well, frankly, honey, your father and I are concerned. You seem so wiped out at the end of the day, and when you get home you just disappear into your room."

"Mom, it's the first week! I mean, what's there to say? They spend the beginning reviewing and relearning the basics. Imagine me practicing *pliés* for hours on end. Dull, huh?"

Rhonda shifts her feet and frowns.

"Does Madame DuPres give you any feedback at all?"

"Mom, do you know what the other girls call her? The Sphinx. After that Egyptian thing. That's because no one knows what she's thinking. The other girls say she doesn't even know their names! And they've been there for years."

"See, now that's another thing. The other girls. Who are they? You've told us nothing about the other students."

The smell of the chicken is making me crazy. Stirring

long-buried hungers. I not only imagine chewing; I imagine talking to my mother. About something real.

Like this afternoon. I had fifteen minutes to kill before *pointe* class, and I dialed Henry. I was standing outside the school, watching as clusters of dancers quick-stepped along the sidewalk and up the stairs, returning from their lunch breaks. Sisters-in-arms, laughing together. Missing Henry in that moment felt like physical pain, even worse than the worsening sore toe I've been trying to ignore.

Someone picked up her cell phone. The Yolanda person.

"Oh, hi, Eva!" she exclaimed when I told her who I was. Oh-hi, like she knew me. "Henry is working out and left her phone here in the room. How's it going? She told me all about your ballet school. It sounds so amazing!"

"Uh, yeah. It's amazing," I replied. For some reason the fact that she knew all about me but I didn't know a thing about her made me want to cry. I got her off the phone, asked her to ask Henry to call me.

"Did I tell you I spoke to Henry yesterday?" Rhonda's eyes widen slightly, indicating boredom. If we're not talking ballet, my mother finds it hard to pay attention to what I'm saying.

"How is she doing?" Rhonda asks politely.

"I miss her," I say instead. "These other girls . . . I don't know. It's competitive."

Her eyes brighten.

"Are they competitive with you? Have you been singled out in some way?"

"No, I'm just one in a faceless mob," I tell her. "It's more

 107

like everyone is competitive with everyone else. Doesn't exactly encourage warm and fuzzy friendships, you know?"

Rhonda frowns.

"You know, honey, some of these other girls? You might end up in the same company with a few of them. Keep in mind that these are good contacts for you."

Henry called me back that night. It sounded like she was talking from inside a tin can.

"Where *are* you? A submarine?" I asked. She laughed.

"It's this totally cool place called the Overlook. It's a lounge, up some stairs, and looks out over the indoor courts on one side and the outdoor courts on the other. Totally sweet for watching matches or checking out other players."

"Ooh, like full-of-himself-blondie-with-the-good-teeth?" I asked.

"Actually, there is way better scoping to be had," she said meaningfully. "But give me your news first."

"Nothing to say unless you want a detailed description of how it feels to twist your limbs until the connective tissue squeaks, then leap, turning, across an enormous room over and over until sweat flies off you like a sprinkler."

"Sounds like fun."

"Sorry to make you jealous," I said. She laughed.

"I miss you," she said.

"No, you don't," I countered. "You've already made a new best friend. Your roommate, Linda. She answered your cell phone and knew who I was. Confess: you've told her all our secrets."

 108

"Oh, yeah, right," Henry said easily. "And by the way, it's not Linda. It's Yolanda. Yoly for short. She's Cuban. And I've told her all about *you,* my best friend, who is going to be a world-famous dancer someday."

"If someone doesn't put strychnine in my Dasani bottle first," I muttered.

"What?" Henry asked.

"Oh . . . nothing. It's just this place isn't conducive to making friends. I swear, Henry, some of these girls would slit my Achilles tendons if they thought it would give them a leg up on me. They are intense, focused, killer ballerinas."

"Like, ax-wielding killers?" she asked.

"Murderous zombies in tutus," I said. She snorted.

"But enough of my uplifting news. What's your latest? Who'd you massacre today?"

"Actually, I had a close match. This girl from North Carolina. She actually broke me once." I know what that means.

"So you beat her 6–1, 6–0."

"Yeah. Moved me up the ladder a bit. I'm two away from the top. By Friday I'll be there." I get this, too. A ladder is just that: all the players challenge each other until the best ends up at number one. Henry was moving into the top spot at the academy.

"Sounds like you're doing great, Hen," I said.

"So far so good," she said, but I wasn't fooled. She could brag to me, but she never does.

I want to tell my mother that if I have to imagine being surrounded by ax-wielding killer ballerina contacts for my entire grown-up life, I'll pass on growing up, thank you. But I don't get the chance. She stands, ready to leave.

"Well, I should see to the dinner dishes. Bring your tray down when you're finished, okay?" She exits. She leaves the bedroom door open, heads down the stairs . . . eight, nine, ten . . . and when she reaches the first floor I whisk the covers back, leap out of bed and cross the room. I shut the door. The latch engages with a whisper of a click.

The chicken breast has been basted with teriyaki marinade. You can smell the ginger and the soy sauce, see the caramelized glisten of something sugary at the slightly singed ends.

I want it so badly I could cry. It's all I can do not to grab it in my hands and take huge, wolfish bites. I can taste the sweetness of it. . . .

A whole breast. It looks like it weighs half a pound. Nobody eats eight ounces of chicken in one sitting. At least, nobody should. Only a total pig would.

I go to my closet, and push aside the big, plastic tub on the floor where I've stored my old American Girl doll stuff. Samantha. I had chosen Samantha Parkington, the rich Victorian-era girl with the dark, glossy hair and the amazing clothes. Well, *all* those dolls had amazing clothes, even Josefina, who supposedly cooked bread in an outdoor mud oven and took care of goats. Henry chose the Depression-era doll: Kit. Sassy. Strong. The girl who could tough out the hard times. We spent hours with Kit and Samantha and all their expensive gear.

As I move the tub, I see her. Samantha's face is pressed

against the bottom corner. She stares at me through the opaque plastic.

Behind the tub I find what I was looking for. It's a big Ziploc bag, the gallon size. I hold my breath as I pull it out, but luckily the seam has held and nothing leaks. I can't stop myself from gaping at the contents: three nights' worth of decomposing dinners.

I prop the bag on my desk and carefully pull the plastic tab across the top. I breathe through my mouth so I won't smell anything (a babysitting trick I learned that helped me get through changing poopy diapers), but something thick wafts from the bag. I feel it just under my nose: the hunk of salmon, the baked potato, the slice of quiche. A tofu "hot dog." Trying not to gag, I spear the chicken breast and deposit it with the rest. I shovel a few forkfuls of salad greens in as well, then zip the whole mess shut.

I replace the bag on the floor of my closet and slide Samantha's box in front of it. Then I take a swig of milk. Allow myself two forks of salad greens before getting back into bed, shivering. Stupid air-conditioning.

I pull the covers over my head, curl into a tight ball and wait to feel warm. My stomach rumbles, spurred on by the smell of food, but it's quiet in my head. I rest one hand on my hip. Hard, the bone just beneath the surface. I close my eyes, my heart slows and my last waking thought is not a thought at all, but a picture. A perfect picture of me and Samantha, safe inside our quiet little boxes.

Chapter Thirteen

HENRY

When I press "end," the Overlook seems strangely silent without the sound of Eva's voice in my ear. Stark change from this afternoon, when just about every student and instructor crowded up here to watch David Ross play the guy from Greenlake Academy.

Greenlake. Chadwickians say it as if they're spitting. It's just another tennis school, but for some reason the folks here get all worked up about it. As if there's some honor to defend when a student from one plays a student from the other. Like, "Hey, man! My academy rules your academy!"

They'd announced at breakfast that the "big" singles contest between Chadwick's number one boy and Greenlake's number one would be held at two o'clock, and everyone was pumped. I'll confess: I was dying to see David Ross play. To see if he approached all the hype about him.

I was blown away. So were all the Chadwick fans. And the Greenlake reps. And, particularly, the poor Greenlake guy who had to play him. He didn't win a single game, and the few

 112

points he earned were on David's errors. But other than a couple of errors, he was amazing. He had power. He had soft hands for the drop shots and short angles. He could pound indefinitely from the baseline, but he could finish at net. He had topspin. He had slice. He had a bullet of a first serve, and a mean kick-spin on his second serve. Most importantly, he was fit. The guy was practically dancing out there, that's how fast he moved and positioned himself to hit the ball.

When it was over, he and the Greenlake dude came up to the Overlook for this little postmatch party. Everybody was cheering, patting both of them on their backs. But basically treating David Ross like a celebrity. Even his opponent acted like he wanted to hang out near him and soak up some of his aura.

I was standing off to the side, near the drinks table, watching this all play out, when for some reason he looked my way and our eyes met. Normally, when I'm looking at somebody and they catch me looking, I do the usual thing and . . . look away. But not that time. Something about him just pulled me in, held me there, and I felt my lips twist into this really stupid shape which I hoped resembled a smile. Must have been, because next thing I knew he was smiling back and walking right toward me.

Frozen, I watched him approach.

"Hey," he said easily when he reached the table. He pulled a bottle of Poland Spring from a big bowl packed with ice. He unscrewed the cap. "It's Henry, right?" he said.

"How do you know?" I asked, surprised.

 113

"T-shirt night." He smiled. "You had the best. 'What Exit?' I loved it." He tilted his head back and took a long drink.

"Thanks," I said, wondering what he would have thought of the shirt I hadn't worn. Instead of Eva's tomatoes I had opted for a tee that simply read "What Exit?" As in the Garden State Parkway. As in, "Hi, I'm from Jersey," and the reply almost inevitably is "What exit?"

He hadn't really participated in T-shirt night. Just wore a plain blue shirt and hung out on the periphery, watching. Laughing with everyone else, but mostly just watching.

"Awesome match today," I said. Like he hadn't already heard it forty times. Yes, I'm *that* original. He glanced quickly behind him. The paparazzi were closing in.

"Useless, actually," he muttered to me.

"Huh?" I said. He frowned.

"Greenlake is a school. A real school," he said. "They train people who want to play in college. And that guy is a year younger than me. It wasn't a fair match." Before I could ask him what he meant, the adoring crowd pressed in. He smiled at me once more, made this "oh well" sort of shrug, and moved to another end of the room.

As I'm leaving the Overlook now, just fifteen minutes shy of lights-out, something rustles on the stairs. Footsteps. I figure it's maintenance, here to vacuum the celebratory confetti strewn everywhere and pick up crushed plastic cups. I head for the opposite stairway exit when someone clears his throat.

"Hey, what's your hurry?"

It's Jonathan Dundas. Aka, the Perv.

It hadn't taken Jonathan Dundas long to convince every girl in the camp that he is totally bad news. Not simply full of himself: Dundas is a pervert. He makes a point of staring at your boobs if he's talking to you. He's let the "secret" out that he brought porn with him to camp. And he thinks it's really funny to twist everything someone says into some sort of sexual reference. Like, the other day Yoly and I were at breakfast and she was telling me that it's hard for her to hit a lofty ball with topspin.

"I like to hit a flat ball, low over the net," she was explaining. "That's always the way I've played. But these coaches want me to totally change my strokes."

Dundas just happened to be sauntering by with his tray as she said this. He could barely contain the smirk on his face when he stopped at our table.

"I'll show you some new strokes, Yolanda," he leered.

I think my jaw dropped when he said that. Yoly, however, didn't flinch.

"Beat it, perv," she snapped, loudly. "Nobody loves you."

He laughed, like he thought it was all some big joke, but he did move on, and found a seat at a table at the farthest corner of the room from us. Yoly leaned across the table.

"That is one bad dude," she said, wagging her finger. "And let me tell you: I know bad dudes. I can smell them a mile off. There's only one way to deal with them. Let them know that if they mess with you, you'll cut off their *cojones*."

"Their *what*?" I asked.

"Sorry. I keep forgetting you don't speak Spanish. Their

balls." Yoly looked at me with this dead-serious expression on her face, and for a moment I absolutely believed she was capable of the proposed surgery.

"Figuratively speaking," she hastily added. Which made us both crack up.

So here I am, mere moments before lights-out, in a dimly lit, deserted room with an oversexed jerk. Great. Where's a good, sharp scalpel when you need it?

"Uh, no hurry," I say to him. "But it is almost lights-out. Good night." I keep walking, but Dundas quick-steps across the room and is at my side before I've reached the stairs. I imagine this is how he covers the court, sprinting swiftly to catch short drop shots just before the second bounce.

His hand closes around my elbow.

"C'mon, Henry! No one checks rooms for, what? Another half hour? Let's get acquainted."

He's tall. Way taller than me, and broad. Something catches in my throat. A panicky feeling I've never experienced before. It occurs to me that even if Jonathan Dundas is a jerk, he's also a top-level athlete. The guy is jacked.

Time to rely on brains.

I glance quickly around, in search of an idea. I see a small couch, not far from the stairs.

"Why don't we sit over there?" I say, smiling at him. I step toward the couch, pulling him with me, since he still has ahold of my elbow. His face relaxes into this confident grin. The way I imagine a hyena looks as it closes in on its prey. I'm thinking if I can get him to release his hold on my arm, I'll

 116

make a dash for it down the stairs. I'm thinking I'm pretty fast myself.

This, of course, is not what he's thinking. He presses up next to me as we lower ourselves onto the couch. I feel his breath on my face when he speaks.

"So, what're you doing up here all alone?" he asks.

God, he had the tacos for dinner. I think I'm gonna yak.

"I come up here to call home. More private than the dorms, you know?" He laughs softly.

"Man, I never call home," he says. "You must be one of those good girls, calling Mommy and Daddy." He leans forward, his face brushing the hair behind my ear. I instinctively jerk back, but there's not much room on the couch.

"Actually, I call my boyfriend. We've been going out for almost a year now and . . . uh, I'm really committed to him, Jon. I hope you haven't gotten the wrong idea."

Like, who would have given him any idea? I've barely spoken to this guy. What a perv!

Dundas is undeterred.

"C'mon, Henry. You're what? A thousand miles from your boyfriend? What he doesn't know won't hurt him. Besides, I'll teach you some things he'll appreciate later. Trust me: the guy will be so thankful." He leans forward again, lips parted, and takes aim at my neck.

Not often, but at key moments in my life, I am reminded that I am, indeed, Mark Lloyd's daughter. Sometimes those are low moments, and I see things in myself of which I'm not particularly proud. Other times, I'm grateful that my father

 117

has taught me to take garbage from absolutely, positively no one.

I curl myself into a little ball, plant both feet directly on Jon's chest and push-kick him as hard as I can. He flies against the opposite arm of the couch, his eyes round and wide.

Hah. Take that, jerk. Bet now you'll think twice before you hit on a girl who spends time in the weight room.

I jump up, balling my hands into two fists.

"Dundas, you touch me again and I'll kick you so hard you'll be singin' soprano."

To my utter amazement, the guy grins.

"You're a bad girl, Henry," he says softly. "I like bad girls." He jumps up from the couch, grabs my fists and pulls both of my arms behind my back. He presses his mouth against mine, and I can feel him trying to force my lips open. I want to scream, but the sound is muffled against his face. I am so mad. Scared, too, but mostly mad. I've never had a boyfriend. Never kissed a guy before, and now this? This creep is going to be my first kiss? I take aim with my knee.

Cojones. The word flashes through my brain at the same moment that Jonathan Dundas crumbles. My new favorite Spanish word—thank you, Yolanda—surpassing even *taco* and *empanada.* An important word, and surprising, especially given Jonathan's dramatic fall and the fact that I didn't think I kneed him all that hard. But hey, whatever works, and I'm about to turn tail and run, when I see him. Standing over Dundas. As if *he* just delivered a blow.

David Ross, aka Little Andre. Wearing a look of pure fury.

"I think she said no," he says quietly.

Jonathan rolls over, grimacing. His combined expression of pain and surprise is sweet to see as he struggles to stand up. He's a big guy, Dundas. Bigger than David. But I can tell: he's afraid of him.

"Hey, no worries, bro," he says nervously. "Just a little misunderstanding. Everything's cool. Right, Henry?"

I suddenly feel like I might throw up. All I want at this moment is to get as far away from Jonathan Dundas as possible. So I nod silently, look away and swallow hard.

"Okay, then, we're good. Okay," Dundas says uneasily. "I'll be going then. Almost lights-out, you know?" He limps away from us, quickly, across the Overlook and down the stairs. David and I listen to his retreating footsteps, until we hear the clubhouse door open and shut. That's when I yield to the weakness in my legs, and plop down on the couch. I hear this sound, like bees buzzing, and I put my head between my knees to ward off the faint that's coming on.

A few minutes pass before the queasy feeling fades. When it does, I realize David is sitting beside me on the couch, his hand resting gently on my back.

"You okay?" he says when I glance up. He looks at me intently, a little frown forming between his eyes. I nod. He takes his hand from my back, and shifts, slightly, away from me. As if he's trying to put a respectful distance between us.

"That guy? He's a creep," David says.

"Tell me about it," I sigh. "He's a stalker. He followed me up here."

 119

"Well, you were next on the Hickey Hit List," David says matter-of-factly.

"The *what?*"

"Hickey Hit List. Dundas has made it his personal goal this summer to plant a hickey on every girl at camp. You were next in line."

"And you know this how?" I demand. Outrage rises in me.

"Common knowledge," David says, shrugging. "It's all he's talked about since camp started. The guy's a vampire wannabe. Frankly, I think he should spend less time leaving his mark on the ladies and more time on his backhand. It sucks."

I'm speechless as I try to absorb this open secret that all the guys seem to know. In my head I do an inventory of necks, trying to recall telltale bites.

"Listen, Henry," David continues. "Warn your friends, then let it go. Dundas is a joke, okay? Someday he'll play for a second-rate college, then run Daddy's company and hit on all the women at his country club. End of story."

A thought occurs to me.

"What are *you* doing up here?" I ask.

"What do you mean?"

"Did you know he was going to follow me tonight? Or is this a coincidence?" David shrugs again.

"Let's just say I've got your back, okay?"

I shake my head, still disbelieving. I don't know what's weirder: Dundas coming on to me, or David Ross looking out for me.

"You're not stalking me, too, are you?" I ask. Half joking. I see the color rise in his face. I don't know him well enough to identify this as annoyance or a blush.

"Just doing my duty," he replies lightly. "Like I said, you were next in line. Pretty typical. Kinda like your game."

I freeze. An insult. Out of nowhere. Or is it?

"Excuse me? Are you dissing my game?"

"God, no. Don't take offense, Henry. Typical at Chadwick is fairly good everywhere else." He yawns. An exaggerated, I-don't-care yawn. And for the second time that night, I feel capable of surgical excision. David stands. "We'd better get back to the dorms," he says.

"Oh, no, you don't. You don't just lay that on me and walk away. Define 'typical.'"

He's not much taller than me, and as he stands there, his hands buried in the big, loose pockets of his wrinkly cargo shorts, his mouth a bare suggestion of a grin, I feel this horrifying urge to . . . kiss him. To wipe the smirk off his face with my lips.

Is it possible to want to kill a guy and kiss him at the same time? Something is seriously wrong with me.

"You're a grinder, Henry. You've got solid strokes and an overall good game. But basically, you win off other people's errors. You grind 'em with consistency." He says this coldly. Analytically, all teasing gone from his voice.

"You mean *force* other people's errors," I correct him.

"Force, wait around, get lucky," he says impatiently. "Whatever. Fact is, it'll only get you so far. If you want to dominate at this level, you have to hit put-away winners."

"You don't think I hit winners?" I ask, incredulous.

"You're capable of blasting winners all day, but for some reason you play patty-cake from the baseline and occasionally come to net on short balls."

"Sounds like you've been spending a lot more time watching me play than working on your own game," I say. Acid in my voice. This is partly a dig. Partly a revelation. David glances at his watch.

"Nah," he says, the smirk returning. "I figured you out in five minutes. Listen, it *is* lights-out at this point. So nightie-night, Henry." He's walking backward, away from me and toward the stairs, as he says this. Hands in those big pockets. "And, uh, by the way. You're welcome. For saving your neck."

David Ross turns, and disappears quickly down the steps. I fall back onto the couch, breathe deeply and shut my eyes tight. I don't care how late it is, or how much trouble I get into. I'll stay here as long as I have to, and if they give me a hard time I'll just shrug. Go ahead. Expel me.

'Cause I'll be damned if anyone is going to see me cry.

Chapter Fourteen

EVA

Rhonda is absolutely convinced it's an omen of future fame. The call tonight from Madame DuPres has sent her rocketing into Proud Parent Hyperspace, and she's pulling out suitcases. Because this weekend I'm moving into the dorms. Madame found room for me, and "someone" (she wouldn't say who) is paying for it.

"We value students like Eva," she said to Rhonda.

Earlier today, I had thought I was getting kicked out. So I guess it just shows you what I know.

Let me back up: Friday afternoon, following *pointe* class. I was leaving the studio and walking to the dressing room, when Madame waylaid me by the door. She spoke to me over the cluster of tightly coiffed heads.

"Eva, after you change, could you please come by my office?" she said. No smile, no expression. Just the regal command, then the *click, click* of her heels as she disappeared down the hall.

Naturally, this sent a shock wave through the rest of the class.

"What's going on, Eva? Why does she want to see you?" The questions buzzed around me as I honestly answered, "I have no idea."

Why? Why Eva? Subtext: Why you and not me? Should I be jealous? Should I feel sorry for you? Are you moving up or heading out?

My mind scrolled through the just-completed class. I thought I did fine. Nothing spectacularly brilliant or devastatingly awful. It was an hour of *relevé*, rising on the tips of your *pointe* shoes from first, second, fourth and fifth positions. We did it French school style, then Russian. Over and over. A solid hour. I don't know. Maybe I looked bored?

In the dressing room, Marguerite body-slammed me against the wall. Figuratively speaking, that is. She zeroed in on me with such intensity that I felt body-slammed.

"You don't have *any* idea what she wants?" Marguerite demanded. I shrugged weakly. I felt weak; it was no act. My right toe screamed at me from inside the ballet slipper, my mouth felt papery with thirst and half my mind was still in the *relevé* zone. An hour of balancing the full weight of your body on your toes, which are encased in a box as hard as wood. All wrapped up in girly satin, but don't kid yourself: *pointe* shoes are to the feet what thumbscrews are to the hands.

"Honestly, Marguerite, I have no clue what I've done," I said, lowering my bottom onto the changing bench and unwinding the ribbons around my ankles. When I offered no other information, she retreated to her locker. I concentrated on not falling over. I didn't know whether it was nerves at the prospect of seeing Madame alone, or postclass fatigue, but the room around me swam and shifted from bright to shadowy, then bright again. The voices of the other girls sounded like buzzing bees.

When I knocked at Madame's door, I was packed to go. For the weekend, or forever. It was Friday afternoon, Rhonda was due in thirty minutes to pick me up and I was feeling fatalistic. I removed every single thing I owned from my dressing-room locker. Normally, I'd clear out whatever needed to be laundered, leaving my shampoo, conditioner, deodorant and other toiletries neatly arrayed in order of size and sequence of use. Not then. If I was to be "uninvited" to the New York School of Dance, there was no way in hell I'd take a valedictory lap through the locker room to collect my stuff.

"Come in," I heard, and I pushed the door open.

Madame DuPres's narrow lair seemed a more likely place to find a high school guidance counselor than the artistic director of one of New York's leading ballet schools. Yellowing framed photos and old ballet posters covered the walls. Two metal filing cabinets, stacked high with folders, occupied one end of the room; a battered wooden desk at the other end faced out the one long window. Madame was seated on an off-gold couch. It reminded me of the beat-up sofa in my grandmother's playroom, which clanks open into a metal-framed bed.

She gestured to the unoccupied end. I dropped my stuffed backpack onto the floor and sank into the cushions.

 125

Your thighs are so fat. Look at that flab, all spread out on the couch.

"Can I get you something to drink, Eva?" I shook my head. The water I chugged in the locker room roiled like a tidal wave in my stomach. I willed myself to concentrate on what she was saying to me. To not think about how my thighs were stuck together. I hadn't taken a shower. I had hurried and now felt sticky.

"I'm fine, thank you," I replied.

"Is someone waiting to pick you up?" Madame asked.

"My mother will be here at three-thirty," I said. She looked at the clock on the wall. How long does it take to kick someone out of a school and destroy a lifetime's worth of dreams? I wagered that Madame could do it in five minutes flat.

"How did your first week go?" she asked.

They chafe, at the top. Your thighs. They rub together when you walk.

"Good," I said, calibrating the right amount of enthusiasm in my voice. "I mean, I've already learned so much." She nodded. Waited.

"Such as?"

"Well, I guess turnout. I think you were absolutely right when you noticed I was using my knees too much." She nodded again.

"The hips. It really comes from the hips," she said. "What else?"

The carrots were around 35. The yogurt was 140. That's 175 calories for lunch. Seventy for the apple you eat on the drive home.

 126

"I've learned a lot from doing basic things slowly. It helped me improve my technique."

"Absolutely. A solid foundation, the perfection of the basics, is essential to any success in ballet," Madame said. "Now let me ask you: are you having fun?"

"Fun?" The word hung in the air. It had been a long time since I'd used "ballet" and "fun" in the same sentence.

"I don't know. Do you think Michelangelo, lying on his back on the scaffolding of the Sistine Chapel, paint dripping in his eyes and his arms aching, was having fun?" The words escaped my lips before I had a chance to think.

Now you've done it, smart-ass. Don't let the door hit you on the way out.

To my utter surprise, Madame DuPres laughed. Her face contorted into something I'd never seen on her before: a bona fide smile.

"Brava!" she exclaimed. "I suppose you think I had a lot of nerve asking such a question."

Oh, I thought no such thing, Madame. Believe me.

I said nothing. Just smiled back at her. When Madame DuPres finished laughing, the trace of a smile remained. Somehow, miraculously, I'd broken through. I wasn't sure where I'd landed, but it was different from where we'd started.

"Eva, you must know that I've been watching you."

Hmm. Actually, I didn't know that. But now I'll be sure to be extra nervous and paranoid. That is, if I'm not getting thrown out today.

"You have potential. True, you come to us with many

 127

deficits, but those are more the fault of your teachers, not your abilities. So we can overcome those. Especially because you work hard. You work very, very hard, don't you?" I nodded. It dawned on me that this might not be the big kiss-off speech after all.

"But Eva, I sense a fragility about you that troubles me."

Fragility? Bad word. Does she think I'm weak?

"I'm not sure what you mean," I replied cautiously.

"Are you tired?" she asked.

"What, right now? Sure. We just finished *pointe* class," I said. She waved her hand dismissively.

"I mean generally. I mean when you arrive in the morning. Eva, you seem exhausted to me, even when you are dancing well. You push yourself hard, you execute beautifully, but I sense you might collapse at any moment. Do you eat breakfast?"

Half a grapefruit, fifty calories. Black coffee. Egg white, no yellow. None of that gross fatty yellow.

"I always eat breakfast."

"What about sleep? You don't stay up late watching television, do you?"

"I never watch TV."

Television? Is she kidding? You know you are not allowed to sit for longer than fifteen minutes without compensating. Fifteen minutes of sitting equals thirty minutes of exercise.

Madame sighed. She looked at me quizzically.

"Why aren't you staying in the dorms this summer? This

128

commute from New Jersey must be hard on you as well as your parents." I shrugged.

"Madame, staying in the dorms costs two thousand dollars. We can't afford it."

She pondered my comment for a few moments, then went to her phone. She dialed.

"It's Gloria. Quick question. Are we at capacity in the dorms?" Pause. "What does 'over capacity' mean? Are students sleeping in the hallways?" Pause. "When might we know about that?" Pause. "Tell him to call me this evening. I don't care how late." She hung up.

"Well, we are apparently 'over capacity' in the dorms now, whatever that means. They're trying to free up some space in our annex, but it's not clear how much space or when . . ." She trailed off.

I wondered what part of we-can't-afford-it she didn't *get.*

"They'll call me tonight, at any rate," she concluded briskly, rubbing her hands together. I sensed the audience was over. I began to gather my belongings.

"Just one more thing, Eva. Did you attend the nutrition class this week?"

The nutrition class. I had no clue what she was talking about. I shook my head.

"The Wednesday-afternoon seminar is always on nutrition, and I highly recommend it."

Once again, I tried to explain my reality to her.

"You know, those seminars," I said haltingly. "They start at

129

three-thirty? My mom tries to hit the road before that to avoid rush hour."

Madame shook her head, frowning.

"Now that is precisely what concerns me. Valuable information you are missing because of the commute." She rose. "Perhaps we can do something about it. Good evening, Eva. I'm glad we spoke." Madame held the door open for me. As I walked out, I noticed, way at the end of the hall, Marguerite. Leaning against the wall, her ballet bag at her feet. Poised to extract from me every word that passed between Madame *et moi*. My heart sank as I anticipated the interrogation.

Then the elevator doors on our floor rang open, and quickly, frenetically, Rhonda emerged. I couldn't remember the last time it felt so good to see my mother.

"We've got to hurry, hon! I'm illegally parked," she said.

I couldn't help lovin' the expression on Marguerite's face as Rhonda and I hurried past.

"Have a great weekend!" I called to her with a smile. As the elevator doors slid closed, Marguerite's mouth dropped open slightly, the very picture of disappointment.

I leaned against the walls of the elevator, feeling the bottom drop from the soles of my feet as we descended. Madame was right: I'm always tired. I was too tired to even talk to my mother, to tell her about the Audience. It did occur to me, however, that something very, very important had happened.

"We value students like Eva."

Subtext: I've noticed her. Picked her out from among my

130

legions of robotically perfect ballerinas and decided she's worth watching. Worth moving into the dorms.

Marguerite was right to hover; she sensed something. Something big.

Yeah, right, Eva. Who are you kidding? She wants you to see the nutritionist. She thinks you're fat.

Chapter Fifteen

HENRY

With both hands, Yolanda cradles a steaming, bowl-shaped cup. It gives off the near-burned smell of strong coffee beans.

"Ooh, a latte," says Maney, staring enviously at the concoction.

"*Café con leche*," Yolanda corrects her. "A little bit of strong espresso, lots of hot milk and sugar."

Maney rolls her eyes. We're at that stage at camp where we don't know each other very well, but we do know each other's annoying habits well. For Maney it's Yoly's Latino thing. (Actually, for Maney it's a lot of things, but this is a particular irritant to her.) Personally, I'm entertained when Yoly describes how you make *sofrito*, or tells us how you can distinguish among Cubans, Mexicans, Dominicans and Puerto Ricans. Maney, however, only likes to talk about the other players at camp. Or herself.

I've never met anyone like Yolanda. She's like two different people inhabiting the same body. When she speaks Spanish, she's transformed. She moves differently. Looser. More

132

animated. Then, when she switches to English, it's without a trace of accent, and if you closed your eyes you'd assume you were talking to any Miami gringo.

Maney shrugs. "No diff," she says. "Latte, *café au* whatever." Yolanda shakes her head.

"Big difference," she says. "*Café au lait*, which is French, is first cousin to *cappuccino*, which is Italian. *Café con leche* is totally Latino. The coffee is very strong, and the milk is *hot*. We're talking *muy caliente, chicas*. And it's mostly milk, you know? Like, 'Have some coffee with your milk, girl.' And sugar? You want to *shovel* it in." As if to demonstrate her point, Yolanda dumps two more heaping teaspoons of sugar into her cup.

We've just come back from a "Feeding the Athlete's Body" lecture, where we heard all about the dangers of refined sugar, among other things. So Yolanda's shoveling is looking pretty rebellious.

"Feeding the Athlete's Body" is one of the afternoon seminars. Right after we knock off the day's on-court work, we have an hour to shower, change and attend a mini class on some topic related to training and nutrition. Yesterday I went to the one on cross-training. Tomorrow it's "Yoga for Tennis." After the lectures, a bunch of us usually drift over here, to the snack bar, for a little predinner refueling.

"I grew up drinking *café con leche*," Yolanda continues. Almost to herself. "We all do. When we're little children, it's pretty much hot, sugary milk with only a splash of coffee. Every day after school I would go to my *abuela*'s house and we would have our *café con leche*."

 133

"Yeah, but Yoly, you're supposed to be training now," Maney says. "All that caffeine is, like, poison. And the sugar is just empty calories."

Yolanda shrugs.

"If I had to give up coffee to play tennis, then I wouldn't play tennis anymore," she says. As if she means it. As if this is something she's been thinking about.

I can't help it, I laugh. Snort, actually. Eva calls it the yeah-right contemptuous snort, halfway between a laugh and a rude remark. It comes out of me, unbidden, usually at inappropriate times.

"Gimme a break," I say. I wave my hand, gesturing at the snack bar around us, the drop-dead-gorgeous courts arrayed outside the windows, the sun-kissed players drinking their healthy juices and eating granola bars. "You'd give up all this for a cup of coffee? Hello? How 'bout decaf?" Maney laughs. Yolanda looks serious.

"When you put it that way, sure it sounds stupid," she says. "And I should probably drink decaf and cut out the sugar. Although I don't think my grandmother would ever buy her Café Naviera in a green decaf can!" She smiles, but I don't get the joke.

"No one is asking you to give up afternoon coffee with your grandmother," I say. "I'm just saying that caffeine and sugar are inconsistent with what we're trying to accomplish here."

"I know. I know," she says quietly. She stares into her cup. She seems less enthused about drinking it now. Maney gets up to buy another juice. I feel bad about the snort.

 134

"You seem to have a very clear idea of what *you're* trying to accomplish here," she continues, kind of wistfully. "You're playing great, by the way. Didn't you make the top of the ladder today?"

"Yeah, Yochenko went down this morning," I say, grinning. "Thanks. But hey . . ." I kick her lightly under the table. "You ended up at seven. Dead center. Not shabby."

The words feel awkward. I'm not used to complimenting a rival player. Because even if Yoly is my roommate, and as close as I've got to a friend here at Chadwick, she's still a potential opponent. It's strange having a nightly sleepover with someone you may have to massacre.

A shadow falls across our table. Before Yolanda can reply, a familiar male voice cuts into our conversation.

"Good afternoon, ladies."

It's Jon Dundas. Unbelievable. The jerk has been doing an excellent job of staying out of my eyesight and earshot for the past week, thank you very much, but now he strolls right up to our table and says hi? Something's up.

I glare at him. He pulls out Maney's vacant chair, spins it 180 degrees, straddles it and crosses his arms nonchalantly over the back.

"So, I hear we've got a date," he says to me.

"A what?" I say. Jon's eyes open wide in mock surprise.

"You haven't heard about our big date?" he replies. Loudly. Predictably, heads turn.

"Dundas, you must be on those drugs again," I fire back, matching his volume. "Because I can't imagine a life that

 135

would include a date with you." Whistles. Male exclamations of "Ouch!" Yolanda bursts out laughing. Amazingly, Jon smiles. Like he's in on some joke. He turns to a table of guys across the snack bar.

"Hey! Doesn't the number one guy on the ladder always play a match against the number one girl?" he asks. A couple of the guys nod.

"It's a Chadwick tradition," one of them says. "The top players on the girls' and boys' ladders do a challenge match. Usually on Saturday night."

"Yeah, right," I call back. "I've never heard of that." I look at Yolanda. Her smile has faded. Her expression is not reassuring.

"It is a tradition here," she says. "I read about it in the orientation packet."

Once again, I find myself wishing I'd taken the time to actually read through the whole orientation packet.

"But if I'm supposed to be playing the number one boy, why am I matched up with Dundas?" I ask the room, which draws more loud cries of "ouch" and a few snakelike sizzle noises.

Dundas doesn't flinch.

"You're lookin' at number one, baby," he says, smirking. Despite my bravado, I feel sick.

"*You* beat David Ross?" I fire back at him, managing to keep the shake out of my voice. For an instant, Dundas wavers. This little cloud passes over his smug expression. *Stung, didn't it? You know he's better than you. Take that.*

"Ross didn't play the ladder," Yolanda says. "He's too good."

"So you're second best?" I sneer. "I don't know if I want to play the second-best guy."

"Afraid of me, Henry?" he says. Quietly now. This time, he isn't playing to the room. He stares at me, and this queasy realization washes over me that Jon Dundas has a score to settle.

"You're going down, Dundas," I reply evenly. It's an Academy Award–winning performance. No one would ever guess that I feel like throwing up. Dundas shakes his head carelessly, flipping the golden hair out of his eyes. He rises slowly, and his eyes rest on Yolanda. In addition to the round cup of milky coffee, she has a big banana-nut muffin on a plate before her.

"I'd watch the calories if I were you. Roly," he drawls, before sauntering out of the snack bar. I look across the table at Yolanda, expecting to see a hurt, stricken expression.

Instead, I see fury.

"Promise me you're gonna kick his ass," she says.

* * *

Later that evening, after no answer on her cell, no reply to my text messaging, and two solid hours of busy signals on the landline at Eva's house, I finally decide to give up. Yoly and most of the girls on the hall went to the rec room to watch some chick flick. I wish I were more of the gal-pal type, and enjoyed crunching popcorn in my jammies in front of the tube with the girls, but that's just not me. Never has been.

A packet of books arrived from Mom today, so I decide to give literacy a chance. I pull on my T-shirt and boy boxers, tuck myself into bed and have just decided that this is indeed a fine way to spend the last hour before lights-out when someone knocks.

"It's open," I call, too comfy to get up.

David Ross steps into my dorm room.

Did I neglect to mention that I'm wearing Eva's T-shirt? I pull the covers up over my tomatoes.

"Hey," he says. "Mind if I come in?" He glances around the messy room. Of course, there is a bra on the floor. Naturally, there is an open box of tampons on the desk. Shoot me now, please, someone.

David pulls a chair out from one of the desks, swivels it so the back faces me, and sits, straddling. I'm wondering if this posture is something they actually *teach* guys at Chadwick.

"Make yourself at home," I comment. To his credit, he blushes. A little. Hard to tell, he's so tan. A little color seems to darken two patches beneath his cheekbones. He has these high, sculpted cheekbones.

"I heard about your match. With Dundas," he says.

"And I heard you're too good to play the ladder like everyone else," I reply. He frowns.

"Only campers play the ladder. Since I'm not really part of the camp, it wouldn't be fair," he explains.

"Hmm. You sure look like you're part of the camp. You eat with the rest of us commoners. Play on the same courts. If you're not part of the camp, what are you?"

David locks his eyes on mine and doesn't blink. The blush has faded.

 138

"I'm a nationally ranked junior who's planning to go pro next year, and it would be a waste of my time to drill with rich-kid summer campers who Chadwick hauls in here to pad the budget," he deadpans. His gaze doesn't falter. He's not bragging; he's simply stating the facts. Setting me straight. And he's ice-cold honest about it.

David Ross is an assassin.

"Well. Thank you for explaining that," I say, struggling to regain my composure. "And to what do I owe the honor of this visit?"

Before answering me, he leans over. Leans way over, tilting the chair forward, and with these long, tan fingers he plucks the bra from the floor, then nonchalantly places it on the desk. Alongside the tampon box.

"Sorry," he says. "That was distracting me."

My turn to blush. He waits, lets it burn real good before continuing.

"I thought," he says carefully, "you might like some help."

"Help?"

"With Dundas."

"Oh. Well, you know, he's being a jerk . . . big surprise . . . but I think it's okay. He stays away from me pretty much, and when we play our match, there'll be a million people around. So it's cool. But thanks." I'm surprised that I feel a little disappointed. I'm not sure what I want from David Ross, but it isn't personal bodyguard service.

"Actually, Henry, that's not what I mean. I'm talking about on-court help."

 139

"Do you think he'd try something *on court?* With everyone watching?" David shakes his head.

"No. I'm talking about . . . some coaching. I'm talking about beating him."

Brilliant, Henry. This guy must think you are a total ditz. And a slob. With boring underwear. Bet now you wish you were one of those girls who wear lacy undies from Victoria's Secret instead of sports bras from Sears.

I struggle to keep my game face on.

"I thought I'd just play him in my . . . typical way," I say. "You know, grind from the baseline and wait for him to mess up?" A hint of a smile crosses David's face as he shakes his head at me.

"Okay, can we call a truce? Please? I'm sorry I insulted you. I didn't think you'd take it so personally. I actually think you're good. Very good. And if you'd come off your high horse and take a little advice, you could beat Dundas."

He means it. Bra-plucking, almost-pro, too-hot-to-be-in-my-dorm-room David Ross thinks I'm a good player and wants to help me win. Okay. I can do this. See? Stepping down from my high horse right now . . .

"What sort of advice?" I say. He leans forward again. There's eagerness in his eyes.

"Dundas has been coming here for three summers, and I know his game inside out. I spoke to Missy, and we've got the pro court tomorrow. I reserved it. All morning, just the two of us. We'll map out a strategy, and I'll run some classic Dundas

 140

moves by you. I know what he does and I can imitate it. What do you say?"

I am so completely surprised that I can't respond. David Ross . . . *the* Little Andre . . . has gone to my coach? Is giving up his morning practice time to drill with me?

David must have some deep, abiding grudge against Jon Dundas. The number one girl has never beaten the number one boy (yes, I finally got the lowdown on this delightful Chadwick tradition), so for me to take out Dundas would be a serious blow to his manhood. It would be the best, most humiliating way to bring the guy down.

And even in the worst case, say I lose to the Perv, at least I'd have gotten the morning alone on the pro court with the famous David Ross.

"I say let's do it." I smile. He smiles back. Awesome smile.

He gets up, and rubs his hands together briskly.

"Great!" he says. "So how 'bout we start right after breakfast? Actually, why don't I meet you at breakfast? Seven-thirty?"

"Sounds good," I say. I am processing the concept of eating breakfast with David. Chewing in front of him. Being with him, while the rest of the camp watches. He flashes another killer smile at me before turning to leave. Hand on knob, however, he wheels around.

"Henry, just so you know. I think you have a good chance of beating him *without* my help. I just think if I give you some pointers, you can seal the deal."

Okay. I could get used to this guy. I could forgive him for han-dling my bra and using the word "typical" in reference to my game. Wow. I could fall, hard and fast.

Watch it, Henry.

"Thanks, David," I manage to say. "See you tomorrow."

He treats me to one more smile before turning, and then . . . his eyes drop. To my chest. During our conversation, I've inadvertently lowered the covers.

"Nice shirt," he says, then walks out, quickly.

Forget what I just said. I hate him.

Chapter Sixteen
EVA

The annex hums, like a hive. I've never lived anywhere besides our colonial on four-fifths of a wooded acre, so signs of life from other floors seem strange to me. I want to concentrate on my book (Henry's mom gifted me with a stack of new paperbacks; she knows I love to read), but I'm distracted by strains of music. Canned sitcom laughter. Doors slamming.

While most of the other students, like Marguerite and Co., live in the dorms adjacent to NYSD, the annex is home to the "overflows." The building screams sixties, and what might have seemed "mod" back then just looks tacky and cheap now. But it's clean, and you have to buzz to get in, and there's a doorman who keeps vigil all night. Dad spent about an hour talking to him about crime in the neighborhood.

He didn't want me to board. Was dead set against it, in fact, he and Rhonda having their first-ever "ballet fight" over this move to the annex. Unlike the Lloyds, who seem to squabble constantly over what's best for Henry, my parents are usually on the same page. The Rhonda page, that is.

After we unpacked all my stuff, he and I had a rare minute alone.

"House is going to be quiet without you," he said. He looked grim.

"Hey, you've still got Rhonda," I said. Trying to tease a smile out of him. But he wasn't having any of it. He cleared his throat.

"Eva, promise me you'll eat properly." I stiffened.

"Of course," I replied quickly. He shook his head.

"No, don't just say 'of course.' Promise me. You know what I'm talking about. I don't want you dieting while you're here."

God, why can't everyone just get off my back? GET OFF MY BACK!

"Daddy, don't worry about me, okay? I'm not stupid." I willed my face into a relaxed smile. I stifled the scream building inside me. He sighed. He didn't look convinced.

"Honey, if you need anything . . . anything, don't hesitate to call. Even if you just want to talk. I'm here for you."

Something inside me threatened to break. I could. I could tell him. Anything, really. He's always been that sort of dad. The big-bear-hug type. The listening, smiling type. I just don't have the words. If only I could start, with one word. . . .

God, you are SUCH a baby! Grow up, you homesick little loser, and let the poor man go home. Get them out of here and stop being such a wimp.

"I know, Daddy. I love you."

Go. Go now, please.

After they left, I curled up in my bed and fell instantly

asleep. At some point I heard the door open and close, and my roommate, a dancer named Hannah, came in. Whispering voices, rustling, as she searched for her ID card. You need to bring your ID to the canteen. When she came back, about an hour later, I was sitting up in bed, reading, and she invited me to go down to the common room to watch TV. She and a little clutch of friends have some show they all watch together on Saturday nights.

That's okay. I'm waiting to hear from Henry.

Today was the day she played that Jon guy, the full-of-himself hottie who turned out to be a stalker. And the day she spent the morning hitting with the school star, David Something-or-Other, who they all call Little Andre. But apparently not to his face. Henry says she doesn't think he has a clue that he's known as Little Andre. I wonder if she'll tell him.

'Cause she's crushin'. Big-time. I've never heard her sound like this. Almost . . . girly. Giggly. Henry is no giggler, let me tell you, so something's up.

She's also no early riser, so when my cell went off at seven this morning, I knew it had to be immense.

"Eva, it's Hen. Did I wake you?"

"No, I've been up for hours. I mean, it's Saturday morning. I wouldn't dream of sleeping in."

"I'm sorry! I kept trying you last night, but your cell was off and the home number was busy! I think your phone was off the hook."

"Might as well have been. Rhonda was dialing the entire

145

New York metro area with the latest news. But let's not go there. What's up?"

Then the blizzard. A blizzard of words from my usually not-so-forthcoming-when-it-comes-to-guys friend. True, it was all mixed up with the usual tennis talk, but what came through loud and clear to me was that Henriette Lloyd, Most Lethal Teen Girl Athlete in the Garden State, was seriously smitten.

"Is he cute?" I interrupted. She was describing, for the umpteenth time, how embarrassed she was when this guy picked up a bra she'd left on the floor.

"What?" she said.

"This Little David guy. Is he cute?" She giggled.

"It's Little Andre, and his real name is David," she says. "And yes. Very."

"How cute? Mike Adams cute?" I decided to run through our list of high school hotties.

"Cuter, but shorter."

"Jon Dundas cute?"

"Yuk. I can't think of Dundas as cute anymore. Too pervy."

"Joey Wilson cute?"

"No, more like Troy Blaine cute."

"Hen, they're the same kind of cute."

"No. Joey is like a good boy who dresses up as if he's taking a walk on the wild side, but he's not really. Troy is truly, deeply rebellious. Joey is a match that just went out. Troy is hot coals."

"My god, Hen. Poetry! What's gotten into you?"

"Eva . . . I like this guy."

"I can tell."

"No, I mean, I *like* this guy."

"Be careful, Henry."

"What do you mean?"

"I think you like him."

Then off she went, to meet him for breakfast and a little carbo loading. I imagine the two of them tucking into bucket-sized bowls of hot cereal, then jet-propelling themselves to the tennis courts, where they slam balls at each other for hours. Sweat pouring off their bodies. Calories burning. It doesn't matter what Henry eats. She burns it right up.

I told her to call me on my cell, tonight, after her match. She was so busy gushing about the Little David guy that I didn't have a chance to tell her about my big move to the annex. But I'll tell her when she calls tonight. Which should be pretty soon. Her match started at seven; it's already eight-thirty.

I reread the paragraph I've already reread. I am amazed at how my eyes can scan, and in some compartmentalized way comprehend, words, while another part of my brain races off in a completely different direction. I see the words on the printed page, but I'm thinking: *Someone is making microwave popcorn.* The fake, super-buttery smell oozes beneath my door. My stomach roars in response, and I have this urge to hurl the book against the door. I can't read with all this noise.

I jump off the bed, lie on the floor and begin crunching. Fingers laced behind my head, knees bent, I curl and touch one elbow to the opposite knee. Uncurl, lie flat, breathe. One.

Then crunch up again, this time touching the other elbow to the other knee. Uncurl. Two.

Your stomach is so flabby. What did you do today? Anything? Oh, yeah, right: you carried a couple of duffel bags from the car and heaved them into the elevator. Some exercise, you slug.

Fourteen. Fifteen. Sixteen. My abs begin to burn. Just a little.

Did you know that every time you walk, you jiggle? All that loose flesh hanging off you, pouches of fat, jiggling with each step.

I keep counting. The television sounds far away now. The elevator down the hall dings. Doors slide open. The girdle of muscle that wraps around my lower back, connects with my abs, is on fire. Forty-five. Forty-six. Forty-seven.

You are so out of shape. Push through this, you wimp. You fat wimp.

Sixty. Sixty-one. Sixty-two.

Someone bangs on my door. I hear girls' voices.

"Eva? Hey, knock knock!"

Marguerite. I hold my breath, hold my bent knees, mid-crunch, suspended. Word travels fast. I've been in the annex, what? Five hours? And already she's tracked me down.

"She must be out," I hear. Anna. Are they all there? The three of them must be handcuffed together. Another knock.

"Eva?" Then the sickening sound of a hand rattling the doorknob, and I realize, too late, that it never occurred to me to lock my door. I jump up from the floor, and when the fluorescent light from the hallway pours inside, I'm standing. I wipe beads of perspiration off my upper lip.

"Oh, hey! There you are! Were you asleep or something?" Two of them: Marguerite and Anna. They walk in.

"Sort of," I say. "I was reading, and drifted off. What's up?"

They both settle, uninvited, on my bed. Which I had just made, the blankets stretched tight and perfectly flat across the mattress.

"Welcome to the neighborhood is what's up!" Marguerite exclaims. "We heard about you at dinner. Why didn't you tell us you were moving in?"

"We only got the call last night that space opened in the annex." I sit. On the floor. I spread my legs in a V and stretch, gripping one heel with both hands and pressing my forehead against my knee.

"So that must have been what Madame wanted to talk to you about on Friday afternoon," she says. Half question, half statement. Of course she wants to know. That's why she's here. Screw the welcome-committee thing: Marguerite needs info.

"Yup," I say into my leg. This would be so weird for anyone who is not a dancer. But if you have muscles like overused rubber bands, it's perfectly acceptable. This girl I knew at Sonia Fleisch's would interrupt herself, midsentence, face the wall, place one heel against it at about shoulder height, then slide, slide, slide forward until both legs were splayed flat. A perfect split from a standing position.

Anna joins me on the floor. She opens her legs wide, until they form a straight line with her torso smack dab in the middle. She leans forward and touches her forehead to the ground. Meanwhile, Marguerite checks out my room. Her eyes light on

149

the framed photos I've arranged in a neat row on the little shelf above my bed. One in particular catches her attention, and she takes it down.

"Who's this in the picture with you?" she asks. She holds the photo out toward me.

"That's my friend Henry," I reply.

"What is she, like, a model?" Marguerite says. Anna, curious, gets off the floor and joins Marguerite on the bed. She peers over her shoulder at the photo.

"That girl is really, really pretty," Anna says.

"I know," I say. I stand up. I hold my hand out for the photo. It's of Henry and me, taken last summer on Long Beach Island. Paige's mom had driven a bunch of us down, after we'd finished our final exams. It was a cloudless, hot day, and they'd all cooked themselves lobster-red, moaning in the van the whole way back. Everyone except Henry and me. She was already tan; I'd stayed under my big beach umbrella most of the day. I can't remember who took the picture. We have our arms over each other's shoulders, grinning at the camera.

"She could be a model," I tell them. "But she is the most un-model-like person you'd ever meet. She's a total jock. Guys follow her around, panting, and she doesn't notice. She's too busy playing tennis." I hold the picture in both hands as I say this. I like bragging about Henry to them.

"Tennis?" Anna asks.

"With a capital *T*," I say. "Believe me, someday we'll be watching Henry in the Wimbledon finals. She's amazing. She's at this camp right now, in Florida? One of those places where . . ."

Marguerite bursts out laughing. She's sprawled across my bed now, staring at the ceiling and laughing.

"Oh my god," she exclaims. "I know this is so random, but do you know that girl from Wisconsin who wears her bun practically on the top of her head, like she's balancing an apple? And, you know, her hair is brown? Well . . ."

This girl has the attention span of a flea. Or a Rhonda. Maybe if you had some juicy ballet gossip for her, she'd actually listen.

My cell phone rings. It's on the shelf above my bed, just over Marguerite's head. It rings three times before I can get my hands on it and snap it open.

"Hello?" I say eagerly.

At first I think it's a wrong number. It sounds like lots of yelling on the other end. Chanting even, like "Wump! Wump! Wump!" Male voices *wump*ing. I'm about to press "end" when I hear Henry.

"Eva! Eva, are you there? Hey, everyone, pipe *down*! I can't hear a thing!"

"Hen?" I shout into the phone, as if that would help. "Is that you?"

The *wump*ing subsides and I hear Henry, her voice slightly softer, as if she's turned away from the phone.

"Hey, guys! Eva wants to know what's going on!" Henry says. Screams follow. Shouting, cheering, thumping. Then a voice I recognize, clearly excited.

 151

"Hello, Eva? It's Yolanda. She won! Henry won! Woohoo!" A pause. I imagine Henry snatching the phone back, because it's her voice I hear next.

"Eva! I'm sorry, this is so crazy. But I *had* to call you!"

"You beat him? The Perv?" I say excitedly.

"Straight sets!" Henry shouts, and I hear more riotous noise. Marguerite and Anna stare at me with these very confused expressions.

"It's Henry. She just won a huge match," I explain. Marguerite stands. She raises her arms in a big, V-like stretch. She practically yawns.

"Cool. Tell her we said congratulations," she says, then heads for the door. Anna smiles and follows. "Catch you later, Eva," she says. They leave.

The noise from the cell phone has diminished. Maybe Henry has moved to another room.

"Hen?" I say.

"I'm here. Phew! That's better. I couldn't hear myself think. Eva, I won! I beat him!"

"Of course you beat him!" I say. "You are amazing. He never had a chance."

"No, you don't understand. He doesn't suck. He hits the ball really, really hard. Guy hard. I have never played anyone who hits like this."

"Henry, you play against guys all the time."

"Not like this. These guys are at a whole different level. They're not just high school jocks slamming the ball at you. It is an entirely different game."

152

She is soaring. So, so happy. Something wells inside me. Tears.

"I am really proud of you," I say.

"I wish you were here!" she shrieks. "This is so cool!"

"I guess all that coaching from Little David paid off," I say. She laughs. Then I hear her say to someone else, "She wants to know if Little David's coaching helped." She giggles. A sound I'm still not used to. I hear a male voice in the background.

"Tell her I'm Big David, okay?" A pause. Rustling.

"Henry?"

"I'm here, I'm here. Sorry. Look, Eva, I have to call my parents, and then these *people* have to throw me into the pool. Another Chadwick tradition. This place is so crazy! But I'll call you tomorrow, okay? I love you! I miss you!"

"I miss you, too. You are the best."

Henry is gone before I say another word. I press "end" and the phone jingles its closing theme. The annex hum seems strangely muted now. My room feels like an insulated box. There's a crack of light at the base of the door, and I can make out the passing shadows of people walking by. I feel so tired. I place the phone on my night table, crawl into bed, still dressed, and pull the covers over my head. I wrap my arms around my body and rest one hand on the hard, reassuring bone of my hip.

Chapter Seventeen
HENRY

David reaches around me. He came up behind me as I signed off with Eva, and as he gently pulls the phone from my hand, his lips brush my ear. I hear him breathe, feel him rest his cheek, briefly, against my hair, and I turn in the circle of his arms. There's no time to look into his eyes. I'm kissing him, melting into this sweet, dizzy kiss that just . . . happens.

When it ends, he looks at me, one corner of his mouth turned up in this teasing smile I'm starting to recognize. He rests his forehead on mine and whispers:

"You taste salty."

"How romantic of you to notice," I say, and kiss him again.

He moves on to my neck. The spot behind my ear. The place where my neck becomes my shoulder. Little kisses, exploring, like butterfly wings. I stifle the urge to laugh.

He doesn't know I'm ticklish. He doesn't know anything about me, really. And right now, at this moment, I don't know anything about me, either. Not this part, anyway. This swooning, crazy part that finds me sliding my hands down his chest, past his belly, to the belt loops of his shorts. Big baggy cargo shorts he always wears when he's not on court. I hook my fingers in the loops and pull him in close to me. He makes this little "ummm" sound, and his lips return to mine. Press harder against mine.

*   *   *

It had been building since breakfast. When I got down to the cafeteria at seven-thirty he was already there, sitting at a table for two near the windows. He was writing on a small dry-erase board, and his empty dishes were pushed to one side. As I came up behind him, the sun shone brightly on the back of his head, igniting these red highlights in his brown hair.

"Hey. D'you already eat?" He looked up at me. The smile. *Oh, help.*

"Yeah, I got here early. Couldn't sleep. Go on, get your breakfast. I'm plotting our strategy."

Our strategy. Couldn't sleep. *Up thinking about me all night, David? Yeah, right. Don't get ahead of yourself, Henry.* As I shoveled scrambled eggs onto my plate and threw a couple slices of wheat bread into the toaster, I tried to redirect my thoughts. Refocus. *Tennis. Eyes on the prize. Not on the guys.*

When I got to the table, I slid my tray next to the dry-erase board, unzipped my Windbreaker and draped it over my chair. David looked up and his eyes went straight to my chest. One corner of his mouth turned up and his eyes crinkled into laugh lines.

"Last night's T-shirt was friendlier," he said. I glanced down at the words printed on the front: "Boys Are Dumb. Throw Rocks at Them." I shrugged, trying to look all innocent.

"Just want to get in the spirit of the match, you know? The whole battle-of-the-sexes thing?" David leaned forward. He leveled his gaze at me, and spoke quietly.

"Don't forget: I'm a boy, too, Henry. You don't want to hurt my feelings." I held his look, and leaned in farther. I dropped my voice to my closest approximation of husky.

"Actually, David, you're no boy. You're the *man*." His eyes grew round. A flash, just a hint, of genuine surprise flickered across his face. For one deeply gratifying moment David Ross was slightly off balance. *Yes! Point goes to Miss Lloyd. Fifteen–love.* Then it disappeared. He moved on without a comment, returning to his plans.

As I wolfed down eggs, he drew sweeping lines on the dry-erase board and talked. Dundas, he explained, was impatient. He liked to finish points early, go for winners when he should still be hitting rally balls.

"His attention span doesn't extend beyond four shots," David explained. "The trick is hanging with him for those four, 'cause he hits really hard. Too hard, actually. He's not fit enough to sustain that level of effort for five sets. Which is why he tries to finish points quickly. But people who can hang with him always beat him."

"Is that how you beat him?" I asked.

"No. But I think that should be your strategy."

"Well, how do *you* do it?" David hesitated.

 156

"I hit harder than him, I'm fitter, and I don't lose focus," he finally said, shrugging.

"Oh, right. If you do say so yourself," I smirked.

David sighed and tossed the dry-erase marker on the table. It skittered onto the floor. He didn't bother to retrieve it.

"Listen, Henry, can we get serious for five minutes? This is not about me. It's about *your* match in"—he glanced at his watch—"eleven hours. Now, do you want to talk tennis, or flirt? Because frankly, I canceled my morning drill session to work with you, and if you're not serious, then I'm gonna go find my coach and . . ."

"Whoa. Hold it right there, cowboy. Flirt? In your dreams." I willed my face to remain cool, but it was useless. I could feel the crimson spreading over my cheeks like a brush fire. David held the thought for a good ten seconds, until I turned completely red.

"I stand corrected. I thought you were flirting outrageously with me instead of concentrating on the business at hand."

"I don't flirt." He raised his eyebrows.

"Really?"

"Really."

"That's a shame. Because despite having a boy's name and playing tennis like a man, you could be a really, really good flirter."

"Don't make me hate you, David." That earned me another killer smile.

"Now *that's* more like it!" he said. He pushed his chair back and stood up. "I think we're ready to hit some balls!"

157

I'd never stepped foot inside the pro court before. That's because it's not intended for the general scrubs. Ringed with palm trees, screened with forest-green windbreaks secured to the high metal fence, it was like stepping into someone's private living room. There were the stacks of fresh white towels. Icy water in an insulated cooler. A teak bench. *Teak.*

For the first hour, we drilled. First short balls, using exaggerated topspin so that they dropped three feet beyond the net. Next, net shots: sharp, hard. Then we moved back to the baseline, for fifty high, deep crosscourt forehands, catching them on the rise. Fifty backhands. Fifty down-the-liners. If the ball went out, we'd start the count over.

When we finally took a break, I was drenched. As I sat on the bench, swallowing a steady stream of icy water, I felt something cool on the back of my neck. David had soaked a washcloth with cold water.

"Behind your ears. Your wrists," he said. "Pulse points. If you press something cold there, you can actually get your body temperature to drop." I pulled the washcloth from my neck. It was already hot where it had touched my skin.

"I think I need complete submersion in the pool," I said. "Or a dry shirt."

Hmm. There's an idea. A shot he doesn't expect.

I went over to my bag, rummaged and pulled out a sleeveless, wicking tennis shirt. And a dry bra. I turned my back to David, took a deep breath and pulled the sodden clothes over my head. I dropped them on the ground and slipped the dry shirt and bra past my shoulders. When I turned, David's shocked look greeted me.

Point to Miss Lloyd.

"What?" I said, willing myself to sound nonchalant. "Nobody can see in. The windbreaks are like privacy curtains." He gestured toward himself.

"Am I nobody? Jeez, Henry."

"Oh, c'mon. I turned my back. And besides. You're already familiar with this bra." I picked up my racket and started walking back onto the court. When I got to the baseline he hadn't budged. He stared at me, hands on hips.

"What?" I repeated.

"You play mind games. You are completely, totally awesome at it, aren't you? It's one of your weapons. It has to be. I've never seen anyone more expert at getting under another person's skin." There was no trace of a smile on his face when he said this.

Game over, Hen. You overplayed that one. What must he think now?

I was silent. I hadn't intended to make him mad. I was only joking around. Okay . . . flirting. I should have stopped. He'd asked me, at breakfast, to stop.

I walked back to the bench.

"I'm sorry," I said. He didn't reply. Just looked at me with this quizzical expression like he was trying to sort something out.

"You're right. I'm the queen of mind games. It's, like, this really, really bad habit." His face relaxed.

"Apology accepted," he said.

"I shouldn't have changed in front of you," I continued. "You must think I'm some sort of teasing slut. God. I don't know why I did that. I've never . . ."

Once I got started, it was hard to hold back. There's something about being forgiven so easily that greases the skids for further confessions. David finally held both his hands up in "I surrender" mode.

"Whoa. Stop, Henry. Stop." I stopped.

"There is a time and place for mind games. Just . . . not with me. Let's make you and me a game-free zone, okay?"

You and me. I nodded, incapable of speech at the moment.

"And let's . . . compartmentalize. Right now, tennis. Later, we'll talk about all your outrageous flirting. Deal?" That sweet corner of his mouth turned up for the second time that morning.

Oh, who's playing mind games now, David?

"Deal," I managed to say.

"Then get to the baseline," he said. "I'm gonna shoot some hard ones at you."

* * *

I wish I did it on good tennis alone, but the fact is the mind games were what finally pushed Jonathan Dundas over the edge.

The guy didn't suck. He had a great second serve, really mean kick. I had a tough time returning it, but he didn't seem to notice, and kept trying to blast me off the court with a big first serve, which, unfortunately for him, rarely landed in.

 160

Then, if he couldn't slam a winner off me within the first few balls, he'd lose his composure and do something stupid to blow the point. So I won the first set 6–3.

As we toweled off between sets, I moved in for the kill.

I walked over to his end of the net. His face was beet-red and he was sitting.

"Wanna quit now?" I said. Loudly. Most everyone was watching from the Overlook, draped over the balcony rail, spilling in and out of the lounge, where the staff had set up cool drinks and snacks. But a few of the pros and coaches were sitting courtside. They whooped when they heard my comment. "Hey man, don't let her get away with that!" someone said. "You tell him, Henry!" another called, laughing.

It was circus time, and I had decided to give them a show.

Dundas wasn't having any of it.

"Just go back to your side of the court," he said between his teeth. No trace of his usual attitude. *Oh, yes, Henry, this one's yours.*

"Would you at least like me to tell you what you're doing wrong?" I replied sweetly. He jumped to his feet.

"Would someone please *make her* go back to her side of the court?" he demanded, looking at the coaches. Missy motioned to me to walk away. I complied, but as I sauntered off I turned toward the crowd assembled on the balcony and gave them all a royal wave. One of those pivot-at-the-wrist jobs. Screams of approval, especially from the girls.

David was standing not far from where I'd parked my water bottle and tennis bag.

 161

"Okay, Attila. Enough," he muttered. I looked at him. The expression on his face caught me up short.

Disapproval. Disappointment. I felt something leaden in my gut.

"Play it pure, Henry," he said. "You can beat him on your game alone." He gave me one short, reassuring nod. Then David went to sit with the coaches.

All I can say is I must really like this guy. Because even though a million little snarky comments and crowd-pleasing, mind-game-playing moves popped into my head, I buried them beneath killer forehands and point-ending overheads. I made my face impassive on every stroke. I forced my tone to be neutral every time I called the score, and as I watched the Perv self-destruct on the other side of the net, I focused on finishing him off with the best tennis I've ever played. When it was over, 6–4 in the second set, and we shook hands at net, Dundas didn't make eye contact. He looked sick, literally.

I didn't care. I was too busy trying to catch David's eye. When he did look my way, he didn't just smile. Didn't just wink, or flash me a thumbs-up. He stood up and started clapping. Standing ovation, totally, and within seconds the whole crowd joined in.

It was a sweet first for Mark Lloyd's daughter.

* * *

Someone pounds on the door. We had slipped in here, the kitchenette off the Overlook snack bar, so I could hear myself talk to Eva. Now the natives are restless. They want to party. Celebrate my straight-sets win over Jon "the Perv" Dundas, my

 162

overturning the repeated humiliation of number one girls losing to number one boys, and throw me, still in my tennis whites and sneakers, into the pool.

I would *so* prefer to be kissing David Ross in the kitchenette, but . . . duty calls.

"We should go before they break it down," I say. He sighs but doesn't argue, which is . . . disappointing. Maybe I want him to say, "Let them all go to hell; I'm here with you." But he doesn't, and when we open the door to a wall of chanting people and pointed wolf whistles, I have to confess: I feel a little drunk on the energy.

"Grab her!" somebody yells, and I'm swept off my feet, lifted and somehow carried. Hands all over me, but I'm laughing too much to really care. I feel like one of those concertgoers who falls back into the crowd and gets passed over everyone's heads.

Out of the Overlook, down the stairs . . . "Do *not* drop her!" I hear Missy's voice . . . across the campus to the Olympic-sized swimming pool, and with an enthusiastic "One! Two! Three!" I'm hurled into the deep end. I make an enormous splash, I sink beneath the aquamarine chlorinated coolness, and once I get over the weird sensation of being fully clothed, with shoes, underwater, I realize what a welcome break the silence is. I open my eyes. I can see them, above me, ringing the pool, and while I can't hear them, I can tell they are chanting, jumping, yelling. I hold my breath, savoring the final seconds before I emerge from this baptism. Because when I come out, everything will be different.

Chapter Eighteen

EVA

I know something is wrong the instant I land. I know it's not possible to hear the crack, but I swear, I hear it. The infinitesimal, unmistakable crack of small bone travels from my toe to my ear, the way an electric current travels along copper wire. It's instantaneous, invisible and true. A light flickers on, and hidden objects reveal themselves.

It's already been such a not-great day.

It began with breakfast in the canteen with the zombie ballerinas from hell. They came, as usual, splay-footed and bunned, into the big, fluorescent-lit room, wrapped in leggings and loose, soft sweatshirts. They lined up, yawning, for egg-white omelettes, filled cups with black coffee and selected their grapefruits. They watched each other chew and swallow, measured and compared each morsel the others put in their mouths, not unlike the way they measured and compared the height of each other's jumps.

For some reason the Three Musketeers (Marguerite, Anna and Caitlin, thus named by *moi* because they are as laughable

 164

and lethal as the original Dumas trio) have decided to adopt me, so even though I'd gotten down to breakfast before everyone, and had assumed my most convincing Do Not Disturb posture, engrossed in my coffee and magazine, down they sat. Wonderful. Every damn morning. It's always the same: Marguerite eats yogurt and granola; Anna eats toast, eggs, juice and fruit; Caitlin eats a sizeable portion of everything, getting up three or four times to refill, then bolts from the table before the rest of us have cleared our trays.

While she's off worshipping the porcelain god, the remaining two zero in on yours truly. And the morning of the not-great day, they had their knives out. Freshly sharpened.

That's because the day before, Madame DuPres made an example of me. We were practicing *chassé*, this step where one foot literally chases the other foot out of its position. Like ballet skipping, with graceful arms making a round, open sweep over your head while your tutu bounces. Of course, in Madame's class, no one wears tutus. But when I was a little girl in Sonia Fleisch's class, I wore tutus and loved *chassé*.

Madame was frustrated. You could hear it in her voice. Sighing with exasperation as dancer after dancer skipped inexpertly across the studio. Finally, she called my name.

"Eva, step forward, please." She called me out of sequence. A choice not wasted on the other zombies.

"*Chassé* across the room."

Obediently, I *chasséd*. I thought, *Light! Bright! Arms sweep!* My imaginary tutu bounced. I could feel my own smile.

I could feel the eyes bore into me.

 165

"Yes!"

Madame's excited voice.

"Precisely! Eva, again, please. I want you to watch her arms. In one sweeping, fluid motion she tracks her progress across the floor. Even down to her fingertips, she is one complete thought."

Once more, across the room, and I couldn't help it: I showed off. I skipped higher, kicked one foot before the other just a bit more sharply, and for effect, doubled the length of the run and circled my arms completely, twice. I turned to Madame when I finished, I leveled my gaze at her and I allowed myself to think, to speak, with my eyes.

She smiled back.

"Thank you, Eva." She didn't need to say more. I rejoined the clutch of staring dancers, willing my face to appear neutral. Eyes downcast, demure. But irresistibly, I looked up, where I knew Marguerite stood.

Let's just say, if looks could kill, I'd have been a splattered, gory Capezio mess on the hardwood floor.

I managed to evade her the rest of that day and evening, but there's no escaping them at breakfast. Especially not after *chassé* day.

"So," Marguerite begins. "I wonder what Madame will have you teach us today."

I am dissecting my first egg. I tap it gently against the table until hairline cracks, like a web, spread across the shell.

"Excuse me?" I say politely.

"Frankly, I don't know why she didn't ask Hillary to demonstrate *chassé*," says Anna. "I think she does it best."

 166

"So do I," agrees Marguerite. She waits for a response from me. I give her none.

Tiny shell fragments fall from the egg as I run my thumb over the smooth surface of the white. I skim the rubbery flesh until it is absolutely clean. Not a pinhead of shell remains. I place the egg in an empty white bowl and move on to egg number two.

"Where did you study before coming here, Eva?" Anna asks. "Donna tells me you went to Nutmeg."

"No, I've never done a camp before this," I say. Tapping, tapping. Little cracks begin to form. We all watch my egg.

"Really? Donna swears she saw you there last summer," Anna insists.

"Must've been my stunt double," I say, without thinking. It's the type of comment that would make Henry laugh.

The zombies don't even attempt a smile. Meanwhile, egg number two is deposited in the bowl. Next comes the surgical removal of the dastardly yellow. The source of all evil, artery-clogging fat. I take a knife and run it longitudinally down the egg, a perfect slice from tip to toe. The egg splits neatly in half, and the yellow falls out in two intact demi-spheres. I deposit them in a second empty bowl.

Sitting with these people makes me want to scream, but it's like I'm glued in place, and as I sit I feel my thighs spreading over the plastic, institutional cafeteria chair. I need to get out of here, need to move.

You fat pig! You pathetic, sorry excuse for a dancer. You tub of lard. That yellow is like the flab hanging off your big fat butt.

 167

"I didn't know Donna went to Nutmeg," I struggle to say. "That's really cool. Why'd she come here this summer?"

"Are you kidding me?" Marguerite says. Like she can't believe how stupid I am. "This place is the *best*. Everyone wants to be here."

I shrug. I take one tiny, mouse-sized bite of egg white. I can't swallow.

"I guess," I say. I have to get out of here. I pass a napkin over my lips and spit out the white. I start to gather my things, but my indifference to the unquestionable greatness of the New York School of Dance is too much of an affront to Marguerite. My shrug has had the effect of waving a red flag in front of a gored bull. And yesterday my *chassé* gored her good.

"You guess?" she says. "You *know* it. Here's what I don't get about you, Eva. We're trying to be your friends, but you avoid us, you're practically rude, and you hide the fact that Madame has singled you out. I mean, be honest. Has she invited you to the full-year program?"

Ha! What a joke! Who would invite a gross loser like you?

The primal scream that has been building at the back of my throat is so close to emerging that I feel actual, real panic. Screw the tray; if I don't vacate this room immediately, I'm going to totally lose it. Now. I pull myself into a stand, heave my thighs off the chair.

"Since you've been here for *three* summers, you know those decisions aren't made until August. So don't accuse me of being dishonest." I grab my magazine and push my chair back

168

with my foot. "See you in class." I leave the canteen before she has a chance to reply.

The three of them don't speak to me from then on. They don't change with me in the locker room. They whisper and glance my way until the moment I look *their* way. Then they turn their heads.

I want to hurt them in ways that show. Like, with a machete.

Instead, I dance.

I flash Madame my brightest smile and loudly say, "Good morning!" to her when we all file in for class. The sphinx startles. Who is this putty, she wonders, addressing me? This clay, meant only to be twisted into lovely shapes of my design? But then our eyes lock and she reflexively replies, "Good morning, Eva." A smile begins to form before she catches herself and smooths the lines of her face back into expressionless.

I've hurled my first grenade. And when I glance at Marguerite and Co., I can see it was an accurate throw.

It goes on all morning. A glorious morning of dance. The sun shining through the high studio windows is bright, one of those perfect, cloudless New York summer days when light glints off the skyscrapers like diamonds, city birds soar and colorful banners flap outside the Met, along Fifth Avenue, in front of Lincoln Center. New York is the city of dreams on mornings like this, and I'm in the zone. I'm there, but not *there*. The space I inhabit is pure movement, insulated from every competing noise: from Marguerite's sneering questions;

sounds of traffic on the streets below; the relentless, CNN-like ticker tape of doubt and fear that plays inside my head all day.

I don't think I've ever danced like this before, and I allow myself to feel Madame's approving gaze. I allow myself to imagine that come September, I'll be one of the chosen. Granted a coveted spot in the full-year program, the gateway to the *corps de ballet*. A brilliant career. A brilliant life. I allow myself to relax in the promise of my abilities, and dance as if I'm already there.

Then it cracks. Of course. Who was I kidding?

The pain, and the freakish sound that I swear I hear but that everyone later tells me could not possibly be heard by the human ear, take me right out. I collapse like a fistful of little sticks dumped from a bag: inelegant, askew. I hear my bones rattle on the smooth wood floor. Fresh pain shoots up my elbow. The room starts going dark, then light, then dark again, and bees are buzzing. Miraculously, I don't faint. But everything from that point on seems dreamlike.

I remember sounds: the muffled staccato of *pointe* shoes and high-pitched exclamations; Madame strident, ordering, asking me to tell her my name, count to five. Strong arms scoop me up, carry me from the studio. There is a cab ride, and I'm taken to a hospital.

By the time Rhonda arrives from Jersey, the verdict is in: I've broken the big toe on my left foot. And not just a hairline fracture. This baby's broke good. The doctor suggests that perhaps there already was a hairline, and the pressure of dancing

 170

on it simply made it worse. Of course, there is good news: it will heal and it's not serious. There is also bad news: I have to stay off it for it to heal correctly. And worse news: I probably won't dance for the rest of the summer.

And finally, the worst news, contained in lab results the doctor holds. Papers which have caused this worried crease to form on her forehead. We're still in the emergency room, where I sit on a high hospital bed, my foot elevated, my toe securely wrapped. Rhonda, poker straight, sits in a chair beside me. The doctor speaks.

"The X-rays confirmed that the toe is broken," she says. "Then, because she complained about pain in her elbow, we x-rayed her arm. Good news there: no break. But I saw things that concerned me, so I ordered a bone-density test." She pauses. The crease deepens.

"Eva is suffering from a condition known as osteopenia, or low bone density. It's a precursor to osteoporosis, and it makes her more susceptible to breaks." Rhonda gasps.

"What could have caused this?" she asks. Doc widens her eyes.

"A nutritional deficiency, most likely." Rhonda makes another sound. A scoff that reminds me of a Henry snort.

"That's ridiculous. We are very nutritionally conscious in our home."

The doctor turns to me.

"Eva, when was the last time you got your period?"

Silence. A cold ball of panic begins to form in my stomach.

171

"I don't remember." Rhonda stares at me. She doesn't answer for me. That's because she doesn't have a clue, either. My period is not something that's been foremost in our minds.

"Within the last year? Last summer?" the doctor persists. My mind scrolls back. What did I do last summer, and did I have my period? I can't remember.

"I don't think so," I say. The doctor nods.

"And when did Eva's menses begin?"

"Excuse me?" Rhonda asks.

"How old was Eva when she first got her period?"

"Oh, young. So young! She was in fourth grade, only ten years old. But, that's Eva. She's always done everything early!" Rhonda's high-pitched laugh sounds maniacal to me.

"And Eva, how tall are you?" the doctor asks.

"Five-one," I reply.

"Do you know how much you weigh?" she continues.

Too much! Too much, you pig! You're so huge your bones are cracking from the sheer weight.

"I don't know. There isn't a scale at the dorms where I'm staying."

Rhonda stands up swiftly.

"May I ask the purpose of these questions?" she demands.

"How much did you weigh last time you got on the scale at Mom's house?" the doctor persists. I hesitate. I can't make myself say it. The feeling, that dark-to-light feeling, descends on me, and the bees are buzzing again.

Pig! Elephant! You are disgusting.

"Stop this! Can't you see you're upsetting her?"

172

The doctor whirls on Rhonda.

"If Eva were a dog, you'd have been charged with animal abuse by now," she says icily. "But because she's your daughter, I'm going to have to discharge her to your care, where I predict she will continue to starve herself. In your nutritionally conscious home."

The doctor takes a step closer to me.

"When was the last time you ate, hon?"

Chapter Nineteen

HENRY

Mark's voice feels like a slap. Even a thousand miles away and through a cell phone. I have this overpowering urge to press "end."

I've just told him I'm playing in Miami this weekend. A junior invitational tournament, the type he has kept me away from. Apparently one of the players had to drop out, and the tournament officials invited Chadwick to fill her spot. After the Dundas performance, the coaches decided there was only one girl to choose: me.

Predictably, Mark explodes.

"Who the *hell* signed off on that?" he demands.

I'm in my dorm room. Yoly is seated at one of the desks, writing a letter to her family. She looks up. She can hear Mark yell all the way from Jersey.

"My coach," I say calmly. "The school. I'm going with a group from Chadwick."

Okay, Hen, since when does two equal a group? You and

David are the only players going. Plus two coaches. So four. I guess four's a group?

"Yeah, well, I've got news for them. You don't have permission to play in semipro tournaments."

"Dad, there's no such thing as semipro. And you guys signed a form giving Chadwick permission for away tournaments."

"Bull*shit*, Henry. I signed no such form."

"Well, Mom did. It was with the stuff giving the school permission to use pictures of me on their website."

He swears loudly. Yoly doesn't look up this time, but I see her eyebrows rise.

"You see, *this* is the sort of crap I'm talking about! They are exploiting you. Not to mention it's like an open invitation to predators. I'm calling them, right now. And Henry: you will *not*, I repeat, *not* play in that tournament this weekend. Do I make myself clear?"

"As a bell, Dad," I reply. My voice is controlled. It gives no hint of the adrenaline-induced rage that makes my hands shake. I press "end."

Weeks without Mark, the freedom of No Mark, has softened me. While I was home, I was used to his anger. Ever ready for it. Now, a few weeks into doing my own thing, the taste of the bit in my mouth again is harsh.

"You okay?" Yoly says softly. I shrug. I throw myself onto my bed.

"He doesn't want you to play in the tournament?" she persists.

"Nope," I say flatly. She shakes her head.

"Why not? It's such an honor. Doesn't he realize you were singled out?"

She doesn't get it. How could she? Yolanda Cruz's father . . . her entire family . . . orbits in a completely different solar system from Planet Mark. She is in the middle of the pack here at camp, and the way her family acts, you'd think she was a Wimbledon champion. They call her every night, telling her how much they miss her, how proud they are of her. You'd think she'd moved to China, and not just gone to some camp up the highway.

For the first time in my life, I'm envious. Not because I want a huge family. Not because I want to live above a restaurant in a hot, crowded city, although I could get used to Cuban food. Not because I want to get applause for playing mediocre tennis. I envy their simple enjoyment of her. The way they laugh together. I think if she told them she wanted to quit tennis and enter a nose-picking contest, they'd all show up to cheer her on. Armed with boxes of Kleenex.

I know my parents love me, and miss me. But I wonder if they would be so obsessed with me if I were ordinary.

"My dad's complicated," I begin.

"All dads are complicated," she says. "Especially about their daughters."

"Yeah, well, Mark's the President of Complicated," I say. She frowns.

"Who's Mark?"

"Oh, my dad. I sometimes call him Mark. When I'm annoyed with him. We do that, Eva and I. She calls her mother Rhonda whenever she gets too over-the-top. Which is, like, always." Yoly gets up from the desk and sits, cross-legged, on her bed.

"You white girls have no clue about over-the-top," she declares. "Try living in a Latino family, with Grandma in the apartment next door, and *tell* me about over-the-top. Try making it through a *quinceañera* with your sanity intact, and then, maybe, I'll listen."

"Keensy-what?" I ask. Yoly's eyes grow big.

"Do *not* tell me you've never heard of a *quinceañera*." I shrug. She gives a little scream of shock and horror, and jumps off the bed. She goes over to her dresser, rummages around in the bottom drawer, and pulls out a large manila envelope. She turns to me, holding it tightly against her chest.

"What I am about to show you stays between us, understand?" she says seriously.

"Sure," I say.

"I mean it, Henry. This is not very . . . Chadwick."

"I promise." She sits next to me and pulls an eight-by-ten photo from the envelope.

It's her. Dressed up like Glinda the Good, the nice witch from *The Wizard of Oz*. More like, stuffed into a Glinda the Good costume, without the wand. She's wearing a little diamond tiara in her hair, which is swept up into this high, fancy do. An enormous white dress billows around her. She wears

 177

diamond-drop earrings, a diamond necklace, dark red lipstick and plenty of eye makeup. She bears no resemblance to the sweaty, tennis-ball-pounding girl I know.

"You clean up real nice, Yoly," I say. She slaps me on the arm, but her face relaxes.

"This," she explains, "is the formal photo for my *quinceañera*. My 'sweet-fifteen' birthday party. Like a sweet sixteen, only more. For Latinas, when a girl turns fifteen, it's like she's officially a woman."

"Sounds cool," I comment. She doesn't answer right away. She looks thoughtful.

"There are a lot of expectations," she says carefully. "A lot of traditions. Expenses. It's like throwing a wedding. There's a band, a sit-down dinner. Drinks. Clothing. You plan for months, all for this one huge party. My family actually has sponsors to help pay for it. Like, the Gonzalez family who owns the cigar shop down the street from my parents' restaurant? They sponsored all the soda, beer, rum, you name it. My *tía* Blanca donated all the flowers. My *abuela* bought my dress. Do you get the picture?"

"Uh, it sounds like you're planning a big, fun party and people are being generous?" I say. Yoly flops backward onto my bed. She stares at the ceiling.

"They *own* you, Henry," she says. "They chain you with their love and generosity. Whether you want it or not, and I never wanted it. I'm a jock, always have been, and I'm not into the whole retro-Cinderella thing. But what do you do when your grandmother says she's emptied out her bank account and bought you the most beautiful *quinces* dress in Miami? And she wants you to go to the dress shop to see it and have a fitting? And next thing you know, you're standing in front of a full-length mirror decked out like a Disney character in a dress two sizes too small?" Yoly is talking faster and faster. She's approaching a rant.

"You say, 'No thanks'?" I suggest. She rolls over and looks squarely at me.

"You compromise," she says. "You swallow the urge to say, 'Sorry, Abuelita, but I'd rather be shot at sunrise than seen in public like this.' Instead, you tell her she's the best grandmother in the whole wide world. Which she is, despite her need to parade you out like a Barbie in front of everyone you know, and quite a few you don't. Then, after she dries her tears from crying over how beautiful you look in your *quinces* dress, you go to your parents. And tell them the only way on earth you'll subject yourself to this torture is if they let you go to a really cool tennis camp over the summer." Yoly smiles at me knowingly.

"And *that's* how you got to Chadwick," I say.

"When the Miami Grocers' Association offered to sponsor the band for my *quinces*, I told Papi we could hire a DJ instead and ask the grocers to pay for camp. He asked, they agreed, and here I am. Compromise."

I look at the picture again. Despite what she says about Barbies, there is radiance in Yolanda's eyes. She looks overweight and overdressed and overly made up and . . . happy. She wears a smile I've never seen on her at Chadwick.

"You look beautiful in this picture, Yoly," I say quietly, handing it back to her.

She looks at me curiously. Silently, she replaces the picture in its envelope, returns it to the dresser drawer. Returns to the bed and gives my shoulders a squeeze.

"Can't you compromise with your father?" she asks kindly.

She is trying so hard to be nice, but the fact that Yoly cannot possibly *get* Mark only makes me suddenly miss Eva. Terribly, like a stab of missing. I realize I haven't spoken to her in days, and I make a mental note to call her, tonight, before lights-out.

"'Compromise' is not a word in Mark Lloyd's vocabulary," I say grimly. "But listen. I don't want to be negative. Maybe the Chadwick people will convince him to change his mind when he calls." *Yeah, right. Not in your lifetime, Henry.*

"Well, in that case . . . I have some big news," Yoly says brightly. "Guess who's going to your match this weekend?"

"Andy Roddick?" I say hopefully.

"So much better: me. And my mom. And my sister Carolina. I asked Missy if I could come down to watch on Sunday, for the finals, and she got us tickets. And afterward, if you all want, my parents said everybody should come to the restaurant for dinner. We'll make a real *fiesta* out of it!"

"Yoly, you do realize I might get knocked out during the first round Friday night?"

"Henry, you are going to win this tournament. I feel it in my bones. I feel like this is going to be a very, very big weekend for you."

 180

That's when I surprise myself. I throw my arms around her in a big, grateful hug. It's all good with Yoly. Positive energy gushing from every pore in her body. Just the sort of karma I need right now. I need to focus on all the good stuff. An exciting tournament. A new girlfriend and dinner out at a real Cuban restaurant. David. Who, it turns out, kisses as well as he plays tennis. Maybe even better.

"Okay, but promise me one thing: you have to help me order from the menu. The only Cuban food I know is rice and beans. And your mom's *empanada* thingies."

Yoly sits up straight. She doesn't need more encouragement.

"Let me tell you about *cerdo asado*," she begins.

Chapter Twenty

EVA

"Yes, she actually used *that word*! In front of Eva! I have never experienced anything more . . . thoughtless. Irresponsible."

Rhonda is ranting to my father on the phone. I listen from the den, where I recline on the overstuffed couch. My cracked toe is elevated on one of the embroidered pillows strewn there; my head rests on another. They are part of a collection my aunt brought back from her trip to India last year.

"And then, as if we weren't upset enough, she ordered an EKG for Eva. Refused to release her until they'd monitored her *heart*!"

My family hardly ever takes vacations, let alone zips around the world to an exotic place like India. The last semivacation I remember taking was to Cape Cod, last summer, for a long weekend. We stayed at a little inn, in a town called Wellfleet. I remember on one side of the Cape the ocean was cold, way colder than the Jersey Shore, and on the other side the beach was littered with razor clams.

Here's what I don't remember: getting my period. Not last

 182

summer, or last fall either. I vaguely recall that at some point my period was late. Then really late. Then gone. But since I knew I couldn't possibly be pregnant (I've never even *kissed* a guy), I didn't bother mentioning it to Rhonda. She continued to stock my bathroom with sanitary pads, and I just kept shoving the unused packs farther and farther into the back of the cabinet under the sink. I wasn't worried. I mean, it felt like a gift. Especially since I've always loathed, hated and despised my period.

I still remember the first time. I was ten. It was fourth grade, and I got it in school. I had no clue what was happening to me; Rhonda and I still hadn't had the "becoming a woman" talk, and when I went to the girls' room after lunch, my underpants were soaked with blood. I was petrified. I figured I had cut myself down there . . . maybe I sat on a splinter on the playground during recess? . . . and after I rolled my bloody underwear into a ball and shoved it into the trash can, I ran, crying, to the nurse's office.

She was very kind but didn't enlighten me much. I guess she felt that was a mother's job, so she called her to pick me up and I left school early. I have to admit, Rhonda did her best, and was very sweet and frank and factual about the whole thing, even though it had totally taken her by surprise as well. I mean, I was ten.

But the fact is all the signs were there. My mother should have noticed. Should have prepared me.

Our family doctor gave it a name: early-onset puberty. When a girl grows faster and develops earlier than the growth chart says she should. It explained a lot. I was the class giant in

 183

second grade. I had pubic hair in third grade. I had breasts in fourth grade. I had jerky boys staring at me and whispering. I had cramps. More than anything, I had the feeling that I was the biggest, fattest, hugest elephant on the face of the earth. I was a little girl stuck in a woman's body, and I wished there were something, anything, I could do to change it.

Rhonda continues ranting.

"Well, I want a second opinion, and tomorrow we are going to speak to a *reputable* doctor." Pause. "Yes, of course I called the school. They've been very nice." Pause. "She's relaxing on the couch right now."

Relaxing. There's an interesting word for how I feel. All floaty and light. The painkillers the hospital prescribed have turned me into cotton candy. I look like I occupy space, but in fact, I'm mostly air. This is good stuff. My thoughts belong to someone else; my mother's voice emerges from a dream. Which is fortunate. Because reality sucks.

Basically, I'm out. Bye-bye, New York School of Dance. At least for this summer. The doc says I need to take a month off for my toe to heal completely, and while the rational side of me thinks that is just not a big deal, the catastrophizing side of me knows it's the end of my career. All those years of ballet lessons and classes, all those summers when the schedule and the budget didn't allow for a vacation . . . for nothing. Madame will forget me like yesterday's headache. The Three Musketeers will probably *help* them move my stuff out of the dorm. . . .

I can't think about them. I can't think about what they're

doing right now. Because if I start looking at my watch and imagining *pointe* class proceeding without me, I may start crying so hard that I'll never stop.

My mother's voice is suddenly close. She's carried the phone into the living room.

"She's right here. I'll put her on." She holds it toward me. "It's Dad."

Inconveniently enough, my father is in Chicago on business. Quite a bummer, because the only thing that stands between me and a complete Rhonda-freak-out-fest is my father's low-keyed presence. The man doesn't have a pulse, and is very, very good at hugs. As my hand reaches out in drug-induced slow motion for the phone, I suddenly feel an overpowering need to hear his voice, to close my eyes and curl up against him here on the couch and feel the low rumble in his chest as he speaks.

"Daddy?" I say, and to my astonishment, my voice breaks. Something inside my chest splits open, and I'm not floating anymore; I'm drifting, cut loose in space, and there's no air to breathe, no sound, nothing to tether me. I'm so lost.

"Honey, everything is going to be okay," I hear him say. He sounds solid. Grounded and sure. I want him to hold on to me, keep me from disappearing.

"Okay," I say quietly. Tears slide down my cheeks.

"We love you, Eva," he says firmly. I look up at my mother. Her mouth forms a determined line.

"I'm sorry!" I burst out. "I'm so sorry I've wrecked every-

 185

thing, Daddy!" My shoulders begin shaking. I don't think I can make them stop. It scares me, being this out of control.

"Eva! You have nothing to be sorry about!" he says. I'm crying too hard to reply. My mother pulls the phone from my hands.

"Bob? She's gotten herself all worked up. I'll call you later." She turns the phone off. She crouches beside the couch, her face level with mine. She puts both hands on my trembling shoulders, and speaks fiercely into my face.

"Eva, listen to me. First thing tomorrow we'll see your doctor, and he'll put all this in perspective. Do *not* overreact."

My heart pounds wildly in the gaping hole inside my chest. I've gone from floating to frantic in under a minute, and that scares me, too.

You are going to get so fat.

No dancing. Not even walking, except with crutches, for a month. Your ass is going to balloon. And when your toe does heal, you'll be too enormous to ever dance again.

"Eva, stop it!"

Horror, panic, in her voice, startles me. I open my eyes . . . when did I close them? . . . and see her staring at me. She's gripping my wrists, hard.

"Stop hitting yourself! Why are you hitting yourself?"

You are such worthless vomit. You are such a pig.

The cover's blown off the shaky ground we've been dancing on. Some subterranean explosion, kindled by a long fuse that leads to barrels of dynamite, has blasted the house of cards to smithereens. Floating, floating, the small singed cards are

 186

floating . . . while someone screams in the background. What ignites something like this? An injury. A disappointment. A missing friend. A missing period. A body that betrayed me. And finally, a word. A word my mother hopes some second-opinion doctor will diagnose away. A word the doctor in the emergency room didn't hesitate to speak aloud.

Anorexia.

Chapter Twenty-One

HENRY

I'm a bottom-feeder. An unseeded, unknown player at the junior invitational tournament in Miami. And I'm *winning*.

Not only am I winning: I'm upsetting. Because I'm a sub, they've slotted me in as a wild card draw, which means I'm pitted against the top seeds right away. On Friday night, the opening-round match? I defeat number three. In straight sets. She was this college freshman from California who threw her racket when she didn't like a line call. Bad move. 'Cause after that racket flew across the court . . . I owned her.

Not with words. Not with attitude or drama. I beat her with game, pure and simple.

It wasn't easy. She kept giving me all these wonderful opportunities to crush her, to play with her head and make her feel like a loser. Like, the first time she double-faulted, and swore (a big no-no), I could hear a few gasps from the audience.

The old Henry would have rolled her eyes. Made some face that drew laughter. Maybe even shaken a finger at her and said, "Now, now, none of that!" The possibilities were endless, and hard to resist.

Instead, I wiped the emotion from my face. I wore a mask of concentration and pretended I didn't notice her self-destructing, and the only sounds from my mouth were the grunts I made when I hit the ball. I turned myself into a robotic tennis machine, which, it turns out, is way more lethal than a smart-mouthed jerk.

Afterward, Missy hustled me straight back to our hotel. We ended up in a dim corner of the restaurant's lounge, down-loading with David and his coach, Harvey. David wasn't scheduled to play until Saturday morning, so he and Harvey had just arrived. As Missy entertained them with descriptions of the reactions following my upset win, I tucked into a chicken-salad sandwich.

"What'd I say?" David commented smugly to Missy. "Didn't I tell you she was going to kick ass?" Missy smiled thinly.

"Our girl is very good, David. But let's not forget that Carly is a head case and routinely blows matches she should have won." Carly was the California racket thrower.

"Oh, please. Please!" David looked at Harvey entreatingly. "Can you get her to admit that I was right? For once?"

"Admit that he was right for once, Missy," Harvey said, grinning. Missy shrugged.

"If Henry beats Stephanie tomorrow, I will admit that you were right. *For once*," she said. David smiled knowingly at her. They have some ongoing jokes, these two, which makes sense. David spends more time with the coaching staff than he does

 189

with his own family. He's been living full-time at Chadwick since ninth grade.

* * *

As it turned out, I beat Stephanie, the number four seed, in straight sets the next morning. Two hours later, during the hottest part of the day, I took out number five. That involved some work. We went to three sets, one of them a tiebreaker. But when it was over I was lined up to play on Sunday. In the final.

That night, alone in my hotel room, I'm just about to turn the lights out when I hear the soft knock. I climb out of bed, pull the door open until the chain checks it and through the crack see David. His tennis bag is at his feet. He and Harvey must've only just returned.

I push the door closed, slip the chain and let him in. He wastes no time wrapping his arms around my waist. He keeps stepping, I stumble backward, and when we fall on the bed he covers my giggles with his mouth. I move my hands to the back of his head . . . I love to touch his hair . . . and it feels stiff with dried salt and sweat. He's definitely smelled better.

He rolls back on the bed, so we're side by side, our eyes inches apart.

"Guess what couple from the same club is playing in the finals tomorrow?" he whispers.

I jump up, with a little yelp of glee.

"You won?" I ask excitedly. Although I shouldn't be surprised. He was seeded first.

"Yup," he grins. "Took me four sets, but I'm there. And I hear, gorgeous, so are *you*."

 190

I'm dying to tell him about my mind-game-free wins, how I beat every one of those girls on pure tennis; but he has other ideas. He pulls me down again, rolls on top of me, and starts the kissing at my neck, just behind my ear. Slowly, his lips slide lower, come around, until he reaches the hollow at the base of my throat. I can't help it; I feel it coming, and despite my best efforts to control myself . . .

I whoop. My body jerks involuntarily, and I dissolve in hysterical giggles. David rolls away from me, onto his back, and sighs impatiently.

"I'm sorry! I really tried this time!" I say instantly. "But you *know* that is my most ticklish spot." I'm truly sorry, but the laughter creeps into my voice nevertheless.

This annoys him.

"It's, ah, kind of a mood breaker, if you know what I mean?" he replies sourly.

"I know. I'm sorry, David." I place my hand on his chest. I lean over and kiss him lightly on the lips, once. Again. I look into his eyes, trying to convince him of my sincerity. This has been emerging as an issue between us: my knee-jerk laughter whenever he makes romantic overtures. Especially near my neck. His grouchy expression relaxes slightly. Another kiss, one he returns.

"You taste salty," I comment softly. He murmurs in agreement.

"I need to shower," he says. He sits up.

"Join me?" he asks. Only a trace of a smile.

He's serious.

 191

At this precise moment the last person in the universe I want in the room with me and David would be my father. But that's whose voice speaks in my ear. His paranoid words of wisdom accompany the semisick feeling that spreads in my gut as I realize what David is suggesting, and I'm transported back to that breezy outdoor restaurant in Boca on the first day of camp, and Mark is telling me to trust my instincts.

I don't think this is what my dad had in mind when he told me, "Never be afraid to say no."

I don't want to say no to David. But I don't want to shower with him, either.

"I . . . don't know if that would be such a great idea," I say softly. Hesitantly, as if I'm actually considering this suggestion. So I'm not saying no. Or yes.

To my incredible relief, David shrugs.

"Yeah, it's probably not. We'd never get any sleep, would we?" He's looking at me with this confident smile. No worries or rejection. He thinks I've got tomorrow's games on my mind, and the importance of a good night's shut-eye.

He leans over and gives me one last, chaste kiss on the cheek before rising from the bed. He picks up his tennis bag and heads for the door. Then he pauses, his hand on the knob.

"I'm half tempted to knock at Missy's room, just to say, 'I told you so!'" he declares.

"Huh?" I ask.

"You know, about you. Kickin' ass?"

I smile at him. "I guess that means you were right. For once."

"Damn right I am!" he says, laughing. His white teeth flash

 192

in his tan face. Movie-star-bright teeth. A random thought crosses my mind: has David had his teeth done, or does he just brush really, really often?

"See you at breakfast," he says breezily, and walks out. I wait one moment, listening to his retreating footsteps and the rustle of his tennis bag, before jumping up and opening my door just a crack. His room is way at the far end of the hall. I see him stand before it, pull his key card from his pocket, insert it and go inside. His door clicks shut.

I rechain my door, then fall back on my rumpled bed. One cleansing yoga breath. Then another. It takes a few minutes before my heart slows its wild beating.

* * *

He clinches it in three straight sets the next day, out of which I only get to watch two. That's because they start the boys' final moments after my opponent and I finish the girls'. I'm in the locker room, toweling off from my shower, when Missy calls in to say he's already up 3–love. I race to get dressed, but then I'm held up by the reporters. The Chadwick "communications" people have set up a mini press gathering in one corner of the refreshments tent. There are two aluminum chairs, circled by six more chairs, but I end up sitting alone because my opponent decided to beat it, no comment.

You can't blame her. She lost to an unknown, unseeded nobody two years younger than her. Some Jersey Tomato who doesn't have a full-time coach, an agent or a sponsor.

"I'm just a teenager who likes to hit tennis balls," I reply to their questions. The handful of reporters laugh, on cue. Missy, standing off to one side, obediently smiles in kind, the fake smile I've learned to recognize. She is stressed because this happened way too fast, too unexpectedly, for her to script what I should say.

I tell them I'm from the Garden State and proud of it, and that I learned to play in my backyard, coached by my dad. They're lovin' it. It's so Cinderella story, and these guys are bored with the usual suspects. Then the questions get more complicated.

"Henry, the girls you beat have been playing the junior circuit for years. How do you explain your win here?" asks one. I shrug.

"I guess three weeks at Chadwick is like three years on the circuit?" I suggest. Laughter, especially when Missy calls out, "Yes, we told her to say that!"

"Maybe it's not so complicated," I continue. "I mean, whether you hit a million balls in your backyard or on an expensive court in a private club, it's still a million balls, right?" Nods, followed by scribbles. I wonder, if I started reciting from Dr. Seuss, would they quote that, too? "One fish, two fish, red fish, blue fish . . ."

"What do you think is the best part of your game?" another asks. I pause.

It occurs to me that the answer to this question, the honest-to-goodness answer, would have been different only one short month ago. Back then, someone might have said, "Her strokes are okay, but she wins by being bitchy and breaking her opponents' concentration."

 194

Not today. Not this tournament, not tomorrow . . . not anymore. I feel this rush.

"Self-control," I answer seriously. They pause. Frown.

"What do you mean? Do you mean mental toughness?" one asks. I shake my head.

"I prefer to think of it as control. That I'm controlling the point," I reply. My *shots*. My *skills*. My *conditioning and foot speed. Not my mouth.*

Missy steps forward.

"Thanks, everyone, but we have to wrap this up. Chadwick is playing in the boys' final, and we want to watch. If you have follow-up questions, please refer them to our communications office." She leans close to me and whispers, "Let's go."

By the time we arrive and find Yoly, her mom and her little sister Carolina in the stands, David and his opponent are sitting. The scoreboard reads 7–5, first set to Ross. My heart does this little skipperdy beat, and I fight the urge to flash him a thumbs-up, a blown kiss, *something.* But I know it wouldn't be welcome. He is staring at the court a few feet ahead of him, oblivious to the packed bleachers.

David's in the zone. There is no breaking that concentration.

General applause from both sides of the court signals the resumption of play, and David and his opponent head back out to the field of battle. I pull on my sun visor and settle in for the match.

It's the best tennis I've ever seen, not counting pro matches on television. His opponent is good, but David is . . . incredible.

His racket-head speed and flawless technique result in these withering, barely returnable shots. He is so quick to the ball that he never seems rushed; every stroke looks like a demonstration for an instructional video, or like he's posing for a *Tennis* magazine cover photo. Click.

When it's over, people stand. The applause is loud; there's even some cheering, which is unusual in tennis. David's won in three sets, and while it clearly wasn't hard for him, there were plenty of opportunities for him to show his stuff. He strides quickly to net to shake his opponent's hand, and makes a point of pausing, speaking with him briefly.

Guys with cameras have spilled onto the court, as well as tournament officials, scurrying around to set up a mike stand for the courtside trophy ceremony. Amidst the chaos, David scans the crowd. When he finds me, he flashes the best smile ever. My heart does a 360.

"Go down to him," someone murmurs, giving me a gentle shove. I turn. Missy.

"Is that okay?" I'm surprised.

"Absolutely. He'll love it," she says reassuringly. "Go on."

I don't need a second invitation. I shoulder my way through the spectators, stepping carefully down the bleachers. I push through reporters. I find David near his courtside chair, rummaging through his enormous tennis bag. As he pulls out a dry shirt, he sees me approach.

"Hey," he says, aiming a heart-melting grin in my direction. I can't help it: I close the last five feet between us with a skip, a little jump, and my arms are around his neck. I hear him laugh softly, feel my feet lift as he swings me around, and I experience this nanosecond of completely perfect, golden happiness.

Then I hear it. The metallic whirr of digital cameras. The buzz of lenses maneuvering into focus. Clicks. David puts me down, and we both turn to face a gauntlet of people taking our pictures. I recognize the *Tennis* magazine guy I met after my match, saying something to one of the photographers. I look at David, a ready apology on my lips, for getting in his way. But he's glancing over my head. Back in the stands, toward Missy and Harvey, and he looks at them questioningly, nods slightly, then winds one arm around my waist.

"Smile, Henry," he says, aiming one at the growing hive of photographers and onlookers. The clicks increase as I obediently pose; they rapid-fire when I shyly lean my head against David's shoulder.

I fell into this moment. Spontaneously skipped to his side. So why does it feel staged?

* * *

The air inside La Cubana is thick: heavy with garlic, roasted meat, fried bananas. Actually, not bananas. Yoly tells us they're *plátanos*, and even though they look like bananas, they aren't. A few small plates piled high with them, thin golden rounds that crunch oily in your mouth, line the center of the long table before us now. David and I sit at one end with Yoly and her cousin Enrique.

The Cruzes' restaurant is the sort of place my mother would describe as a hole in the wall. Mark would call it a dive.

197

It's packed with Formica tables and booths upholstered in red vinyl. The walls are a crazy quilt of hand-painted murals depicting island scenes (I'm guessing Cuba), old concert posters and framed, yellowed news clippings about baseball players.

Even though the menu is written in English and Spanish, David and I yield ordering to Yoly and Enrique. Yoly insists on *empanadas* to start, followed by lettuce-and-tomato salad. Dinner will be the restaurant's famed *cerdo asado*, or roast pork, along with *ropa vieja*, which is Spanish for "old clothes." Yoly explains it's actually spicy shredded beef. We'll also have black beans and white rice, plus something I've never heard of: *yuca*.

"It's a root vegetable, like a potato," Enrique tells us. "Cook it with a few pounds of garlic, and it melts in your mouth."

Enrique smiles easily at us across the table. He's older, almost twenty, and is handsome in a sort of not-tall, square-jawed way. He studies business administration at Miami University, but comes home lots of weekends to work at the restaurant. "Better money than my campus job," he explains, "plus free food." His mother, Yoly's *tía* Blanca, does a lot of the cooking at La Cubana. It's her pork we're destined to eat.

"Best pork in Little Havana," Yoly tells us after the waitress gathers the plastic menus and hurries off to get our drinks.

"Which means best pork in Miami," Enrique adds.

"Which also means best pork in Florida," Yoly counters.

"And that means best pork in . . . the country?" David suggests.

"More like the world," Enrique corrects. "Excepting Cuba, of course."

"Well, I'm psyched," I declare. "Even for the yuck-thing. Bring on the garlic." As if on command, my stomach makes a low, audible groan. Everyone cracks up.

"Someone needs to feed this girl," David says, smiling. "She's earned it."

"Oh, we'll feed you, all right," Enrique says. "When we come out with the *flan* for dessert, you will both be begging us to stop." Everyone laughs.

Mr. Cruz, from the end of the table, says something in Spanish to Yoly. She lowers her eyes as a blush spreads across her cheeks. "*Sí, sí*, Papi," she says, a little dismissively, and waves her hand at him. Enrique stares at her, his eyebrows raised.

"Why not? I think it's a great idea," he tells her. Yoly sighs.

"Let's not push this," she says to him. Undertones of "drop it" in her voice.

"What?" I press.

"Nothing," Yoly says at the same time Enrique replies, "The *quinces*." They glance at each other, then Yoly sighs in resignation.

"My dad would like to invite you to my *quinceañera* in a few weeks," she explains. "Please. You are under *no* obligation to attend."

"Even though you would miss one of Miami's best parties of the summer," Enrique adds.

 199

"I like parties," David says agreeably.

"You would *love* this," Enrique tells him.

As Enrique tantalizes us with descriptions of the extravagances planned for Yoly's *quinces*, I try to ignore the growing distress on her face. She trusts me with all this Cuban-tradition stuff; David is unknown to her. Enrique's unabashed enthusiasm for the family's celebration stands in sharp contrast to her demand that I tell no one about her very "not Chadwick" *quinces* photo.

"Wait," I hear David interrupt. "You go to church?"

"Before the party," Enrique explains. "There's a big mass, and everyone comes. The girl walks to the altar, led by both parents. She looks like a bride, you know? All dressed up in this very fancy gown? Her mother places a tiara on her head; her father gives her a ring. In turn, she hands them a plastic doll, which is usually dressed just like her. It's meant to symbolize her growing up and giving away the things of her childhood. Then the parents hand her flowers."

"Red roses," Yoly prompts him. She seems resigned to the narrative.

"It doesn't have to be red roses," Enrique argues.

"*I'm* getting red roses," she says, a tinge of irritation in her voice.

"Fine," Enrique says. "Then everybody sits for the mass, and the girl makes a speech."

"Speech?" I say. Yoly is resting her chin in her fist. She rolls her eyes at me and nods.

"A big, formal thank-you to everyone in my whole life," she says. "I haven't started it yet."

"Better get going," Enrique says, poking her in the shoulder. She glares at him, just as three waitresses armed with platters of food flank our table. There's barely enough space for all of it. It smells incredible, and my stomach roars in appreciation again.

As we shovel superhuman portions onto our plates, Yoly speaks.

"If you guys would like to come all the way back here for my *quinces*, we would be honored to have you," she says graciously. "But I also know you two are way busier than I am with the tennis schedule, so please, no pressure." Before I can reply, David jumps in.

"We'll check to see if there's tournament play that weekend, and if not, we'll try to come," he says easily. He takes his first bite of pork. He chews, and his eyes widen with an expression just this side of amazed.

"That was the best thing I have ever put in my mouth," he says sincerely.

Chapter Twenty-Two

EVA

For the first time in our long, unblemished friendship, Henry and I are fighting.

Basically, she wants the Obnoxious Parent of the Year trophy mailed to her in Florida, pronto. I refuse, insisting Rhonda's recent behavior makes *me* the uncontested recipient. And dammit, I tell her, I deserve to win *something* right now. She's got enough real trophies.

"Let me set this scene for you," Henry persists. "Sunday night, way past curfew because we left Miami really late. Note: Yoly and I are *not* crammed into the stupid Chad-bus, but cruising in David's totally sweet ride. A Porsche Cayenne SUV, which . . . get this . . . Porsche has lent him. I know, control your amazement. They can't give it to him, because that would be considered payment, and he's still an amateur, but he can *borrow* it."

"And why would a major, high-end car manufacturer do something so ridiculous?" I ask. It's not like Henry to embellish to the point of lies. She must really want the trophy.

"Free publicity," she answers. "They want David to be conspicuous about the car when he plays tournaments. When we were leaving for the Cruzes' party, and this random reporter was tailing us in the parking lot? David told me to stand alongside the Cayenne and smile at the guy."

"That's not about the car. That's about having a hot girlfriend," I counter. Henry ignores me, and continues to make her case.

"So, we're pulling in to the school after this totally perfect day? We've got kick-ass trophies in the trunk, we've been listening to this awesome mix Yoly's cousin gave us for the ride back . . . remind me to tell you about Enrique, you would *love* this guy . . . the temps have finally dropped to a civilized eighty degrees, these amazing flowers are blooming all around the entrance to the school, so when we get out the air smells like perfume, and I have just closed the door to the Cayenne when I hear, 'Henry? Is that you?' And there, sitting alone in the dark parking lot, is my father."

Despite my resolve to not budge, I feel a shiver down my spine as I picture Mark skulking in the shadows.

"Eva, it was beyond awful. He started out all quiet, comes up to me and just says, 'Pack your things. We're leaving.' I'm, like, in total shock."

"Fine. I'll give you that. Mark wins the shock-value and fear-factor points," I say.

"No, wait. It gets better. David, who doesn't know my father, comes racing around from his side of the car. He thinks Dad is some nut job who's wandered onto the campus. So he yells, 'Yoly, run to security! Get help!' then sticks himself between me and Dad. 'Buddy,' David says, 'if you know what's good for you, you'll turn around and leave quietly.'"

"Oh," I reply, deflated. This is indeed trophy-winning drama. Hard to imagine how Mark and the new boyfriend will bond after this. "That's pretty bad, Hen."

"Ha!" she exclaims. "It gets worse! He starts yelling at David. Who-the-hell-are-you-step-away-from-my-daughter sort of stuff, then I'm yelling, 'Daddy! Stop it! Just stop it!' Then David turns to me and says, 'This dude is your *dad?*'"

"Ugh," I say. "Proper introductions were a bit awkward after that?"

"Yoly, I thought for sure Mark was going to hit him. It was so scary."

"Excuse me. What did you just call me?" I say.

"Huh?"

"You just called me Yoly."

"No, I didn't," Henry replies.

"Henry. I may be listening to you from a cell phone a thousand miles away, but the reception is perfectly clear, and you called me Yoly."

"Well, I'm sorry. It's probably because she's part of the story. See, she's taken off, and we can hear *her* yelling, and people are coming out of the building. One is this guy I've never seen before, and he goes right up to Dad, saying, 'Mr. Lloyd, we asked you to please not do this.' So now I realize he's already been at the school, stirring up trouble."

"What was Little Andre doing?" I ask. I've finally figured out that "David" is not "Little."

"At first he was stunned, like me. But finally he realized we had to get out of there. So he begins to lead me into the main building, which makes Mark go totally wild. He tries to come after us, and these burly Chadwick guys . . . I guess security got there by this point . . . sort of circle around him, and I hear someone say, 'Mr. Lloyd! Are we going to have to call the police?' and Eva, I just started bawling."

"Henry, this sounds over the top, even for Mark," I say. "What set him off?"

"The tournament," she says. "When he realized Mom had already signed papers giving me permission to travel off campus to play, he decided to drive down by himself and pull me out. He was so angry."

I sigh. It's the first time I've heard the complete, unedited version of the story, gory details included. And I'll admit: Mark's a madman.

But the trophy is mine, nonetheless.

"Granted, your father has some serious anger-management issues. But let's be honest: you've worked things out. Your dad and the Chadwick people sat down the next morning, and not only are you still at the school, but he's agreed to the tournaments."

"Yeah, and how long is that gonna last?" she grumbles.

"You also have an adorable, doting new boyfriend with a cool car and a new best friend who can supply you with endless

205

amounts of greasy ethnic food. And also a growing fan base," I continue.

"Eva. I do not have a new best friend. Stop that."

But I'm on a roll. A downhill roll, actually.

"I, on the other hand, have an injury that, while probably not career-ending, has certainly reshaped the landscape of my future. My scholarship has been rescinded, although I can try out and reapply once I'm better. Plus, I'm facing a long, lonely, boring summer with nothing to do but hang out with my foot elevated."

"I know things really suck for you right now—" Henry starts to say. But I cut her off.

"Before you think I'm whining, let me assure you: I'm not. These are the facts, and depressing as they are, I can live with them. What I *don't* think I can tolerate for another stinking second is the insufferable pity party my mother has decided to wallow in. You'd think I *died*, the way she's carrying on! Do you know, after someone from the school called and said if we didn't move my things out of the annex they'd be deposited on the sidewalk, she got on such a crying jag that her doctor has prescribed meds for her!"

"Why would the school dump your stuff?"

"Because they've called *three times*! Rhonda just can't let go of it. Can't accept that I'm out, and she has nothing to brag about all summer."

I can tell how harsh this sounds. I can tell Henry is taken aback. But I'm not worried about what she thinks.

"So you want to know why I deserve the trophy?" I continue. "Because as far as my mother is concerned, I *am* dead. She doesn't know who or what I am without *pointe* shoes. If I'm not her perfect performing Eva, I'm nothing. If that doesn't deserve an OPY, then I don't know what does."

There's a long silence as Henry and I listen to each other breathe from a thousand miles away. Finally, Henry speaks.

"Do you miss it?" she asks.

"What?" I ask. She sighs.

"You know," she says quietly. I flinch. I've been trying so hard not to go there. "Because if it were me," she continues, "I know how much I'd miss tennis."

Something wells up inside me. Miss it? I want to scream. There's a hole the size of the Grand Canyon in my chest. There's this big, black void where my heart used to beat. There is nothing inside me. I am . . . nothing. Empty, without dance.

I feel so awful. I'm so angry. Even at Henry. And she doesn't deserve it, which makes me mad at myself, too. I am a horrible person, and it's no wonder she's moved on. She's better off without such a loser for a friend.

"Keep the trophy, Eva," Henry finally says when I don't reply. "Rhonda is definitely more obnoxious." Pause, then we both burst out laughing. Although in my ears my laugh sounds more like choking as I try to contain the screams behind my words. Lurking there. Always threatening to break out.

"And listen to me," she continues. "I am not . . . repeat *not* . . . looking for a new best friend. I really like Yoly. I wish you could meet her. But Eva, you are the sister I'll never have. No friend could replace you. You know that, right?" I take a deep breath.

"Yes. Of course. Same here, Hen. I'm sorry. I'm just . . . sad. You know?" I feel them now. Tears, running down my face. I need to get off the phone.

"You're entitled to be," Henry says sympathetically. "Wanna know what I do when I'm in the pits? I run myself a soothing bath with nice, smelly salts, and soak in it while I read a cheesy romance novel and eat Dove dark-chocolate bites." She laughs. "Come to think of it, it's a fun thing to do even if you're not in the pits."

Chocolate bites. Once upon a time Henry and I ate an entire bag at one sitting. . . .

Yeah, now there's an idea for you, blub butt. An entire bag of Dove chocolates. You'd be waddling for sure after that.

"Hen, I've gotta go."

"Sure, Eva. I'll talk to you tomorrow, okay? Hang in there, tomato. I love ya."

"Love you, too," I reply. Then the line goes quiet, and Henry is gone.

No clue. She has no earthly idea how lucky she is. Lucky to have a metabolism like a power plant. A game like Sharapova and a bod like Kournikova. A thousand miles' worth of highway between her and her toxic father, who promised to return to Jersey tomorrow. A hot boyfriend and a new girl-friend. Most of all, she's lucky to be far away from me, the most worthless friend anyone could ask for.

Or maybe I'm the one who's lucky. That she doesn't know what a loser I am.

Chapter Twenty-Three

HENRY

If I can focus now, I'll be able to focus anywhere, anytime. Cat-calls from spectators, bad line calls from opponents, a little sun in the eyes . . . those will be nothing compared to the nuclear-holocaust level of distraction generated by Mark, seated on the sidelines, as I drill with Missy and two other Chadwick coaches.

This is what they worked out with Mr. Congeniality: a day in which they will prove to him that his precious daughter is not being mistreated, poorly coached or exploited. Likewise, he gets to prove that he's not a certifiable lunatic who presents a threat to himself and others.

I *so* love being in the middle of this.

Sunday night had ended with security escorting Dad off the grounds and David pulling me into the quiet of our dorm lobby. I couldn't stop crying. When I finally calmed down, he placed his hands on both sides of my head and lifted my face toward him. His brown eyes seemed darker than usual, the easy smile they always seemed to contain replaced by a question.

"Tell me," he said gently.

So I did. To the extent that I could. How do you explain hating your father and wanting desperately to please him at the same time? How do you explain his volcanic emotional eruptions followed by genuine affection and praise?

Harder still: how do you explain your growing fear that being around him is turning you into some sort of monster yourself? Yeah, right. You *don't* say that to the hot new boyfriend. You say things like "my dad's a control freak" and "he has anger-management issues" and "I'm lucky my mom's really nice." And you let him listen with those patient, gorgeous eyes and kiss the tears off your face, and you pretend his hugs make you feel better. And you eventually head up to your dorm room to sleep, but you don't.

"Things" were worked out. There was a prebreakfast meeting, including Mom on conference call (she'd had no idea where Dad had gone), and he seemed way calmer. The Chadwick people were also calm, but in an unsmiling, watchful way. Made you wonder if they'd posted a SWAT team in the foliage, ready to pounce if Mark so much as hiccuped. I'd come down to breakfast early: still red-eyed, hesitant. The place is such a rumor mill that I knew everyone had probably heard about Henry Lloyd's crazy father.

I was stunned to find him standing at the entrance to the dining room, alongside a grim-faced member of the coaching staff.

"Your dad's going to be joining you for breakfast today," the coach said as I approached. "You can eat in the private dining room next door if you'd like." I stared uneasily at them.

 211

"It's okay, Hen," Mark said, trying to smile. He put up both hands, like he was surrendering. "They shot me with the tranquilizer gun and I'm as tame as a kitten this morning." He laughed, although the coach and I didn't join him. I shrugged and walked into the dining hall. I loaded a tray with scrambled eggs, oatmeal and fruit and slipped into the room off the main cafeteria. Dad trailed me and we sat.

As I squirted ketchup onto my eggs, he began.

"I'm sorry about that little scene last night," he said. I snorted.

"That's a first," I said sarcastically.

"What?" he asked.

"You. Apologizing. You probably shouldn't get started, Dad. We'll be here all summer." He frowned but contained himself.

"Yeah, I probably had that coming," he said quietly. "But I do mean it, Hen. I'm sorry."

"And one more thing," I continued. "Last night? That was not a 'little scene.' It was huge. It was *awful*."

To my amazement, he nodded. He cleared his throat.

"Honey, one of these days you're going to be a parent, and you'll understand . . ."

"No, Dad. I'll *never* understand how you get so crazy. This is a good place. I'm learning tons and playing great tennis." *Real tennis, Mark. Mind-game-free, trash-talk-free tennis.*

"Why can't you just be happy for me?" He didn't answer. He took a bite of his toast. A swig of coffee. The tears started welling again. *Damn, dammity damn damn . . .*

"When are you leaving?" I said.

 212

"Tomorrow," he said. "I'm invited to sit in on your lessons and join you at meals today. As long as I behave," he added, the corners of his mouth turned up slightly. Something between a sneer and a smile. I stared at him.

"What if I don't want you hanging around?" I continued.

"That's not up to you," he said shortly. He picked up his napkin and wiped his mouth carefully. He'd run out of patience. "Let's not forget that you are a minor and you are here with my permission. If I don't like what I see, you go home."

His words felt like a light blow to my brain, and I finally got it. He was behaving so the Chadwick people wouldn't have him forcibly removed from the property. They were appeasing him so he wouldn't pull me from the school. It was an elaborate game of give-and-take, over me.

And it was depressingly familiar.

* * *

Standing on the baseline of the pro court, a basket of balls behind me, I try to erase Mark from my sightline as I work my serve. I'd forgotten how much it sucks to play while he's watching. Luckily, he sits outside the court, peering in between the windbreaks. Missy has invited these two other Chad-pros (that's what we call them) to join us today: Paul and Scotty. It's great to have all the attention, but not lost on me that this is intended to impress my father.

The three of them watch and offer suggestions as I concentrate hard on each phase of the serve: the loose, muscle-sleepy moment before you coil; knees bent, racket back with the head dropped behind you; the ball tossed high, hovering in the air; the hurling, whipping motion of the racket face, flung like a baseball; the *pock* of contact. *God, it feels so good to hit something.*

Thirty minutes into it, I'm bathed in sweat.

"How 'bout a water break, Henry?" Missy suggests. Paul nods, and the two of them head to the Igloo cooler parked alongside the court.

"You're a fast learner." Scotty stands next to the basket of balls.

"You guys are good teachers," I concede.

"Next thing to work on is your toss," he says. "You're twisting your hand at the end of the toss, and the ball spins." I nod. This isn't the first time I've heard that.

"I know. I need to place the ball in the air, and finish the toss with my palm open. Pretend I'm catching raindrops." Scotty's eyes widen, and he smiles.

"That's the same visual my coach at Florida used!" We walk toward the coolers.

"His name wouldn't happen to be Ray, would it?" I say jokingly. Scotty stops.

"Ray Giordano," he replies.

Thirty feet away, Missy and Paul sip from little conical paper cups as they chat with Mark. He's stepped inside the fence and stands with them beneath the umbrella.

"Ray Giordano was your coach at Florida State?" I say quietly.

"Until I was a junior," Scotty says. "He left because he had some family problems. Sick mom, I think. He moved back to

 214

the Northeast, and I heard he was doing some private coaching and helping to take care of her. Do you know Ray?"

"Wavy dark hair? Probably my dad's age?" I say.

"Green eyes?" Scotty continues, enthusiastically. "Throws his head back when he laughs?" I nod. "Damn!" he exclaims, laughing. "Who says it isn't a small world?"

"Too small, if you ask me," I reply nervously. "Listen, Scotty. My dad isn't a member of Ray's fan club, if you know what I mean." Scotty's eyes register instant comprehension.

"Check," he says. "But, just out of curiosity, *when* did you work with Ray?"

"A little over two years ago," I say quietly. "When I was fourteen." He does some quick mental calculations, then nods his head.

"Right," he says. "I heard he stayed up north for a year before joining Philmont."

Missy is motioning us toward the water, and it's time to cut this conversation off. Still, I can't resist one more question.

"What's Philmont?" I ask. Scotty chuckles.

"That's like asking, 'What's Bechtel?'" he says. "It's some global corporation that makes everything from widgets to bridges. They also sponsor athletics, and that's the part Ray got involved in. Look for their logo at your next pro baseball game. Or in the Chadwick lobby."

"Chadwick?" I say.

"Philmont's one of our sponsors," Scotty says. "I think we've got three Philmont students this summer. What about you? Do you have a sponsor?"

 215

"I have a scholarship," I explain. He shakes his head.

"There are no scholarships at Chadwick. People either pay full freight, or a sponsor picks up the tab. Make sure you find out who's covering you, Henry," he says. "You'll want to write a thank-you note at the end of the session. Even more important than getting your toss right is making sure to always, and often, thank your sponsors."

We've reached the cooler by now, and Scotty, good as his word, instantly switches the conversation. Mark seems astonishingly relaxed, actually pulling his lips back and revealing his teeth in a canine sort of smile. He obviously likes what he's seen this morning; Missy and Paul, meanwhile, also wear rather self-satisfied expressions. It's a freakin' lovefest under the umbrella, but as I hold my paper cone under the Igloo spout, my hand shakes. And I make a mental note that this afternoon, if I can lose Mark for a little while, I'm going to spend some time in the front office.

I want to know who's getting my thank-you note.

Chapter Twenty-Four

EVA

Rhonda claims it was ants. A curving, determined line of black ants marching into my bedroom. Plus an odor. Whatever. I'm sure she's lying. Lying to cover up the fact that without my ballet to obsess over, she's reduced to rummaging through my stuff.

Paige's mom drops me off from the swim club at three, even though it's the heat of the day and prime time for floating in the pool. Paige whined about leaving early, but Rhonda had scheduled a four o'clock appointment with my new shrink, so I had to come home. Not that I explained anything about it. Nor did Paige ask. It's amazing how little one has to say to be friends with this girl. Just pretend to admire her as she tugs at her bikini and struts repeatedly past the good-looking life-guards, and you're in.

I walk into the kitchen, the arctic air-conditioning doing an insta-freeze on my still-damp hair, calling out, "Mom! I'm back," and from upstairs she replies, "Eva. Could you please come here right now?" There's that special *something* in her

 217

tone, and I know we're in for yet another wonderful mother-daughter moment.

I climb the stairs slowly: Doc's orders. Baby that toe. Of course, I'm not in the mood to get there quickly. And I'm tired. My heart races, as if I'm running bleachers.

Well, what did you expect, whale butt? Three weeks of absolutely no exercise. You are so miserably out of shape that you can't even walk up the stairs to your own room.

The smell hits me at the door. Rhonda stands in the middle of my bedroom, surrounded by boxes, random clothes and whatever else she has disgorged from my closet. She wears gloves, that yellow rubber-chicken kind you put on when you scrub something greasy. She also wears this sick expression. Like she's going to vomit.

She points to a plastic pail on the floor.

"Would you mind telling me what this is?" she says.

I take two timid steps toward the bucket and peer inside. Brownish liquid, moldy chunks floating in it. There's a clear plastic bag mixed in with the liquidy ooze, and it reeks. I see a small blue plastic tab poking from the surface, those Ziploc tabs you pull to seal storage bags . . . and then I know. There are about seven or eight month-old uneaten dinners in that bucket. I had completely forgotten about them.

My mind freezes. I cannot think of a word to say.

"Eva! What is this garbage doing in your closet?"

Garbage. Well, she's right about that, isn't she? The garbage they've been force-feeding you since the summer began. You were right to not eat it.

 218

"I have no idea what that is! It's gross. Get it out of here!" I exclaim. She stares at me.

"What do you mean, you don't know?" she replies. "Eva, it was in *your room*. Behind the plastic storage bins. I've been noticing ants upstairs, and this morning there was a line of them leading into your closet. I opened the door and the stench practically knocked me over!"

"Well, get it out!" I shriek. I turn and race down the stairs, no thought for my toe. Weird floating sensation. My heart bangs against my ribs again, but somehow my legs feel weightless, like I'm flying. It occurs to me . . . in a strange detached way, as if I'm watching myself . . . that maybe I'm falling? But I reach the den, still upright.

She follows. I've burrowed deep within her overstuffed couch, my damp head pressing into the cushions. For once she doesn't reprimand me for wet hair on her precious furniture. She chooses her words carefully.

"Tell me what was in the bag in your closet."

She hates you. You are a pathetic little loser. All she's ever cared about was bragging to her stupid friends about your dancing. Bragging about all the things she's too uncoordinated to do herself. And now you've gone and injured yourself, and she can't forgive you. So she'll get back at you in every way she can, starting with this: making you fat. Don't tell her.

"I don't know!" I scream into the cushions.

"What do you mean, you don't know?" Rhonda replies, her voice slightly higher. "Who else puts things in your closet?"

 219

"Paige," I say. Instant, nonsensical, knee-jerk response. Rhonda looks dumbfounded.

"Paige is putting garbage in your closet?" she says. I sit up. My mind races.

"That was something she wanted me to throw out for her. I remember now. It must have fallen out of my backpack. I forgot to dump it." Rhonda sits wearily on the edge of the couch.

"Eva, this makes no sense," she says quietly.

"It's from her soccer game," I say. "Paige is the captain, and she's supposed to clear the bench before they leave? It's a drag, people always leave their empty Powerade bottles lying around. Sweatshirts. One day there was even a laptop under the bench. So Paige asked me to help her carry all this stuff, and there was a bag of orange slices the team didn't eat. I put it in my backpack and must've forgotten to dump it. It really got gross, didn't it?"

Rhonda stares at me, shaking her head.

"Those weren't just oranges," she says. "There was some sort of meat in there."

"Well, I don't know what those girls eat!" I exclaim. "Why are you interrogating me?"

"I'm not interrogating you—"

"Well, it sure feels like an interrogation! No hot lights, but plenty of suspicious questions." Rhonda reaches out and places one hand on my shoulder.

"Eva, soccer was months ago. We're in July." I sigh, exasperated.

"Paige is captain of her spring travel soccer team. They just played in the regional finals. In *June*."

I watch the confusion play out across Rhonda's face. She wants to believe this story, but she knows damn well there was nothing in that bucket resembling a rotten orange. After a minute, the lines of her face arrange themselves purposefully.

"If Paige is team captain, then she should get the trash, not you," she says, a little indignation brewing. "Friends don't treat each other that way."

"Well, if you don't like Paige, why do you keep pushing her to invite me to the swim club?"

"I don't push her! What are you talking about?"

"Oh, please. 'Eva doesn't have anything going on this week, Paige.' I mean, could I look like more of a loser?"

"Honey, you are not a loser. I . . . I just want you to get out a little. It kills me to see you sitting in your room day after day."

Yeah, that's right. Loser daughter with no social life. Nothing to brag about there.

She glances at her watch.

"Well!" she says briskly, getting up. "I need to fumigate your room. Then we have time for your snack before we head to the doctor's. Okay?" She doesn't wait for an answer. And as she retreats back upstairs, I feel like throwing up.

Yeah, but you can't, can you? You've never been able to. You're such a wimp.

* * *

221

Wendy Koontz looks like a large child dressed as a grown-up. Some organic cotton approximation of professional clothes that come off more like refugee couture from *Little House on the Prairie*. Her long, colorless hair is neatly woven in a French braid that trails down her back. She wears rimless glasses and chunky, colorful shoes that you gotta know are treated with tea-tree oil. She speaks in a girlish whisper. I don't think she could scream if her life depended on it.

I have an overpowering urge to smack her, which is not good, since she's my therapist and I'm supposed to be in here baring my soul. But I can't get beyond the feeling that this gal could use some assertiveness training herself.

We sit in her office, the three of us: Rhonda and I in these deep, cushy armchairs, Wendy in her desk chair with the wheels on the bottom. She smiles serenely. Her expression matches the décor. Muted colors. The walls covered with flower prints. No framed diplomas.

"So how's it going?" she asks gently. Rhonda and I look at each other, unsure who is supposed to answer that question. This is our second appointment. The last one started with both Rhonda and me in the room for fifteen minutes; then I went solo with Wendy for the remaining forty-five. I assume it's the same drill for this visit as well.

"Fine," I reply, at the very same moment that Rhonda says, "A little stressful." Only Wendy smiles.

"Eva, why don't you start?" she says. I take a deep breath.

"Everything's going fine," I repeat. I try to match her flat, emotionless affect. "It's a little boring, since I'm trying to stay

 222

off my toe as much as possible. But I've been able to spend some time with friends. We hang out at the town pool a lot."

"Swimming?" she inquires softly.

"Eva's doctor doesn't want her to swim right now," Rhonda interjects. "But she can visit with her friends at the club."

Wendy acts as if Rhonda isn't in the room. She stares placidly at me, awaiting a response.

"I'm not supposed to swim," I say agreeably. Then stop. Wendy holds my gaze for five full seconds, then moves on to Rhonda.

"Why do you think things are a little stressful?" she asks. Rhonda shifts uncomfortably.

"Well," she begins, "there's definitely some tension. Between us." She nods in my direction. "And even between Eva and her father. They've always been so close, and this is a man who never argues, he's so even-tempered, and last night? Well, they weren't exactly shouting at each other, but he raised his voice because she barely touched her dinner. . . ."

"Pot pie, Mom. You made chicken pot pie. You know I loathe it." So much for serenity. The acid in my voice could burn through reinforced steel.

Rhonda looks hesitantly at Wendy, who says nothing.

"No, I didn't know that, Eva," Rhonda says. "I thought you liked it. I know you won't eat beef, or pork. Just chicken and fish. So I thought pot pie would be a good choice."

"Well, you thought wrong," I say. Silence follows.

"What *did* you eat for dinner, Eva?" Wendy finally asks.

"I had some ramen noodles," I say.

 223

You mean ramen broth. You dumped the noodles.

"And that's it?" Wendy continues. I frown.

"May I ask a question?" I say.

"Of course," Wendy says.

"Why are we talking about what I eat? I thought that topic was saved for the nutritionist Mom's been dragging me to." Wendy purses her lips.

"I'm concerned over your choice of the word 'drag.' Eva, are you going to these appointments unwillingly?"

"Why is it that I have to answer your questions, but you get to answer my questions with another question?" I fire back. The urge to hit her is becoming almost too much for me.

"We were talking about the different responses you and your mom had to my question. You think things are going fine; she says it's stressful and attributes the stress to your conflict over dinner last night. That's why we're talking about food."

I pull my gaze from hers and stare out the window. Leafy foliage presses against the glass. Wendy's office is attached to her house, a tasteful square addition to her suburban Ridgefield home. Last visit, I remember hearing ambulances screaming in the distance. Wendy said Ridge Valley Hospital was only a few blocks away.

"Mrs. Smith, why don't Eva and I talk alone now?" Wendy says. Rhonda dabs at her eyes; she sniffs. Wonderful. More waterworks. Rhonda hasn't stopped crying since Dad came home with all my stuff from the annex. Wendy picks up a box of Kleenex and holds it out to Rhonda, who plucks a tissue, smiles gratefully, then quietly exits.

Wendy returns to me.

"I'd like to get back to the nutritionist. Your choice of the word 'drag' makes me think you don't want to see a nutritionist."

"Well, you have to admit it *is* a little ridiculous," I say.

"Why?" Wendy asks.

"What does a nutritionist know about broken toes?" I reply. Wendy's eyes widen ever so slightly.

"Not much, probably," she says. "But you're not seeing a nutritionist to discuss your broken toe." I shrug.

"Why do you think you're seeing a nutritionist, and seeing me?" Wendy continues.

"I have no idea," I say. "Because it gives my mother something to do besides cry over my lost ballet scholarship?"

"Is that why you think your mother is crying?"

"It was just a guess. You'd have to ask her."

"You sound very angry, Eva."

"Not at all. I love having nothing to do all day, getting dragged around to stupid doctors' appointments and being pressured to eat unhealthy, disgusting food."

Wendy looks steadily at me, digesting this comment. Then she changes tactics.

"Tell me about the bag your mom found in the closet."

They're talking about you behind your back.

"When did she tell you that?" I say.

 225

"She emailed me before your appointment today," Wendy says.

"Well, then she probably also told you it was some trash I had forgotten about."

"Yes, I know that's what you told her. But I want to hear it from you."

"Excuse me: are you calling me a liar?"

"I'm giving you an opportunity to confide in someone. What goes on in this room stays in this room. Priests and doctors. We're professional secret-keepers."

I laugh, in spite of myself. Wendy smiles. She waits. I disappoint her, however, so she tries again.

"What do you think all these appointments are about?"

"I told you, I don't know."

"What do your parents say?"

"I don't know. Ask them."

"Why don't you tell me?"

Relentless. The woman must've completed her residency interrogating prisoners. I look at the clock. Only ten minutes have ticked by.

"They think I need help," I say. Then stop.

"What sort of help?" Wendy presses.

"Eating help," I say reluctantly. Wendy bobs her head, a slight, encouraging nod.

Oh god, look at those thunder thighs squeezed into that chair! She wears those dresses to hide her big lard butt. This is the sort of woman who stows a twelve-pack of Twinkies in her bottom desk drawer. Why would you tell her anything?

"Some emergency-room doctor in New York told them I'm too thin," I finally say. "They've completely overreacted."

"Do you think you're too thin, Eva?"

"No. I've just said, everyone's overreacting."

Wendy picks up a manila folder from her desk and flips it open.

"I'm looking at a memo your family doctor faxed to me. He says at your last weigh-in they determined that you are only at seventy-three percent of the minimum healthy weight for someone your age and height. He says blood work indicates that your electrolyte balance is off. An EKG shows that you have an irregular, slow heartbeat. A bone-density scan reveals osteopenia, which means your bones are thinning, probably caused by a calcium deficiency. Your mother reports that after you shower the tub is full of your hair. You've stopped menstruating, which is what happens when the percentage of fat on your body drops below healthy levels. Eva, this doesn't look like an overreaction. It looks like a very serious condition."

My god, why won't these people let up! Dough Girl here doesn't know the first thing about health. Look at her! Even her ankles are fat.

"Wendy, I'm a dancer. Guys lift me. I leap. The aim is to appear light, to bound across the stage effortlessly. Have you ever seen a graceful elephant bounding effortlessly?"

"Healthy ballerinas menstruate," Wendy replies evenly. "They are not bald. Their toes don't crack during lessons." I throw myself back into the cushions in frustration.

"Listen, I eat, okay?" I half shout. "Maybe not dripping,

 227

bloody steaks and buckets of Häagen-Dazs, but I eat good, healthy food. Everyone is threatening me and saying I have to gain a couple of pounds, and I've agreed to gain a couple of pounds. What more do you want from me?"

"We want you to accept that there is a larger problem here that goes beyond gaining a few pounds, and we want you to accept help," Wendy responds instantly.

"What problem? What's the larger problem?" I fire back at her.

"Eva, you have an eating disorder."

"That's *bull*shit. That's overreacting crap you got from my mother, and I'm not going to sit here and listen to it."

"That's a diagnosis from several different doctors. And it was the last thing your mother wanted to hear."

"Are you my therapist, or hers?" I demand.

"I'd like to be yours. But you need to speak to me. Honestly."

Oh, moo. Go moo, you big cow. Let me tell you something, Wendy-girl: no one is honest. And if they tell you they are . . . they're lying.

I get up. A bit too quickly. The room goes from dark to bright, and the jackhammer inside my rib cage springs into action again. I grasp the back of the chair to steady myself, take one slow deep breath. Then I toss a little "honesty" at Wendy.

"You want to know what was in my closet? It was garbage. Garbage that my parents were trying to make me eat. They know I like steamed vegetables, grains, beans. But instead they slather everything in fatty oils and cheese. So yeah, I dumped

228

the gross food in the bag, hid it and unfortunately forgot all about it. Now you know. What are you going to do? Go tattle to my parents?" I stare, hard, into Wendy's wide, watery eyes.

"I told you: what's said in this room stays here," she answers. "But Eva, I'm really, really proud of you for coming clean with me." She smiles the smuggest, most self-satisfied smile I've ever seen.

So they know about the closet. It's okay. They don't know about your pockets, do they? Half a peanut butter and jelly sandwich fit nicely in your pocket yesterday, compressed neatly into that paper napkin. Bet you can get a sandwich and a half in there tomorrow.

I might burst into tears at this very moment. Time to exit, stage left.

As I concentrate on walking out the door, Wendy says one last thing to me.

"I'll see you next week, Eva."

Hand on knob, I pivot to face her.

"Whatever. It's not like I have anything else to do."

Chapter Twenty-Five

HENRY

"So, how rich *are* you?"

He doesn't look at me. Concentration intact, he keeps his eyes on the road, and the four lanes of Greater Fort Lauderdale drivers weaving aggressively down I-95 south toward Miami. I can read his expression, though. Amused and puzzled at the same time. Interested. David Ross loves a challenge, and I keep him slightly off balance.

"What makes you think I'm rich?" he asks back. "I told you: this isn't my car."

I've reclined the passenger side seat of the Cayenne slightly. I close my eyes and lean into the luxury of an all-leather interior, breathing deeply, loving the way it smells. Not just a new-car smell. A quality scent. Still, if I weren't wearing a formal dress and heels right now, I'd be tempted to prop my feet on the dashboard, a move that horrifies David.

"I know," I say, opening my eyes. "And it's not your baggy-shorts style that gives you away. Although I must say, you have potential. Especially tonight." I turn to feast my eyes once again. He's wearing a black Armani tux. He will turn heads at the *quinces*, no question.

He takes his right hand off the steering wheel and slides it behind my neck, massaging the place where my hairline begins. I press my lips against his forearm, the crisp white of his dress shirt. The jacket hangs neatly on a hook in the back.

"So how did you sniff out my millions?" he asks teasingly. I consider for a minute.

"For one thing, you *own* that tux. Even the richest guys at my school don't own tuxes. They rent them for prom." He nods. He's humoring me.

"And?" he prompts.

"Secondly, you never talk about money. It's like air to you. Open your wallet and pull out a few bills." He shrugs.

"Maybe I'm just not materialistic," he says. "It's boring to talk about money. I mean, isn't it more interesting to talk about . . . tennis?"

I raise one eyebrow and gaze at him skeptically, which makes him laugh.

"Okay, what else?" he asks.

"*This* is the dead giveaway," I say. "You are way too comfortable in high-end, boutique-y stores to be a nonrich guy. Like when you took me to Mizner Park to shop for this dress? I was completely intimidated by the sales staff. You acted like you owned the place."

"I'm just a self-confident guy," he says smoothly. He removes his hand from my neck and places it on my knee. It begins migrating north, slipping beneath the skirt of my dress.

 231

I grasp it firmly and return it to the steering wheel.

"Less confidence, more driving," I say. "Remember: arrive alive."

He sighs, but not unhappily. This is a familiar dance. We keep skating to the edge of some unspoken, invisible boundary. The game intrigues him. At least for now.

"Sorry, but you still haven't made your case," he says. "I'm just your average middle-class jock trying to become a rich and famous professional athlete."

I shake my head.

"I have one more piece of evidence," I declare.

"Shoot," he says.

"You don't have a sponsor," I say simply. "Your family is footing the bill for this outrageously expensive school." He frowns. A real frown.

"How do you know that?" he asks.

"Lacey told me," I reply, but I'm not liking the expression on his face. As if I've strayed into forbidden territory.

"Why are you asking the secretary at the front office about me?" he says. He's mad. Not just annoyed: mad.

"Actually, I was asking her about me. My sponsor. It just . . . came up . . . about you. I asked. She answered. I'm sorry. Are you upset with me?" I'm having a hard time believing that I've done something wrong.

David doesn't answer right away. All the teasing playfulness has left his expression.

"No, I'm not upset with you," he finally says. "But I am upset with Lacey. She shouldn't tell anyone how I pay for

Chadwick. My family has been scrupulous about protecting my amateur status. Controlling information about money is very important."

"David, I'm not going to go blabbing your business. . . ."

"It's not about you, Henry," he says abruptly. "It's about whether Lacey talks to anyone else. Who just happens to wander in and ask."

We're both quiet now. The assassin side of David has reared its head. Scrupulous-about-protecting-my-amateur-status. Anyone-who-just-happens-to-wander-in-and-ask. I forget, sometimes, how serious he . . . and his family . . . are about his tennis.

I don't have a very clear sense of David's family. I know his parents are married and he has a younger brother and sister. But he rarely talks about them. He rarely talks about where he grew up. Friends from home, climbing trees, a favorite pet: not a word. And when he does mention his family, it's almost . . . corporate. Like he's some enterprise, some research and development project into which they've invested eighteen years' worth of time and money.

It's such a contrast to Yoly. I feel as if I know every Cruz intimately, from her notoriously cheap uncle Eddie who didn't want to rent a tux tonight, to her floozy of a cousin Marta, who was threatening to come to the *quinces* with the no-good-boyfriend-that-everyone-hates instead of her mother's-best-friend's-son who just finished his first year at college.

When I mentioned to Yoly how David hardly ever talks about family or growing up, her eyes widened in surprise.

 233

"Sure he does, Henry," she said.

"When?" I demanded. "Except for tennis, his past is practically nonexistent."

"His past *is* tennis," Yoly replied. "He grew up on a court. When he wasn't homeschooled in order to make time for his lessons, he went to private schools that were mostly little-kid tennis camps. You know this, Henry. You're the one who told *me*."

She was right, of course. If he didn't talk about childhood friends, it was because he hadn't had many. If he didn't talk about playing or climbing trees, it was because he hadn't. He hadn't ever really been a little boy.

He'd been a prodigy.

Sitting beside him now, beautiful in his white dress shirt, I try to imagine what sort of little boy he might have been. I think he was sweet. I think he was probably very serious.

I wonder if he was lonely.

"I'm sorry, David," I say quietly. "Please don't be angry with me."

His lips press themselves into a firm line, but he lays one hand, palm up, in my lap. I place mine inside his, and we weave our fingers together.

"Why were you asking about *your* sponsor?" he finally asks.

"Oh, no big reason, really," I reply casually. "Someone just told me it's good manners to write a note thanking your sponsor, so I was getting an address."

David slides Enrique's CD into the player, and as we fly through the concrete jungle of Greater Miami sprawl, pink

 234

light slanting off the glass windows of high-rises, the sun migrating west, we don't talk much. I'm thinking that's okay. We're comfortable with just *being*.

So . . . why don't I tell him? Why can't I talk to David about the sick, cold stone that formed in my stomach the other day when Peg Lacey cheerfully pulled my sponsorship folder and showed me, on the Philmont Corporation letterhead, Ray Giordano's signature, confirming that their company would cover all my expenses for summer camp at Chadwick?

I lean back in the seat and let the music and cold air from the blowers wash over me. I replay the old story in my head. I don't want to, but I can't help it. It's like picking at a scab. Playing with a loose tooth hanging by a thread.

* * *

On Tuesdays and Thursdays I had lessons with Ray, on our court out back.

It was the best part of my week.

Tennis with my father had, at that point, become such a battle of wills that I was starting to hate our practice sessions. The sound of the ball machine made my skin crawl. Mark's constant barking orders summoned a monstrous rage in me. I would fantasize about pegging him with an overhead. I would imagine the look on his face if I hurled my racket over the fence, swore and stomped off the court.

Of course, I never did any of that. Because despite resenting him to the point of violence, deep down I loved the game. I needed it. They needed it. Something positive to point to from their ruin of a marriage: the brilliant daughter-athlete.

 235

So Mom made some calls and found Ray. It was a huge relief to work with somebody who didn't take my missed shots personally. He was fun and encouraging and intense. I would walk off the court dripping with sweat, but never tired. He convinced me that I was an awesome tennis player; he convinced me that he genuinely liked me and enjoyed our time together.

And, as Eva and I agreed, he was cute. For a grown-up. A little younger than my father, he was tennis-pro lean and perpetually tan. I didn't mind when he stood behind me, his chest brushing lightly against my shoulder blades, his hands wrapped firmly around my wrists, shadowing the form I needed to perfect for my serve.

One afternoon, a lesson day, I had early dismissal from school. I must have forgotten to remind my mother, because when I walked in the front door and called out, "Mom, I'm home!" the house was silent. I climbed the stairs to my room, tossed my backpack on the floor and flopped onto the bed.

That's when I heard murmuring. It sounded like a radio playing next door, but then I realized it was a conversation, coming from our backyard patio. I got up and looked out my window, which opened onto the back of the house.

Mom and Ray were seated at one of the round metal café tables she had bought the summer before. She had her arms stretched out in front of her; Ray held both her hands in his. He was leaning forward, and as he spoke, his head bobbed with the force of each word. Mom stared dully down at their hands. Occasionally I'd see her nod in assent.

I stepped back from the glass as if it were hot. I remember

 236

the sharp intake of my own breath, the thrum of blood pounding in my ears. Then I ran. I pounded down the stairs, threw the front door open and raced outside. It felt good to pound the pavement with my heels.

He liked my mom. This whole "wow-you're-so-great-at-tennis" thing he did with me? A big act to get near her. And her? It didn't matter that my dad was difficult. Didn't matter that he never made her laugh anymore, that they went to a marriage counselor, that they bought patio furniture but never seemed to have friends to invite over. They were married. We were a family.

She wasn't supposed to hold hands with my tennis coach.

I returned home hours later, only moments before my father pulled in to the driveway. Mom was pacing in the living room.

"Henry," she said when I entered, her face pale and strained. "Where have you been?"

"What do you care?" I snapped. Shock on her face. I never spoke to her that way. Both of us could hear the electric garage door engage. Mark was pulling in.

"Your father's home," she said, nervously stating the obvious.

"Don't worry, Mom. I won't say anything," I said curtly. I couldn't look at her. I folded my arms across my chest and stared at the carpet.

"Excuse me? Say anything about what? Do you realize you had a lesson with Ray this afternoon?" She looked dumbfounded.

 237

For one moment, doubt flooded over me. This was no act here. My mother really had no clue why I was upset.

Then again . . . she didn't realize I'd seen them. She thought their little secret was intact.

"I'm going to my room," I mumbled, and tore up the stairs. Just before I closed my door, I heard the jangle of my father's keys as he tossed them onto their usual place on the kitchen counter. Heard his hearty greeting to my mother.

I didn't return downstairs until she called me for dinner. Dad was already seated at the dining-room table.

"Hey, there's my girl!" he said pleasantly. "How was your day?"

"Fine." I avoided his eyes. I pulled out my chair and sat. Pasta steamed on my plate.

"D'you have your lesson with Ray today?" he asked. Mom stood behind him. She was carrying her own dish to the table. Instinctively, I looked at her. She stared back, hard, and gave a short, barely perceptible nod.

"Yeah, it was fine," I said. I picked up my fork and a big spoon. I tried to concentrate on twirling spaghetti into easy-to-swallow nests.

"What did you work on?" Dad continued.

My throat constricted. I couldn't eat. I carefully placed my fork and spoon down.

"How would you feel if I said I don't want to take lessons with Ray anymore?" This flush of crimson crept up my mother's neck and spread to her cheeks.

"I thought you liked this guy," Dad said suspiciously. I shrugged.

"Yeah, I like him fine. But the drills are getting sort of repetitive. I don't see why we have to pay him when I could just work with you."

My mother had become a statue. With these huge, unblinking eyes, she stared at the plate she held.

"That's quite a different tune than you were singing last week," he commented. "Last week I heard Ray Giordano was better than sliced bread."

"Yeah, well this week he's toast," I quipped. I tried to laugh, but it didn't quite come off. Mark's eyes narrowed.

"What's really going on?" he said. I shrugged.

"Nothing. I'm just not sure this is such a good fit anymore." He glanced at Mom.

"Do you know what this is about?" he asked. She shook her head. Mark plunged ahead.

"Do you feel uncomfortable around Ray for some reason?" he said.

"Oh, Dad, for crying out loud, don't make a federal case out of it!" I exclaimed. I was incapable of cool. "See? I knew you'd immediately get all paranoid. That was why I hadn't said anything about Ray before. I've been trying to be positive." He put one hand up, cutting me off.

"Whoa, whoa," he said. "I'm not being paranoid. And I have no problem ending the lessons. I'm always happy to save money. I'm just surprised and want to make sure it's not just some mood, or . . . or something else is going on that you're not telling us."

I knew what he meant. It made sense. Why else would I suddenly go so cold on Ray Giordano? What else could turn a kid so quickly?

It was as if I held a grenade, and had a split second to decide whether to pull the pin or not. And if I did, where would I toss it?

Only one thing was absolutely clear to me at that moment: Ray had to go.

The thing is, when you set off a grenade, stuff flies out in a million different directions, ripping into everything and everyone in sight. You set off a grenade, there might not be anyone left standing when the dust clears.

"Dad," I said carefully, "everything is cool. I just feel like this thing with Ray isn't a great fit. Like I said, he's starting to repeat himself, and the workouts are getting boring. Plus I think he's here too much. He hangs out after the lesson is over, and it's like he's trying to be my friend and not just a coach. It feels a little . . . icky."

Dad looked at Mom triumphantly. As if he'd just won a big argument.

"Kids know, Marian," he declared. "They have a sixth sense about this sort of stuff. I told you, I never felt right about the guy. . . ."

"Oh, stop it, Mark. Please," she said angrily. She half dropped, half slammed her plate of pasta down on the table, spattering sauce on the tablecloth. "It doesn't matter who it

 240

was. You never would have liked anyone else coaching Henry. And now she's given you the excuse you were looking for." She looked at me accusingly. As if *I'd* done something wrong.

"Ray Giordano genuinely cares about our daughter," she continued. "She's right. He does linger after lessons. And during those times I've had several conversations with him about the poisonous, destructive dynamic that can develop between an overbearing parent and a talented child. You worry about people who want to ruin Henry? Well, I worry that by the time the two of you are done fighting with each other, she'll never pick up a racket again. Or if she does stick with it, you'll turn her into such a trash-talking brat, no one will speak to her on or off a tennis court!"

She stared, hard, at me. I couldn't believe what I heard. Was she trying to say all that coziness on the patio was about me?

Mark slammed his hands on the table. Mom and I both jumped.

"Who the hell is this guy, that he thinks he can talk about me behind my back to my wife?" he roared.

It was all downhill after that. Pretty typical, actually. No dinner was eaten by anyone; I do remember leaving the table and retreating to my room. That very evening Dad called Ray and uninvited him to our home ever again. He said "the check is in the mail" for the last lessons, sayonara, god knows what else. My mother was so blisteringly angry that she got in the car and drove off. I think I must've been asleep when she finally came back.

The next day, a Saturday, Ray Giordano pulled in to our

driveway. He walked around the house, to the tennis court where Dad was watching as I called the dogs.

It escalated to yelling almost immediately. Dad shouted, "Get off my property!" as Ray was pleading, then loudly insisting, "Shut up and listen!" I felt numb and nauseous and disbelieving all at once. At some point I started shouting, too, something like "Stop it! Just stop it, both of you!" and the ruckus got so bad that the neighbors heard and called the cops.

It was definitely our awfullest, sickest Lloyd moment.

Ray left after the police arrived. My dad didn't press charges. My mother threw together an overnight bag and spent the rest of the weekend at my uncle's, returning by Monday morning. Greeting me, wordlessly, in the kitchen, with a hot breakfast and the smell of fresh coffee before I boarded the bus to school. Somehow, the three of us limped through that day. Then the rest of the week. A month. A year.

My mother and I never spoke about what happened. And until Jerry Goss appeared out of nowhere, Ray Giordano was relegated to the back of the closet. Packed away, chloroformed. A locked box with a DO NOT DISTURB sign taped to the top.

Chapter Twenty-Six

EVA

Sounds and voices float over and around me like a haze. Splashing and little-kid laughter. Faraway conversations. Paige. Paige's friends.

"I mean, could my hair *be* more frizzed? I *hate* f-ing summer!"

"Dude, chillax. Your hair is fine. You just burned it into submission with my straightener."

"Burned? Does it look burned? Oh my god!"

"It looks *fine*, Paige! Jeez, you are so obsessed with your hair."

"You know, I thought I smelled something when I was using your straightener. I think the settings are wacked."

I'm stretched out beneath the shade of a beach umbrella. Wrapped in a towel. Rubbery bands of a folding chair press into my back, my legs. Bounce slightly when I move. It's cold.

"That is a $180 salon-approved, ceramic-paddle hair straightener, and it is *not* wacked."

"Oh my god, you paid $180 for a *hair* straightener! Are you f-ing kidding me?"

"I didn't pay for it. My aunt gave it to me for my birthday. It's a Chi."

"Still."

"Where is Paige going?"

"Probably back to the bathroom to look at her hair." Laughter.

"What did you pay for yours?"

"My what?"

"Duh! Your hair straightener."

"Thirty-seven-fifty at Target."

I'm breathing through a cocktail straw. The air just won't come. There's a line of pain the length of my arm.

"You can't get anything but crap for thirty-seven-fifty. If you want to fry your head, be my guest, but I'd toss that thing in the Dumpster."

"Yeah, well, Paige managed to fry her head on *your* $180 crap, so I'll keep my Tar-zhay special, thank you very much." Pause.

"It was burned, wasn't it?"

"To a crisp." Laughter.

"We should have told her."

"What's the point? You can't *un*burn hair."

Someone is pressing a fist into the middle of my chest. Pressing, right between my boobs. I try to breathe, but the air won't fit. I need to say something, but I can't remember their names. Paige's friends.

"Ouch! What the heck, Paige! You just hit me with a wet towel!"

"I *hate* you guys! Why didn't you tell me I burned my hair?"

"You didn't burn your hair! It looks great!"

"By the time you came out of the locker room, it was too late. You can't *un*burn hair."

"Screw you people! I'm outta here. Eva, are you ready to leave?"

Leave. Move my legs. I can't get up.

"Paige, c'mon. Don't be mad."

"Oh, and *you* wouldn't be mad if you toasted your hair and no one told you?"

Something's not right. I'm not right.

"Dude, she is *white*."

"Who's white?"

"Eva."

"Eva's always white. She hates the sun."

"So she comes to hang out at the swim club . . . why?"

"No, I mean like *sick* white. Look at her."

"Eva? Talk to me. Is something wrong?" Paige speaking. Close to me.

I need air. If I don't get air I'm going to faint. Or throw up. Or both. I feel sick and floaty and my arm hurts.

I need my mom.

I think I close my eyes.

"I don't feel right." Me, speaking. My tongue feels heavy. My voice sounds far away.

"Hey, guys, something's wrong. Something's really, really wrong." Scared voice.

"She's, like, drenched in sweat."

 245

"Should we call her parents?"

"Somebody, run, get the lifeguard." A chair scrapes.

"Eva! Eva! My god, why doesn't she say anything?"

Why can't I say anything?

"I'm calling nine-one-one."

"Just wait for the lifeguard, okay?"

"Girls, is there a problem?" Woman's voice. Splashing. I hear "Marco!" Voices answer "Polo!" "Marco!" "Polo!"

"Everyone stand *back*!" Man's voice.

Someone leans on my chest. Presses my chest so that I can't squeeze the air into my lungs. The pain from my arm shoots up my neck. Someone is crying.

There are sirens, far away. My eyes are closed, I know that now, and I'm slipping, drifting. Everything is muddled. The person sitting on my chest has turned into a mountain. Crushing me. I'm disappearing. Only little puffs of air slip into my lungs. That's all I'm allowed.

At some point I feel lifted, on a cushiony soft cloud. And it's such a relief, to fly.

Then everything goes quiet.

Chapter Twenty-Seven

HENRY

Aida's Reception Ballroom is like nothing I've ever seen. Or imagined.

Gold. Pillars. These little carved trees, in massive clay pots, line the walkway entrance. A fountain, painted gold, spews water straight up so when it rains down it looks like shimmery gold fragments. A white Hummer limo, seven windows long, is parked outside. Women with some serious bling walk arm in arm with men in tuxedos.

"Toto, we're not in Kansas anymore," I murmur into David's ear as we walk from the parking lot. He squeezes my arm, which is wrapped around his. He is gorgeous in his slim black jacket, which smells faintly of aftershave, not his usual laundry detergent.

The vestibule is loud with people speaking Spanish. We elbow slowly toward a double-door entrance at the back. On one side, propped on a large artist's easel, leans an enormous framed photo display of Yolanda. In the center is her formal picture with the white gown and tiara. Around that are less formal pictures, showing all the different "faces" of Yoly. I like one of her standing in front of a tennis net, dressed to drill, holding her racket.

We wander into a massive ballroom. On either side of us, there is a sea of round tables and chairs, elegantly set with white linen and flowers. Before us, a gleaming wood dance floor extends to red-carpeted steps with a curtain at the top. A four-tiered cake is displayed on one side of the steps, and a DJ has set up his equipment on the other.

A waiter carrying a tray of glasses approaches. David slips his arm from mine, plucks two from the passing tray, and hands one to me. Bubbles float dreamily to the surface. I wave the rim beneath my nose. Champagne.

David clinks his glass against mine.

"Cheers," he says. He sips, his eyes smiling mischievously.

"We're underage and supposedly in training," I say dryly. He winds his free arm around my waist. He moves in close and we rotate, dancelike.

"We're celebrating," he corrects.

"What?" I reply. He considers the ceiling for a moment, then looks at me again.

"Yoly's *quinces*," he says, "to start." I narrow my eyes at him. "I don't know. Truth and beauty? Love and friendship?"

My heart skitters. Seriously, an EKG machine would reveal a skipped beat. I feel his breath warm on my face as he speaks. I take the tiniest of tastes. I've never had champagne

 248

before. It's surprisingly unsweet. The bubbles fizz, like Pop Rocks, on my tongue.

"A *real* taste, Henry," he says softly. I lift the glass to my lips and fill my mouth. It's like drinking sparklers.

"You're corrupting me, David Ross," I tell him.

He laughs. He twirls us just a little faster. By the time we find our way to our table, both our flutes . . . he tells me that's what they're properly called . . . are empty.

Yoly has seated us with Enrique, who's already there.

"Hey, Henry! *Cómo estás?*" He's with a pretty girl in a red, shimmery dress. He wears a tux with a light blue vest, indicating that he's family. Yoly told me that light blue would be the unifying theme color tonight.

"*Muy bien, Enrique,*" I reply. "*Y tú?*"

He replies in a pleased blizzard of Spanish, and I put my hands up in surrender.

"Sorry! Hello-how-are-you is as good as I do."

"So far," he says pleasantly. "A little more time in Florida and you'll be fluent. We'll make a real *cubanita* out of you!" He turns to his date. "This is my friend Maria Arreche. Maria, this is Henry Lloyd, who lives with Yolanda at Chadwick, and her friend David. How are you, man?" They shake hands. Enrique looks at me with an expectant smile.

"So," he says, "are you ready for your first *quinceañera?*" Maria's eyes widen.

"You two have never been to a *quinces?*" she asks. I shake my head.

"Until I met Yoly, I'd never even heard of a *quinces*," I confess.

"Where are you from?" Maria asks. I think she half expects I'll say Mars.

"New Jersey," I tell her. She frowns.

"Right next to New York, how could they not know *quinces*?" she says, more to Enrique than to us.

"Well, all I can say is that you're both in for the *fiesta* of a lifetime," Enrique says.

At that moment the DJ says something into his microphone, and the packed ballroom becomes eerily quiet. Then a rhythmic drumming, just shy of a construction-site jackhammer, fills the room. It booms from the DJ's giant speakers and the crowd picks up the beat with enthusiastic claps, swaying hips, cheers. The dance floor clears.

The velvet curtains at the top of the staircase part, and Yolanda appears, to wild applause, holding hands with some tall, dark-haired boy.

Her hair is styled in this updo and held in place by a rhinestone and pearl tiara. In her ears she wears long, matching drops. Someone has done her makeup, and even though I've never given a thought to lipstick in my life, I make a mental note to ask her the name of this color. Acres of cloudlike gauze and satin billow around her; she gleams with pearls and sequins. But it's the perfect smile, the complete happiness, radiating from Yoly that makes her the most beautiful girl in the room.

She and her partner dance-strut in unison to the center of

the floor. They face the staircase and join in the rhythmic clapping themselves.

Couples descend the red carpet to wild applause. The guys are dressed in black tuxedos with blue vests, the girls in floor-length gowns of baby blue. The DJ announces their names as the girls line up on one side of the dance floor, the boys on the other. As soon as they are all in place, the DJ switches gears, the rhythm changes and Rihanna fills the room:

It's getting late
I'm making my way over to my favorite place

Rihanna fans whoop when they recognize the words to "Don't Stop the Music" and the opening dance by the *chambelanes* and *damas* begins.

In and out they weave, in perfect time. Yoly and her partner lead them at the head of the formation and . . . the girl's got moves. I knew she could pound forehands; I knew she could run. But shimmy in a ball gown? Amazing.

David bumps his hip against mine. Laughing, we bump and clap with Rihanna.

"Did they *practice* this?" he says loudly, leaning toward me.

"They hired a choreographer," I reply, trying not to yell. "They had rehearsals and everything." He shakes his head in wonder.

It's too noisy for me to tell him all I know. About the agonies Yoly endured trying to pick this song. "I mean, can you imagine Abuelita rockin' out to *"Don'tcha wish your girlfriend*

 251

was a freak like me?" she had explained, singing to me one afternoon. She'd finally settled on Rihanna, even though some of her friends thought it was way tame.

I look to my left at David. When he feels my eyes on him, he breaks out one of those heart-melting smiles. He is so gorgeous. I want to dance with him . . . can he dance? I can feel the music clear down to the small of my back, and I want to move with it. With him.

Then suddenly it's over, and another, slower tune begins, something Yolanda has played for me. The dance floor clears, and Mr. Cruz approaches Yoly and her partner, who places her hand in her father's and steps away. Strains of "Find Your Wings" fill the room, and the traditional father-daughter dance begins. The DJ plays the Spanish version, but Yoly has told me what the words mean. About a girl becoming a woman, and her father's wish: to give her wings and let her fly as high as she can.

The crowd becomes quiet as they dance. Yoly leans her head against her father's chest. Some people start to gently clap.

It occurs to me that I might truly be in Oz, or on Mars. Definitely not any place I've been before. Where fathers dance with cherished daughters and the rooms aren't big enough to hold all the friends and relatives.

"Are you okay?" David says to me. I put my hands to my cheeks; they come away wet.

"C'mon." He wraps one arm around my waist and leads me toward the exit. I point my face toward the floor. *Don't make a scene. Don't wreck this for Yoly. Don't ruin your makeup.* I try thinking of everything possible to stop the waterworks, but the tears keep coming.

At the far end of the now-deserted vestibule, David finds a small couch. We sit; he reaches into his jacket and pulls out a handkerchief. I take it and dab my eyes.

"Is there another eighteen-year-old guy on the planet who carries a handkerchief?" I wonder aloud.

"Comes with the monkey suit," he deadpans. We both laugh.

"Thanks," I whisper. I ball the hankie tightly in my lap. He places his hands over mine and I notice, not for the first time, that he has wonderful hands. Long, tapered tan fingers. Strong wrists.

"What's making you cry?" he says softly. Which brings on another gush.

"I don't know," I finally manage. "Something about seeing her with her dad." He nods. I don't need to explain more. He gets the Mark thing.

"And the whole party. It's incredible, don't you think? Every relative, every neighbor. Even the priest who did her mass this afternoon is coming, that's what she told me. I mean, my family can't even manage to get a few friends over for a barbecue, but Yoly's can fill a ballroom." David smiles at me and gently kisses the tip of my nose.

"Henry Lloyd, you're a romantic. I never knew."

"What do you mean?"

"I mean, you see this cheesy affair with the Mr. Microphone DJ and you get all emotional. It's sweet."

 253

Something inside me stills.

"What do you mean, cheesy?" I say. His eyes widen.

"Do I need to explain? We're in a reception factory, they're serving cubed Monterey Jack on toothpicks, and I've never seen more sequins in my life. It defines cheesy."

"They think this is a wonderful party," I say haltingly. *I think it's wonderful, I don't say. A party filled with every imaginable person who loves you.*

"Oh, I know," he says reassuringly. "It's just not my style. You know what I mean. I'm sure Mr. Cruz spent a fortune. And that dance number was cool. And Yolanda seems happy. Even if she does look like a meringue." He laughs softly and squeezes my hands. I don't reply.

"Can I tell you something, Henry?" he continues quietly. Seriously. I nod.

"Cheese cubes and bad DJs aside, I'm having a great time. Because I'm here with you. I'm . . . really into you." His mouth forms a teasing smile, but his eyes are anything but. They bore into mine, and I know, absolutely, that this is huge for David Ross.

My mind swirls, abandons me, as I try to take it in, but before I can think of how to react, his lips are on mine. Long, sure kisses that surprise me with their intensity, and I'm kissing him back, this beautiful boy who, like me, has felt different, and alone, for too long.

Loud cheering and applause come from the ballroom now, the father-daughter dance complete, and people drift into the vestibule again. David and I move apart. He looks at me with this expression of pure happiness. I don't know what the question was, but he's obviously thrilled with my answer. He stands, pulling us up.

"So are you ready to dance with me?" he says. I sigh.

"You *dance*, too? I think you may be too perfect. At least for me," I tell him. He laughs as we return to the packed ballroom, gripping my hand firmly in his. There's ownership in that grip. Confidence. A little pride. We reach the vortex of the twirling crowd, David turns to me and we dance. I see only him. I can't take my eyes off him. I want to get lost in this moment, this dance. I want summer to never end. I want everything to work out, for all of us . . . me, David, Yoly, Eva . . . for all of it to wind up someplace happily ever after.

I want so badly to love him back.

Chapter Twenty-Eight

EVA

He's a pig. He's a fat, disgusting pig in a white coat, and he's trying to make me fat as well.

"Eva, we need you to cooperate so we can help you."

Yeah, right, you want to help me. You want to stuff me full until I explode. Don't tell me that bag is water. It's liquid sugar. No way is that getting into me.

"Who the hell are you?" It hurts to speak. My throat has been rubbed raw with sandpaper.

"Mr. Smith, could you try talking to her once more?"

Another face hovers over mine. I'm lying flat. The faces float above me.

My father.

"Eva, honey, please listen to Dr. Miner."

He's not my father. My father would never let them stick a needle in me. Drip poison into me.

Rolling sound. It's rolling toward me again. Swaying bag of water. Clear plastic bag, thick with sugary water.

"What is that?" I croak the words.

"These are fluids to rehydrate you, Eva." *Pig's voice again.* "That's what you were getting before you yanked out your IV. We need to reinsert it now, but you can't struggle."

The father imposter nods. He fakes a smile at me. His lips stretch sideways over his yellow teeth.

I have to get out of here.

"Hold her."

Giant goons in white pin me down. They're coming for my arm, the top of my hand, where they stuck me before. F— you, stupid pigs! I'll pull it out again! I'll pull it out!

A woman is crying.

"Hold up, everyone. This isn't going to work."

The goons retreat. The big pig disappears. He's talking to someone.

"This level of resistance doesn't leave us many options. I'd like to sedate her, get an IV going and, with your permission, intubate her."

"What's that?" *Woman's choking voice.*

"It's a thin feeding tube we'd insert up her nose. She'd get a steady stream of calories, even while she sleeps. We'll do this slowly and monitor her to avoid refeeding syndrome. She could arrest again if she gets too much too fast. But she needs something, immediately."

"I'm sorry. I don't understand." *Fake father's voice.* "Did you just say she could have another heart attack?"

"If we refeed her too quickly, that's a possibility."

"Oh my god!" *The woman.*

"Please, just do what you have to do." *Fake father.*

 257

Pigs! Killers! I won't let you!

"I'm going to have to ask you to step outside."

I've got to get out of here. I try to lift up on my elbows and climb out, but something invisible holds me. I reach, feel a strap, thick cloth, firm across my hips. They've tied me.

"Daddy! Please don't go! Daddy, don't leave me!" The words feel like shouts but sound like the driest of whispers in my own ears. He doesn't hear me.

"Hold her." *Goons again. Pressing me down with such force I expect to feel my own bones break. Pinprick, in my arm, cool, spreading, and they've done it. They've killed me. This is poison spreading through my body. Goons relax their grip.*

"Eva, we're going to try again, okay? You'll feel a little sting on the top of your hand. We're putting water back into your body. You're very, very thirsty, and it's important that you leave this in. Don't pull it out."

Some woman in a white dress wipes, cold and wet on top of my hand, pricks me. I don't fight. They've poisoned the fight out of me. I watch. I watch from a distance, floating outside myself.

What does it matter? It doesn't matter anymore. I don't matter anymore.

Chapter Twenty-Nine

HENRY

Late-morning rays of hot Florida sun sneak into my room around the edges of the drawn blinds. We sleep in on Sunday mornings, and after last night, when David and I pulled into Chadwick at two a.m., I've slept in extra late. I squint at the digital alarm clock perched on the bedside table: 11:37. Almost lunchtime.

I stretch my arms high over my head, stretch my legs under the thin blanket, big sleepy catlike extensions, then kick the covers off. The gears of my brain slowly click into action. Shower. Dress. Dining hall. Early-afternoon drill session with Missy. I can do this. I stand, yawning. Stumble to the dresser in search of clean socks, underwear. Only my turquoise dress, draped over the back of Yoly's desk chair, and the foot-torture shoes tossed against the wall, betray any evidence that the *quinces* ever happened.

In the cold, clear light of day, all the confusion of the night is supposed to fade away. Right? Unfortunately, there's nothing cold or clear about a hot, hazy Florida morning.

He loves me. He said it last night, the l-word, standing outside the Cayenne, parked in the Chadwick lot. He said it as he kissed me, his arms wrapped around my back, pulling me close against the whole slim length of him, the nighttime breeze moving through the palm trees with this dry, papery sound. You couldn't have scripted a more romantic moment, and I felt my heart break open as I wondered, *Is this it, then?*

How can you be in love with someone you've known for a month? But what else could this be? This stupid, crazy, dizzy way I feel if I only *think* of touching him. If I see him across a room, or watch him hit a tennis ball. Or smile. God, that smile.

So why didn't you say it back?

Halfway to the shower, I realize what I need even more than a few gallons of water streaming over my head: a long-overdue chat with a best girlfriend. Who knows you better than you know yourself, and still likes you anyway. Who tells you to put on your big-girl panties and face down whatever scares you, or makes you mad, or thrills you to the bone. Or at the very least, helps you figure it all out.

I dial Eva. We haven't been connecting lately. Her cell has been off and she doesn't answer my messages. When I get her cell voice mail again, I call the Smiths' house.

Someone picks up after a single ring. A woman's voice.

"Smith household."

"Uh, hi. Is Eva there?" A pause.

"Who is this?" she says.

"It's Henry. Mrs. Smith?"

"No, this is Laura Blythe, the Smiths' neighbor. Are you a friend of Eva's?"

"Yeah, I'm a really good friend of Eva's. Is she home?" I'm trying to get my head around this strange conversation. Where are the Smiths, and who is this woman?

"I guess you haven't heard. Eva is in the hospital. Her parents are with her now."

Body blow. Mind blow. No way. I'm not hearing this.

"What happened?" It's all I can manage.

"You should probably talk to her parents. Would you like me to—"

"Was there an accident? Is she okay?" Impatience rises in me. Gives me back my voice.

"Oh, no, nothing like that. But you should talk to Rhonda. Do you—"

I press "end," cutting off the infuriating voice, and dial home. Mom picks up.

"Mommy, why is Eva in the hospital?" I demand loudly, not even bothering to say hello.

"Henry? Honey, calm down. Who told you?"

"What is going on?" I practically yell. "Why didn't anyone call me?"

"It only just happened. I only just heard myself."

"Just heard WHAT?" I am yelling now, for real. My mother sighs.

"Eva had a heart attack."

This is stupid. This is what happens when you drink champagne and stay out until two o'clock in the morning: you hallucinate. Because heart attacks don't happen to fifteen-year-old girls from New Jersey. We're a red state, cancer clusters everywhere, and you'd get skin cancer from lying out at the Jersey Shore before you'd have a heart attack. You'd get in a car crash while cruising down the Turnpike, blasting "Thunder Road," before you'd have a heart attack.

"Eva didn't have a heart attack," I say. Like I'm picking a fight.

"She was at the swim club," Mom continues. "The girls she was with noticed that Eva didn't look well. Thank god they were at the club, because the lifeguard knew what to do. . . ." Mom's voice catches. There's a silence. She's crying when she speaks again. "She had a seizure. By the time the ambulance got there, she'd started breathing on her own again, but at the hospital she went into cardiac arrest, and they needed to use the paddles."

"When did this happen?"

"Last night."

"This is unbelievable! Big fat men get heart attacks. Not kids my age!"

My mother is silent.

"Mom? What's going on?"

"She's gotten very thin, Henry."

"Define 'very thin.' And what does that have to do with anything?"

"I don't know what she weighs. But you'd scarcely recognize her. It happened very quickly, after she had to drop out of the ballet school. She just stopped eating. Rhonda has been hysterical about it."

"When is Rhonda *not* hysterical?" I say fiercely.

"I've never seen her like this," Mom continues, ignoring my comment. "The doctors were warning them that if Eva didn't turn it around, they'd have to institutionalize her."

"Turn *what* around?" I demand.

"The anorexia," my mother says. "It's gotten so much worse."

I'm stunned into silence. Never has anyone actually used the a-word about Eva, although they've all suggested it. Even at school, kids were constantly remarking on how little she ate, how thin she was, the dark circles that often appeared in her pale face. Yeah, she could have stood to gain a few pounds. But she's a dancer. They're thinner than the rest of us.

But this is different. Mom says it so matter-of-factly. How much worse? I want to ask. Why didn't anyone tell me?

Why didn't Eva tell me?

Or did she?

"When were you planning on calling me about this, Mom?" I say accusingly.

"We talked about it. We all agreed that there was no point upsetting you."

"No point? What do you mean, no point?"

"Honey, there's nothing you could have done. Eva is very, very sick. In her mind as well as her body. She's not rational, and the less she eats the worse it gets."

"No! I don't believe that. Mommy, this is Eva we're talking about. *Eva.*" I know her better than I know myself, I want to scream. I can tell her anything. She can tell me. We are there, always, for each other. Even a thousand miles apart, Jersey Tomatoes. Forever.

"Henry, I'm heading over to the hospital this afternoon. I'll call and let you know how she is. Meantime, you need to stay focused. This is a big week for you. You've got a tournament . . . when? Friday? That needs to be your priority right now. Eva's in good hands."

It's a lights-on moment. Of course. That's why they didn't tell me. Because nothing, not even sickness or possible death, should deter Henriette Lloyd from her path to stardom.

'Cause we're all riding on it.

"I can't believe this," I say. I don't wait to hear her response.

I press "end."

* * *

I pound on his door. I wait. I pound again.

When it opens, the room behind him is dim. I've woken him up. I step inside, uninvited, and am met by a wall of musky sleeping-boy smell. He stares at me, bewildered, dressed only in these light blue cotton boxers. His hair is rumpled; there's a trace of pillow crease along his cheek. Reflexively, my eyes strafe the length of him: the hard muscles of his belly. The tan line just above the elastic waistband. He closes the door.

"What's goin' on?" he says thickly.

David's bed is covered with rumpled, still-warm sheets.

There is junk on the floor, a tennis bag, tossed clothes. Maybe eight feet of clear space, but I pace it. Three fierce steps, pivot, three back. Pivot. I am a riot of energy. I want to pound something.

"Henry, what's the matter?" he says. He stares. I seem berserk to him.

Somehow I manage to say it. To admit that while I was drinking champagne and dancing, my best friend's heart stopped beating. That she's so sad she doesn't eat anymore. That everyone kept it from me, even her. Even my parents.

Even me. Why didn't I know?

When I'm done raving, he steps close to me, takes both my hands and pulls me toward his bed. His eyes are fully alert now, filled with concern. We sit on the edge of the mattress, his fingers laced tightly through mine.

"You couldn't possibly have seen this coming," he says.

Our knees bump. His legs are dark from the sun. The hair on his calves looks gold over the tan. Farmer's tan, that's what we've all got, tennis players. I see the line midway up his thighs, the line circling his upper arms. His chest is lighter than his face. Smooth, muscular.

My best friend is in the hospital. Almost died. And I'm checking out my boyfriend.

What's wrong with me?

I pull my hands away, jump up from the bed. Three steps, pivot. Three steps back.

"Henry." Commanding. I halt.

"Stop blaming yourself. There was nothing you could do."

 265

"Who says I'm blaming myself?"

"It's kind of obvious." He sees right through me. I don't want him to. I don't want him to see what I'm really like. I put my hands over my face.

He's up, his arms around me. He rests his cheek on the top of my head.

"David, while we were at the *quinces*, she was in an ambulance."

"And if you'd been in your dorm room reading last night, she'd have still been in an ambulance. Stop guilting yourself out."

I deserve a little guilt, I almost say. I'm a bad friend. A mean, mind-game-playing bad person.

"I've got to go."

I say the words before I fully comprehend their meaning. He pulls back to arm's length, peers into my face, puzzled.

"Go where?" he asks.

"Home. Jersey. I need to see her. Let her know that I'm there for her." He lets go, steps back. He doesn't look happy.

"It's a thousand miles to New Jersey."

"I don't care. I can't concentrate on tennis right now anyway."

"Be reasonable. How are you going to get there?" I take a deep breath.

"Can I borrow the Cayenne?" His eyes widen. An incredulous smile forms.

"Are you forgetting that you need a license to drive?"

"I have a permit. I'd have my learner's license except I've been too busy to take the test." He takes a step closer to me.

"Are you also forgetting that I don't actually own the Cayenne?"

"David, I will be so, so careful." The frown line has formed between his eyes. He realizes I'm serious.

"Do you know how much trouble you will get into for ditching camp? Driving a car you don't own, without a license? Not to mention that it's dangerous to drive that far all alone?"

"It's twenty hours one way if you don't stop," I continue. My mind is working; I'm picturing this drive. "My father broke it up eight, eight, and four hours the last day. I can be there tomorrow morning." I'll need something, I think. Six-pack of Red Bull. Hell, a whole case of Red Bull. I can do this.

"No." Finality in his voice. "If you need to go home that badly, buy a plane ticket. Talk to Missy. Get permission to leave for a couple of days. Don't be stupid about this."

"I already talked to Missy." More surprise on David's face. "Right before I came here. Mom had already gotten to her. She must have called Missy the *instant* I hung up."

"And?"

"Missy says I can't leave campus without parental approval, and they want me to stay put."

David looks relieved. His shoulders actually relax.

"Well, I guess that's the answer then. Keep checking in by phone. If you call Eva a few times a day, she'll know you're there for her."

He takes a step toward me. He's going to touch me again, wrap those gorgeous arms around me, pull me in close to that just-out-of-the-bed scent of him and . . .

I'll forget. Not completely. But for huge chunks of the day. Then days turning into a whole week. I'll start by kissing him, here in this messy room. Maybe we'll end up on those sheets for a while. We'll walk, holding hands, to lunch, late, barely making it in time. We'll go to afternoon drills. We'll cool off in the pool before late-afternoon match play. Showers, then dinner. Sunday dinner is usually pretty good. Steak, or even shrimp.

And a few times during the day I'll pick up my cell phone and press the number next to Eva's little ballet picture. Check in with Mom for the latest updates. Maybe at some point Eva will feel like talking.

There's a word for this: compartmentalize. Concentrate on what's in front of you, right now, and think about the rest of it later. Put the messy junk you don't want to deal with in a box. Like you're doing the right thing by stuffing all these unpleasant feelings, all these unpaid bills, into a file folder marked TO DO.

Gazing at this amazing boy who wants me, I wish I could tumble into this sweet life with him and forget all about the rest of the crap I left behind in Jersey. But it's not possible anymore.

As he steps forward, I step back.

"Don't," I say warningly. He looks confused.

"Don't what?"

"*Don't* tell me you love me," I manage to say. "Just do me that one favor."

I'm out the door before he can reply. I take the stairs, two at a time, to the girls' floor. People wandering around the hall. Somebody asks me how Yoly's party went. Awesome. Great. I don't know what I say before I make it to my room and shut the door. I struggle to control my breathing. I can't control my tears.

It's quiet, everyone's left for lunch, when I hear the soft tap on my door. It's been, what? Thirty minutes? I ignore it. Tap again, a little harder.

"Henry?"

When I open it, the first thing I notice is his hair. Slicked back and wet. He's showered. The next thing I notice is the bag. Slung over his shoulder, a compact, square black travel bag.

He steps into my room. He looks raw. Not like he's been scrubbed on the outside, but scraped out from the inside. He's fully dressed but looks more naked now than when he was wearing only those blue cotton boxers.

He closes the door. Drops the bag on the floor.

"Get packed," he says. "I'll take you."

I'm in his arms before I'm even aware that my feet have moved. Tight. He's holding me, hard, but his words come out tight, squeezed from some deep place in his chest.

"Don't ever walk away from me like that again," he says.

 269

Chapter Thirty

EVA

They say I've been here two days.

I ask if I've been asleep that long and they don't answer. They shift their eyes away from mine and say, "Your parents were here. They went home to shower and change clothes, but they'll be back." I want to ask them, Where *is* here? but I'm so tired. I'm tired like old bones. Like blowing sand.

I think I've been asleep, but it's not like any sleep I've known before. I remember things, like from a dream. And sounds. Especially sounds. A girl. I want to ask them, Who was that girl screaming? Tell them, because they really should know that some girl was screaming. Awful, sad screaming and sobs. I think I cried, too, when I heard it, because sadness like that is just contagious, you know? It makes me sad to hear her, and while I'm sorry for her, I want to tell them to take her away because I can't handle those cries right now.

I try to lift my hand, and it's so heavy. A little plastic tube, like a whisper, traces across the top of my hand and brushes

 270

my arm. It's stuck by papery white tape. It trails up and over and behind me, and I force my eyes to follow where it leads until I see a plastic bag full of liquid, swaying from this tall metal holder. Something trails across my face: from my nose and over my cheek. I want to brush it away, but I'm too tired to move my hand. Too tired to talk. To tell them about that girl.

There's this cloudiness over everything right now, and I close my eyes. Is this sleeping? If I'm sleeping, I wouldn't be able to wonder if I'm sleeping, right? So what is this? It's float-ing. And cool. Where the tape touches my hand I feel some-thing cool, and it spreads throughout my body. Except for my chest, which feels sore. Bruised.

I remember a car, driving fast, and one hot thought stabs through the cloudiness, that I was maybe in an accident? I want to force my eyes open, lift my head just a little and look at my body. Check for bandages. Casts. Missing parts. But it's swirling from cloudy to dim now, and yes, this is sleep coming. Later. I'll figure this all out later.

Dim goes to dark, but just before I disappear into it I real-ize where I've heard those screams before. Those familiar, awful screams.

I own them. They own me. They're the background noise that's been playing at low volume inside my head for so long now I couldn't even tell you when it began. Once upon a time. Way back when I was someone named Eva Smith, who had a doll named Samantha and loved to dance. Soft at first, then louder, more insistent, a steady background screaming in my head.

All out now. Floating in the dim, darkening air above some bed I'm in. My wailing sobs. My screams. And it's okay. Because my head is finally, blessedly empty. Still.

Chapter Thirty-One

HENRY

Somewhere outside Dillon, South Carolina, David begins to disintegrate. We've been driving close to ten hours. He's looking for a McDonald's.

This from a guy who never lets trans fats or caffeine pass his lips. He's a walking, talking sports-nutrition textbook who gives me grief because I always, absolutely, have to eat salty chips with my sandwiches. And now he's craving a pseudo-chocolate shake and a coffee?

"You're hitting the wall, aren't you?" I say quietly.

"Actually, I hit the wall in Savannah. Right now I'm climbing the wall." He says this without a trace of humor.

"I can drive, you know," I say. He sighs. It's the fourth time I've offered.

"No, you can't," he says. "You only have a permit. It's not your car. How many times do we have to go over this?" I don't answer. We don't speak as he turns off the exit ramp and follows the signs with the golden arches.

"Thank you for doing this for me," I say quietly. Also, not

 273

the first time I've said this. He reaches over with his right hand and gently massages the back of my neck.

The pimply-faced teenager who works the cash register at McDonald's looks really put out that we've come in ten minutes before closing, but he manages to sell us two coffees and a tall chocolate shake. David and I find a booth at a far corner of the restaurant. We're the only customers.

He starts with the coffee. He makes a terrible face.

"This is shit," he says, and pushes it away. I don't think I've ever heard him swear before. I take a sip of mine. He's right.

"Maybe there's caffeine in the shake," I suggest. He takes a long draw from the straw.

"That might be the only naturally occurring substance in it," he comments. He stares out the window, into the darkness.

"I'm going to need a break at some point. I can't do twenty hours straight through," he says to the glass.

"Okay," I say. I wonder what he means by "break."

"Let's see how far we get," he explains. "Maybe I can last a couple more hours." We don't speak, both of us lost in our thoughts, as he sucks down the shake. The pimply kid is turning out the lights when we leave.

We make it as far as Smithfield. David simply exits; he doesn't explain why.

"Is this, like, the ham place?" I wonder aloud.

"That's Smithfield, Virginia," he says.

"Really?" I say. "How do you know that?"

"My mind is a dumping ground for useless information," he says. "Result of too much homeschooling." I laugh.

 274

"This Smithfield is, however, the birthplace of the actress Ava Gardner," he continues.

"Wow. I don't know who she is. But now I'm really impressed."

"Don't be. I read it off that sign we just passed."

He pulls into the first motel we see. A Quality Inn. He parks the Cayenne in an empty spot near the entrance.

"Wait here," he says.

I watch him walk stiffly toward the double glass doors. I glance at my watch. One o'clock. We've been on the road more than twelve hours. I crack the window. Instantly the humid North Carolina air seeps in, mixing damply with the car's air-conditioning. I sneeze. I pop the glove compartment in search of Kleenex travel packs and dig through the papers stuffed inside. I pull out the stack and my glance falls on the top, yellow sheet. It's the car registration.

In the dim light I read that the Cayenne belongs to Paul Ross, Denver, Colorado. David's father.

I hear a riotous symphony of crickets. Distant highway traffic. Eva's voice in my head: "And why would a major, high-end car manufacturer do something so ridiculous?"

You are so clueless, Henry.

The sound of the trunk opening startles me.

"We're all set," David says shortly, shouldering his black bag and my backpack. I shove the papers back and snap the glove compartment closed.

I follow him through the glass doors, through the lobby, to an elevator. One lone woman sits at the reception desk. She

 275

doesn't look much older than us. She doesn't look up as we pass.

The room has a nonsmoking sign on the outside. David inserts the plastic key card, the electronic light blinks green, he pushes the door open. Cool air greets us, a sharp contrast to the close, warm air in the corridor. I go in first, flip the light switch.

One double bed.

David walks past me into the room, tosses both bags on the floor in front of the dresser and enters the bathroom. He closes the door behind him. I hear him pee into the toilet. He flushes. I hear the taps open, hear water splash into the sink. Rattle of paper as he unwraps the soap. When he comes out, I'm working the zipper on my pack, searching for my toiletries kit. My toothbrush. The big T-shirt I usually sleep in. With the tomatoes. My hands shake.

"Next," David says.

I look green in the fluorescent light of the bathroom. My hair hangs limp in my face. I feel greasy. I pick up the wet soap, lather my hands, massage it into my forehead, the creases along the sides of my nose. I rinse, and rinse again. I rub my face dry. I peel off my shirt. My bra. I step out of my shorts. I pull the tomatoes over my head. The tee falls just to the tops of my thighs.

When I come out, the room is dark. Before I hit the bathroom lights, I see the outline of his body in the bed, beneath the covers. It takes my eyes a moment to adjust, then I make my way slowly to the bed, hands outstretched. I pull the blankets back, slip between the cool sheets. I lie absolutely motionless, listening for the sound of his breathing. Just as the thought crosses my mind that he's already asleep, he speaks.

"I set the alarm for six," he says quietly.

"Okay," I say back. He doesn't move.

"Good night," I say softly. Too softly for him to hear, I think. But he hears me. The bed moves. The sheets whisper as he slides to the middle. I turn to him and his arms are around me. My hands are on his bare back and for one panicked moment I think he's naked. Then I feel the soft cotton of his shorts against my leg.

I try to say his name, but his mouth covers mine. Our knees knock. He pulls me close, presses his hips into mine. My heart bangs against my ribs. He must feel it. He must feel this wild drumming. I cling to him, my mind in a whirl, and both of us, dog-tired, far from home, not thinking straight, sink into the darkness of a motel room in Smithfield, North Carolina.

At some point, sleep comes.

Chapter Thirty-Two

EVA

She sits in the chair alongside my bed. She fills the chair. She reads from something in her lap, her legs crossed, one ankle resting atop one knee. Her skin is coppery, her hair lightened by the sun. I watch her for a while. Wait to see if this is another one of the dreams.

She flips a page.

"Hey," I say quietly.

She startles, looks up. Her sapphire eyes are wide. She leans forward, eagerly.

"Hey back," she replies softly. She reaches between the metal bars running along the side of the bed and places one hand over mine. I feel its weight, its warmth.

"You're real," I tell her. She laughs. Her teeth look so white.

"Of course I'm real," she says. I sigh. Close my eyes briefly.

"Lately it's been hard to tell. What's real," I explain. She nods her head solemnly, as if she understands.

"You look good," I tell her. You look huge, I don't say. You look like a taller, wider version of my friend Henry.

 278

"How're you feeling?" she says.

"Dopey. They're giving me drugs. I feel thick all over."

"Ugh. Bet that sucks," she says sympathetically. I try to raise my hands. They move an inch, then stop.

"They've tied me, Henry," I tell her. I tug, to no avail. My wrists are secured to the bars on either side of the bed. She looks at me sadly.

"I know," she whispers. Her eyes fill.

"I hate it," I tell her. She doesn't reply. Her eyes spill over, tears running in two straight lines down her cheeks.

"Eva, I'm so sorry," she says.

"Why are you sorry? You didn't do anything." She smiles through her tears.

"I'm sorry that I didn't know how sick you'd gotten."

I turn my head away from her. When I do, I feel it. Brushing against my cheek. A thin plastic tube protrudes from my left nostril, runs the length of my face, over my shoulder, then snakes up and out of the bed until it disappears into this machine. The pump, they call it.

You're disgusting. You look so disgusting, with this thing hanging out of your nose.

A thought occurs to me. I turn my face to her again.

"What are you doing here?" I ask.

"I'm here to see you," she says.

"You're supposed to be in Florida," I say. A summer camp. Henry is supposed to be away for the whole long summer.

"Is camp over?" I ask, panic rising in me. How long have I been here?

 279

How long has this damn machine been pumping fat into me?

"There's two weeks left," Henry says. "I took a break to come see you."

"Oh. Okay," I reply. Deep breath. My chest rises, falls. "You had me worried there for a minute."

"What do you mean?"

"I thought for a second that the summer was over. Time has gotten really weird for me."

"Do you know how long you've been here?" she asks. I pause. It feels like a trick question.

"How long?" I ask.

"Three days." I don't reply. I'm trying to remember what three days feels like. Right now, it feels like a few minutes. And an eternity. That's how long I've been tied to this bed.

"It took me almost an entire day to get here," she continues. "Twenty-two hours, on the road." She waits. I guess I'm supposed to say something about that, but I can't think what. My mind moves sluggishly over all the possible things I might say. These drugs have shifted my head into slow motion. I tug at my wrists.

"Henry." She looks at me expectantly.

"Help me untie my hands."

Her face falls. Instantly I know. She doesn't have to say a word. I can tell from her expression: she won't do it.

She's on their side.

"Eva, I don't think I'm allowed. But if you want, I'll call the nurse and we can ask her. . . ."

 280

"Forget it. Never mind." The words sound snappish, despite my heavy, slow-moving tongue.

"Please don't be mad. Your mother said you were pulling everything out, and that's why they restrained you. I don't think they'll let me stay if I untie your hands."

Rhonda. She's been talking to Rhonda. Where is Mommy Dearest, anyway?

"You probably shouldn't stay. There's nothing for you to do here."

Go. Go run around in the sun with your new friends. Just leave me here to rot, surrounded by psycho doctors and fat-pumping goons.

"Don't say that. You don't mean that." Tears in her voice.

But I do, Henry. I do mean it.

Chapter Thirty-Three

HENRY

Dad's taking me to the airport later this afternoon. I have a one-thirty flight out of LaGuardia, which should land me in Fort Lauderdale around dinner. Missy will pick me up.

Mom and I sit outside on the patio. She's on her third cup of coffee. Necessary medication, after the late night we all had. We sit at the faux-French metal café table. The "Ray table." Sorry, that's just the way it is. Some pictures get burned into your mind permanently.

Like the picture of Eva in that hospital bed. I wasn't ready. Wasn't ready for the shrunken, birdlike size of her. The long, thin plastic tube that snaked from her nose to a blinking machine on wheels. Her complexion, which had always reminded me of freshly washed china, now like ashes. The skin under her eyes sunk into lavender half-moons. Her teeth protruding slightly, as if they'd grown. But, of course, they hadn't. Her face had simply shrunk, the skin of her cheeks pulled back tight so that the teeth and jaws stuck out, skull-like. She barely made a bump beneath the sheets. She could have been a fold in the blanket.

I'd wandered into that, straight off the road. Hadn't called anyone, somehow sweet-talked my way past the guard dogs at the nurses' station, even with the backpack I'd been hauling for the last twenty-four hours slung over my shoulder. One of the nurses led me to a corner of the ICU, with all these blinking lights and scary metal contraptions. To a bed where an old woman slept.

"Where's Eva Smith?" I asked her. She gestured toward the old woman, who, you realized if you looked closely, was actually a fifteen-year-old girl, and this sound came from my throat.

It's like I barked, the pain and surprise were that bad.

"Do you want anything else?" Mom asks. I shake my head. I've just polished off a stack of waffles layered with strawberry jam and drenched in maple syrup. We had a late breakfast.

She cradles her mug in both hands, staring across the lawn toward the tennis court. I've got my head tilted back, eyes half closed, face to the sun. It's gonna be a scorcher. Heat bugs rasp in the hedges. Humidity must be ninety percent.

"I think this is the best thing, hon," Mom says. "Until she's stabilized, and released from the hospital, there's not much we can do." I open my eyes and stare frankly at my mother.

"She doesn't want me here, anyway, Mom." She sighs. She puts the mug on the table.

"That's not Eva talking. It's the eating disorder," she says patiently.

"Oh god, not that again," I mutter. I can't help myself.

Eva's been seeing a therapist . . . something else no one had bothered to tell me . . . and when Rhonda found out that I was at the hospital, having a mini freakout, she set me up with this woman Wendy. A crunchy-granola earth mother who talked psychobabble at me for half an hour. I think Rhonda paid her for her time.

"Think of an eating disorder as an emotionally abusive relationship," Wendy said, in this maddeningly soothing tone. We were sitting together in the "family area," this puke-colored, dimly lit room set aside for the family members of intensive-care-unit patients. As soon as the nurse saw me lose it in the ICU, she hauled me out of there and sat me down in Pukeville. Called the Smiths, who called the Lloyds . . . you can imagine. Henry, who's supposedly in Florida, is actually in Jersey. Before I knew it, they were all at the hospital, with Wendy in tow.

"Imagine that abuser lives in your head," she said. "He talks to you in a voice you might actually confuse with your own internal voice, but this one is extremely negative. Think of him as Ed. As in Eating Disorder. Imagine Ed is a snarky guy dressed in dark leather and smoky glasses. He whispers mean things to you all day. Tells you you're fat. Calls you a loser. Undermines your confidence, convinces you that no one really likes you. And the only time Ed is nice is when you're starving. He compliments that. Makes you feel virtuous for being disciplined and slim. Ed encourages the behaviors that hurt your body and isolate you from others."

 284

I couldn't decide whether I wanted to beat that Wendy senseless with her own Birkenstocks or fall into her arms, crying. She was comforting and infuriating at the same time, drove me crazy. Or maybe it wasn't her at all. Maybe it was Rhonda. Who kept nodding, dabbing at her eyes, gazing at me earnestly as Wendy "explained" Eva's eating disorder.

Worst of all, my own mother has bought into this crap. Now she thinks anorexia is a demonic possession by an abusive guy named Ed.

"I don't think I can stomach the Wendy bull right now," I say.

"Why do you think it's 'bull'?"

"Because Wendy is blaming Ed for Eva's problems instead of laying the responsibility where it belongs," I say angrily.

"And where would that be?" she asks gently.

"Oh, gosh. Let's think hard. How about right smack-dab at Rhonda's feet?" I say. She shakes her head at me.

"It's not that simple," she says. "I've been reading a lot about anorexia. . . ."

"Mom. Please. The woman *defines* the term 'stage mother.'"

"So how come *you're* not starving yourself?" my mother asks. "Is it because there's no pressure on you? No difficult parent to contend with?"

Point to Mrs. Lloyd. I hadn't thought of that.

"Well, for what I do, eating is encouraged. I spend hours in the weight room instead of hours in front of a mirror, in a leotard, comparing the size of my butt to the rest of the girls'." Mom rolls her eyes.

285

"So we blame ballet?" she says.

"No, but it explains a lot. She needs to be wispy thin; I need to be muscular."

"The differences between you and Eva go deeper than that," Mom says. "Did it ever occur to you that part of her attraction to ballet *was* the look it required? The emphasis on perfection? It's an art form that an obsessive, somewhat compulsive person might be drawn to. Which is also the very personality type most susceptible to an eating disorder. Just as certain people are more prone to becoming alcoholics or drug addicts, certain people, if the conditions are right, are more likely to develop anorexia."

"I'd say life in Rhonda's house provides the perfect conditions."

"Honey, you have always been tough. You wear everyone's expectations for you like wings: you fly. For Eva, success and the accompanying expectations are like stones she has to haul up a mountain. They burden her. Deep down, she doesn't believe she's worthy of the praise heaped upon her."

"You're wrong. *I'm* the negative one. The angry one. You know what the other players used to call me on the Jersey circuit? The bitch. That's because I play mind games with my opponents. Mean mind games. My own boyfriend said it. But Eva? She's the nicest person I know." Mom shakes her head at me again.

"It's not a matter of nice versus mean. It's about strong versus vulnerable. Ed would never have had a chance in your head."

Ed in my head. The words create a picture in my mind. I see a smarmy guy, a black-leather version of Jonathan Dundas, wandering onto my tennis court. Standing off to the side, a smirk on his rodentlike face. He watches me serve, and after I hit one in the net, he comments, "That sucked."

I grab him by the scruff of the neck and kick him in the backside so hard he practically flies off the court.

Okay, so Henry Lloyd wouldn't have put up with an Ed, real or imagined, for an instant. But who ever said Eva did? Who was ever negative to Eva? Rhonda, for all her faults, thinks her daughter is amazing.

Is it possible that someone as beautiful and extraordinary and kind as Eva, could, deep down, feel bad about herself? So bad that her negative feelings took on a life of their own and became an ugly voice in her head that she was willing to believe?

I don't know. I'm so tired right now I feel like I've been wrung out. I don't know who's right, who's to blame or what to do, for that matter. So I'm doing what I'm told. Heading back to Chadwick and my own great expectations. There's a tournament on Friday, after all.

"You never told me you had a boyfriend," Mom says quietly, interrupting my thoughts.

"He's just some guy at the school," I say shortly. "No biggie."

She taps her head with one finger, as if she's just remembered something.

"His name isn't David, by any chance, is it?" My stomach does a 180-degree flip.

"And you know that how?" I ask.

"He left two messages on the answering machine. Sorry. With all the drama in the past twenty-four hours I forgot to tell you."

"What did he say?" I ask. Like I couldn't care less.

"He just asked you to call. He said he'd left messages on your cell phone."

The screen door opens, and Dad steps out. He carries his own cup of coffee.

"Thanks," I say to Mom. "I'll call him back later." She eyes me suspiciously.

"That's a lot of messages for 'no biggie,'" she says. Dad pulls up a metal chair.

"What's no biggie?" he says. His hair is wet; he's just showered.

"The David who's been leaving messages is Henry's boyfriend from Chadwick," Mom explains. "Or . . . not," she adds hastily when I flash her a murderous look.

Mark frowns.

"Did I meet him?" he asks.

"You could say that," I reply. I barely hold back the sarcasm. "He was the guy you almost throttled the night you jumped out of the bushes."

An uncomfortable silence follows. Finally Dad clears his throat.

"Henry, I'm very sorry if my behavior has cost you, in any way. If this boy broke up with you because he thinks your father is a nut job, then I'm sorry."

 288

"He thinks you're a nut job, but that's not why we broke up," I say. Mark purses his lips. He knows he deserved that one.

I need to change the subject, fast. I do not want to discuss David with them. Right now they think I spent twenty hours on a bus from Boca to Newark, where I transferred to another bus for Ridgefield. Cabbed it to the hospital. End of story.

As far as they know, Smithfield, North Carolina, does not exist.

"Listen, no offense, but I don't want to talk about David," I say.

"You know," Dad says briskly, "we have some time before we have to head out to the airport. What do you say I run you by the hospital once more?" I shake my head firmly.

"She doesn't want me there," I repeat. "We've been over this, okay?"

"I just spoke with Bob," my father says. "Eva's awake, and he says she's been having a pretty good morning."

"Well, how about we don't wreck it for her?" I say. But he keeps talking.

"I'll bet when she thinks about her visit with you yesterday, she's going to feel bad. Because you're her best friend, and she loves you."

I stare at him. I cannot remember a time, ever, when he ventured a guess as to how someone else felt.

"Everyone deserves a second chance, Hen. Especially a good friend. There's nothing better you can do for someone than give them a second chance." His eyes are full as he looks

 289

at me, and even though I realize he's talking about a hell of a lot more than Eva . . . I get it.

Every once in a while I'm lucky, and something prevents me from making a complete jerk out of myself. Hard to believe, but right now, that "something" is Mark Lloyd. Go figure.

Is it possible, I wonder, to kill a thing with a word? Does just *saying* stuff, dragging it out into the clear light of day, make it better? I honestly have no clue. We three Lloyds were up until the wee hours beating ourselves over the heads with words. About Eva. About tennis. About Mom and Dad. And Ray. Yeah, even Ray got dragged out from his little hidey-hole in our hearts. That was fun.

These therapy types, the Wendys of the world, think all the talk helps. All I know for sure is that keeping secrets never helps. The things we don't say are like slow-acting poisons, eating away at us from the inside. So I don't know if it would have helped Eva to say how sad and scared she always felt. I don't know, if I'd been brave enough to admit to her and to myself that she was too skinny, and that the calorie counting worried me, if it would have helped. But not saying it sure hurt.

And real friends speak the painful truth.

I glance at my watch.

"Sure, Dad. Let's go," I say.

* * *

She's awake, and her eyes are wide, urgent, as I approach. Even though I saw her yesterday, I still struggle at the sight of her. I will myself not to stare at her wasted shoulders. The thick knobs of her elbows.

 290

Her dad is sitting with her when I arrive. He gets up and gives me a tight hug. He's always so nice.

"Thanks for coming back, Henry," he says. "I'm going to go make some phone calls while you girls visit, okay?" He bends over Eva and plants a kiss on her forehead. "I'll be back in a minute, hon." He walks out of the ICU and gives us some privacy.

"Hi," she says tentatively. "Thanks for coming back."

"No problem," I say. "How's it goin'?" She turns her head restlessly. She reaches up to run her fingers through her hair.

"Hey! They untied you!" I say without thinking.

"Only for part of the time," she says. "They put the restraints back when I'm alone." She's glancing nervously around the room. I wonder if she's planning on trying something while I'm here. Her eyes return to me.

"Do you hate me?" she asks quietly. The words feel like a blow.

"Why would you even ask that?" I say. "Don't be a dope." I try to smile at her.

"I'm sorry," she says. "Dad says I told you to leave. I don't remember that." I shrug.

"It's okay, Eva."

"But it's not," she returns fretfully. "I mean, I wouldn't say that to you, would I? And I can't remember. So please, Henry, just tell me: did I ask you to leave?" I sigh.

"Yeah, you pretty much did. But Eva: I'm not mad. Okay?" Her eyes fill.

"I'm sorry," she whispers.

 291

I don't know what to say. I don't know what I can possibly do to help her. Except give her a second chance.

"Apology accepted," I say, "even though you don't owe me one." The tense lines on her face relax.

"Dad says you're going back today," she says.

"Yup. Only place in America that's hotter and more humid than Jersey," I joke.

"Is it hot out?" she says.

"Awful. Like walking into a steam cleaner. You are very lucky to be in all this nice air-conditioning." I realize this is a pretty stupid thing to say to someone in intensive care.

"It's too cold," she says. "I hate air-conditioning."

"Well, maybe you should be going to Florida," I quip. Stupid comment number two. One more and I'll strike myself out. Eva and I are quiet for a while.

"I might, you know. Go to Florida." I look at her in surprise.

"When I get out of here. Wendy wants me to go to this program in Florida."

"What sort of program?" I ask.

"For anorexia," she says. She holds my eyes with hers when she says this. It's the first time the word has passed between us. Mom told me Eva refuses to admit that she has anorexia.

I nod. Accept the word. Allow it to float freely in the space between us.

"That might be good, you know?" I tell her. "Florida's not so bad. I mean, *it ain't Joisey*. But it's okay." I try to smile bravely at her.

 292

"Jersey tomatoes are the best," she says, returning the barest trace of a smile.

"The very best," I agree. "Although, if we both end up in Florida, what will that make us? Hothouse tomatoes?" She laughs. A little. Then she turns, stares at the wall.

"We'll see," she says quietly to no one in particular. She seems very distracted.

I could burst with all the things I need to tell her. But seeing her lying there, a ghost of the beautiful, lively girl I hugged good-bye only five short weeks ago, I'm ashamed of my own need. She almost died. What's a trophy, or a party, or even a broken heart, compared to that?

I miss her. I miss my best girlfriend.

Her eyes are closed; she's dozing off. She's still on some pretty heavy meds. I grasp her now-free hand and squeeze. As far as I went, twenty-plus hours, a thousand miles, she strayed farther.

"Come back to us, Eva," I whisper.

Chapter Thirty-Four

EVA

Someone's played a mean trick on me and replaced Henry with Wendy. I wake to find her, draped in one of those wrinkly, sacklike dresses, sitting in the chair beside my bed.

"Hello, Eva," she says, not unkindly.

My mouth feels dry. I can tell that my own breath is bad.

"Can I have some water?" I ask. She presses a button that slowly raises the head of my bed to a semi-upright sitting position. She holds out a tall paper cup with a lid and a straw. I reach for it. My hands are still unrestrained. Before I sip, I lift one edge of the lid. Peer inside. Sniff. Plain water. I take a long pull on the straw and the cotton lining in my mouth dissolves.

"Is Henry gone?" I ask. She nods. I take another long, cool sip.

"How long have you been here?" I ask. Wendy glances at her watch.

"Not long," she replies.

I hate the way Wendy never answers questions. Why

couldn't she just say, "I've been sitting here for seventeen minutes." Or, "I haven't left your side for thirty years. You've just woken from a coma, and Zac Efron is president of the United States." I mean, if you take into account the creation of the universe, thirty years qualifies as "not long."

They must be backing off on the meds. I'm starting to remember things. Like how much Wendy annoys me.

"How do you feel?" she asks. I consider.

"Less loopy," I tell her. She nods.

"Do you think you're ready to eat something?" I freeze.

Here she goes again, Lard Ass pushing food. What'll it be today, Wendy-girl? Peanut butter Häagen-Dazs sundaes?

"I thought I was being fed by this tube," I tell her.

"Yes, but you want to begin eating normally so that your doctors can remove the tube."

"But I can't eat while I have the tube!"

"Why not?"

"Because that would be too much."

"Why do you think that would be too much?"

Why do you think, fatso? Okay, maybe a pump full of calories plus a full meal doesn't seem like too much to you. Maybe you don't mind waddling around with those ankles. But there's no way I'm doing it.

"Why don't you just answer my question!"

"What question, Eva?"

Throw it. Just throw it at her.

The paper cup hits the floor. Water pools.

"I'm sorry, but that's just not acceptable." Slight trace

 295

of irritation in Wendy's voice. It comes as something of a relief, getting a bona fide human reaction out of her. She stands up.

"I don't recall a question, Eva, but I do have an answer for you. Unless you want to remain intubated and restrained to this bed, you need to eat." She leaves the room.

I feel broken. Brittle. I'm so sick of it all: the restraints, the drugs, the tube, the threats. I don't know what to do. I can't decide. I'm so tired of fighting.

You know what to do. Get the damn tube out of your nose. It's pouring fat into your belly while you lie here on your dead ass. Which, by the way, is spreading while you sleep.

I can't pull it out. If I pull it out, they'll just stick it back in.

They'll take it out if they think you're eating.

Wendy returns. She carries white towels and a small bowl. A familiar smell wafts from the bowl.

"What's that?" I ask. She is spreading the towels on the floor, sopping up the water.

"It's pasta. Plain boiled ziti," she says.

Ziti. Rotini, spaghetti, fusilli, linguini . . . all the "'eenies," I called them. "What do you want for dinner tonight, Eva?" my mother would ask, and I'd cry out, "I want 'eenies, Mommy!" One night when Dad was traveling for business, we went to the grocery store and bought one box of every pasta ending in *i* that we could find. She boiled up a portion of each, and dinner for both of us that night was a ginormous bowl of pure carbohydrate, a melting pat of butter on top. We both decided that good ol' spaghetti tasted best, even though we knew each shape was made from the exact same ingredients.

We ate and ate. We were so full that we fell asleep together, on her bed, while she was reading to me that night. And in the morning, when she started pulling out the boxes of breakfast cereal, I asked, "Wanna eat the rest of the 'eenies?"

She microwaved the leftovers and we giggled like two friends doing something naughty.

I want to love pasta again. I do love pasta. I love . . .

Plain ziti, my ass! Dripping with butter, more like. Can you imagine Wendy eating anything plain in her life?

"Can't I have fruit?" I ask. Wendy sighs.

"You haven't eaten regularly for a long time, Eva. Plain, cooked foods like pasta are best for you at first."

What would that lard butt know about nutrition? Give me a break. She's smeared something on those noodles.

"I don't want pasta. I don't like pasta. I like fruit." Wendy replaces the bowl on the end table. She sits quietly for a few moments before diving in again.

"Your mother told me you like pasta."

'Eenies. They're called 'eenies, and yeah, she would know. . . .

Shut up! Shut up with that stupid 'eenies baby talk! You are such a big baby.

"By the way, I enjoyed meeting your friend Henry."

Hmm. Where's this going?

"I can sense a real bond between the two of you. I was

297

thinking, when I met her, that you're very lucky. A true friend like that doesn't come along very often."

For some reason, her words make me sad. I feel my eyes well up with tears.

"What did you tell her?" I ask.

"I tried to help her understand why you've gotten sick. How she can support you."

There she goes again, with that "sick" stuff. Know what's sick, Wendy? You're sick. Anyone with rolls of fat around her ankles is totally sick.

"She's in your corner, Eva. She wants to see you get out of that bed and smile again."

Guilt rains down on me from every possible direction. Guilt, for making Henry leave her special camp just because of me. Guilt, for the fear in my parents' eyes every time they look at me. Guilt, for what I imagine this hospital costs.

But mostly, guilt over that small white bowl on the end table. Because I'm thinking maybe I should eat some pasta. Maybe I should trust Wendy. Taste food again.

Yeah, that's the spirit, you cow. Pasta today, pizza tomorrow, right? A little pasta, plus the nose-tube crap, and you'll roll right out of ICU. You pig.

Wendy has picked up the bowl again.

"What do you say we start with one bite?" she says softly.

298

Chapter Thirty-Five

HENRY

I had woken to an empty bed. Traces of early morning peeked around the edges of the heavy motel curtains. The digital clock glowed: 6:15. I'd never heard the alarm.

I snapped on the lamp, climbed out of bed and looked in the bathroom: empty. My eyes did a quick inventory of the room. My backpack: on the floor, my junk strewn around it. His sneakers: gone. The keys to the Cayenne: not on the dresser. The square black bag: on the dresser, zipped open, one of his T-shirts poking out. My shoulders relaxed.

I decided to hop into the shower. As I rummaged through my pack in search of shampoo and clean underwear, I caught a glimpse of myself in the full-length mirror over the dresser. Tangled blond hair. Long, wrinkled T-shirt with two tomatoes, like crumpled roses, blooming just over my breasts. I was a mess, for sure.

But I was still me.

Nothing had happened. He'd wanted it to, but I couldn't. I

wasn't ready. *We're* not ready, I told him. We've known each other, what? A few weeks? That's no time at all.

"I feel like I've known you forever," he breathed into my neck. The sweet smell of him, the feel of him, pressed against me beneath the cool sheets, was . . . indescribable. Kissing him, holding him, is wonderful. Perfect. But then it changes. There's this urgency, this insistence about him. I know it's what happens next, but for me, right now, it doesn't feel right. It feels scary.

He rolled away from me in the dark. I heard him breathe out, an impatient blow I recognized. It's what he does when he's trying a new shot and the ball keeps hitting the tape.

I think I counted to ten before sliding toward him. I placed one hand on his chest, rested my head on the pillow next to his.

"Please don't be angry with me," I whispered.

"I'm not angry, Hen," he said.

"Don't be disappointed," I pressed. He said nothing.

"You're disappointed," I said.

"Well, yeah," he said. Impatience in his voice. "You could call it that."

"I'm sorry," I said quietly. He slid one arm under and around me. He wound his fingers through my hair.

"We should get some sleep," he said. "It's a long way to New Jersey."

When I emerged from the steamy bathroom, a towel wrapped around my wet head, he was back. He had opened the curtains. Two Styrofoam cups steamed on the round table in front of the window. There was a paper bag with the Dunkin' Donuts logo on it. He smiled at me.

"I got us some breakfast," he said.

"Ooh, I hope it's sugary and loaded with trans fats," I said, eagerly approaching the bag. He shook his head.

"Nope. Two sesame bagels, cream cheese on the side," he said. I picked up one of the Styrofoam cups.

"Caffeine?" I asked hopefully.

"Oh, yes," he said. He pulled two large Nantucket Nectars from the bag. "And juice."

We didn't speak as we unwrapped the bagels and took our first tentative sips of the hot coffee. I could make out traces of blue sky through the gauzy privacy curtains. It promised to be a good day for driving.

"What time did you get up?" I asked him.

"I don't know. Five? I couldn't get back to sleep. My mind was working overtime."

"Don't you hate that?" I agreed. "It's like you know you have to sleep some more, but you just keep *thinking*." He was quiet when I said that. He cleared his throat.

"Actually, Henry." A statement. I waited. Blew on my coffee. "I've been thinking."

Not a good intro.

"I think we should go back."

My lungs, instinctively, sucked air. Deep, sharp intake of breath. The way, so I've heard, your body clutches at air when you've plunged into icy water.

 301

"What do you mean?" There was a dead look in his eyes. It made me sick.

"I know that Eva is your best friend, and you think she needs you right now . . ."

"I don't think it. I *feel* it. Like, in my bones. This is not a question, David."

"Fine, you feel it," he said. Patiently. Like you would speak to a child. Something dark stirred inside me. "But Henry, be honest. What can you really accomplish up there? She's got her family and a whole hospital's worth of doctors looking out for her."

"I don't want to accomplish anything. I just want to be there for her." What part of this doesn't he *get*? I thought.

"I don't know, Hen," he said softly. "Are you sure you don't want to be there for *you*? Are you sure this isn't just some grand gesture because you feel guilty?"

"Why would I feel guilty?" I demanded.

"Because things are going well for you and not for her," he said. "Because you're happy and she's not. I don't know, you tell me. Because in the cold, clear light of day, this whole thing is starting to look pretty irrational. And I don't think I can hang with it anymore."

I couldn't believe what I was hearing. After making it halfway up the East Coast, he wanted to turn around? A light went on in my head.

"You've been talking to someone," I said. Scripted. It explained the tone. The rehearsed expression. He placed the coffee cup carefully on the round table.

"If we head back now," he said, "no recriminations. No sanctions, no problems. We'll be able to play in the Friday tournament. I mean, I think we'll be a little road-weary, but first round shouldn't be too bad. . . ."

"Who?" I interrupted. "Who told you 'no problems'?" He sighed.

"Harvey," he said. "Missy. I checked my phone messages when I went out. They're pretty upset, but I managed to calm them down."

"Because you told them we're heading back," I said.

"Yes," he said. He took one step forward, eagerly. "Henry, I know how you feel, and I totally respect that . . ."

"No, David, I don't think you have a clue how I feel," I said, my voice shaking. "I can't believe you would go behind my back. I can't believe you wouldn't talk to me first. What else aren't you telling me? Besides, by the way, about the car." It slipped out. Not the way I'd hoped to bring up the topic.

He looked confused.

"What?"

"The Cayenne. I know your dad owns it." David sighed again.

"I'm sorry. I wasn't up front with you about that. I just . . . hate . . . for people to judge me. To put me in the 'rich kid' box before they get to know me."

"You could have told *me* the truth," I said.

"I can tell you the truth now that you know me," he corrected. "But when we were just getting together? Don't say it

 303

wouldn't have colored the way you see me." I didn't reply. I didn't want to give him a single point.

He stepped closer to me.

"Henry, I swear, that's the only, only lie I've ever told you. So please believe me about this Harvey and Missy thing. Please appreciate how much slack they are cutting us. Ditching out of the program like that, without permission? Anybody else would have been sent home."

"Exactly," I snarled. "Chadwick's rising stars. They'd let us get away with murder as long as we keep winning." I couldn't contain the bitterness in my voice. He frowned.

"That's not what's going on," he said.

"Of course that's what's going on!" I snapped. "Why don't you see it, David? Let me ask you something: don't you ever feel *owned* by these people?"

"I feel lucky. These people support me," he said, incredulous. "They support us." I couldn't help it; I snorted.

"Oh, that's bull! You're not their family, David. You're their *investment*. Earn a top-ten ranking someday and they'll love you. But say you break an ankle tomorrow? Then it's welcome to oblivion."

He crossed his arms tightly and stared at the carpet. When he spoke again, I could tell he chose his words carefully.

"I'm going back." Something inside my chest split open.

"David. Please. I need to see her." I couldn't bear the thought of turning around. Not now. He nodded.

"I understand," he repeated. "Listen. We're about thirty minutes outside of Raleigh. You can pick up Amtrak there, which will take you to Newark. From Newark you can get a bus to Ridgefield."

The conversation had changed direction so quickly I actually felt dizzy. I sat on the edge of the bed, still clutching my coffee.

"How do you know that?" I asked.

"I had Missy check the trains. I told her I'd do my best to bring you back with me, but if you wouldn't come, we needed a Plan B to get you home."

I could hear a little "oh" escape my lips. Suddenly the anger I'd been riding evaporated, and I just felt . . . abandoned. My eyes filled.

David took the coffee from me, placed it on the floor and held both my hands in his. He knelt before me.

"Please, Henry. Let's go back. Let the doctors do what they're supposed to do, and we'll do what we're supposed to do."

Supposed to do.

Who the hell decides *that*?

Chapter Thirty-Six

EVA

The tube is out. Breakfast is plain toast and juice. Along with this maroon plastic bottle of something called Boost. I'm trying not to freak out over what must be in it. I read the nutrition information on the label: 360 calories packed into eight fluid ounces. Plus enough vitamins and minerals to sustain a team of Clydesdales. You know, those enormous horses that pull the beer wagon?

The voice in my head shrieks, especially over the Boost. Every time I lift it to my lips, Ed unleashes on me.

Fatty, fatty two-by-four, can't fit through the bathroom door! Here comes chunky monkey Eva drinking her Boosty woosty! Loser. Big baby. Big baby who does everything they tell her.

Only Wendy understands Ed. She tells me she hears him behind my sarcastic jokes and nervous questions and anger. Especially the anger. She says the shrieks are Ed's death cries. When I eat healthy food, it's like pouring holy water on a demon. Make him sizzle, she tells me.

I don't know how to tell her that every bite I take is like

flames to *me*. Guilt that burns all the way down. And on good days, I can believe that Ed is some nasty guy living in my head. But most of the time . . . there is no Ed. It's me. That voice is my own.

If I can't tell the difference between me and this so-called Ed, who do I believe?

Wendy is due in to see me this afternoon, but Rhonda has shown up for breakfast this morning. Wonderful. Someone always sits with me when I eat (they call it "support"), and today I've won the jackpot and get Mommy Dearest. She's slurping something she picked up at Starbucks. Caramel Macchiato, she calls it.

"Would you like a sip?" she offers.

I stifle the impulse to hurl the Boost at her head.

"You really aren't *getting* this, are you?" I say.

"Getting what, Eva? I offered you a sip of Starbucks."

"Right. Trans-fatty, sugary, caramel crapulous whatever." She looks nervously out the window.

"I'm sorry. I just thought you'd enjoy it more than the shakes they're giving you. I mean, those Boosts already have eleven grams of fat in them, so I thought . . ."

"FUCK!" The Boost hits the wall. A brown stain explodes, drips.

Now THAT'S my girl! Next time, peg her.

"Eva, my god, why did you do that?" She looks frightened. She yanks some tissues from the box on my night table and swabs the wall. Smears the brown even more.

"These are not SHAKES! They're supplements, okay? Get

307

with the lingo, Mom. And can you *not* talk about . . . calories? Or fat grams? It is so unbelievably triggering!! Why don't you understand that? Does Wendy need to beat you over the head or something?"

She returns to her chair and stares at the floor. A long minute passes before I notice her shoulders shaking. She is sobbing without making a sound.

"Not this again," I mutter. Her head snaps up.

"I'm sorry. Is it upsetting to you that I'm crying?" she demands, her face streaked with tears. "Are you the only one around here allowed to express your feelings?"

"When have you ever *not* expressed your feelings?" I fire back. "It's been the Rhonda Show in our house since the dawn of time."

She laughs. Not in a mean way. More like I've told a great joke.

"Oh, Eva, how little you see. The Rhonda Show! Starring the Invisible Woman, I suppose. The drudge, whose entire existence is spent in the service of her amazing daughter!" She falls back in her chair, laughing and crying. Which I guess means she's hysterical.

"That is so lame!" I fire back at her. "You are, like, the stage mother from hell, and somehow that's my fault?" She shakes her head.

"Nothing is your fault, Eva. I'm just saying it's been anything but the Rhonda Show all these years. It's been the Eva Show."

 308

"Yeah, and you loved it," I say bitterly. "Every braggy minute of it."

"I did love it. Because you loved it," she says softly. "And we love you."

"You love the way I dance," I correct her. "Face it, Mom. Without *pointe* shoes, I'm not particularly interesting to you." A fierce expression comes over her face. She stands up.

"Someday you'll have a child and realize how incredibly unfair that comment was."

"Hey, you're the one paying for all the therapy. Sorry if the truth hurts."

She folds her arms across her chest tightly, her lips a thin line. I can't tell if she's thinking about what to say, or trying to hold back things she knows she shouldn't say.

"From the moment . . . the moment . . . you were born and they placed you in my arms, I have loved you. I looked into your beautiful little face, and it was as if I recognized you from another life, and you had been returned to me. I loved you naked and screaming and red and helpless, and there wasn't a *pointe* shoe in sight." Her voice trembles as she speaks.

"*You* love dance, Eva. And because we love you, we've done everything we can to give you what you want. I know I'm not perfect, and for the life of me I can't figure out why you're so angry. But here's the truth: if you never, never dance again? I will still love you."

She walks out of the room. I know she's coming back; she's left her bag. She's left her Starbucks. She's left me, with this adrenaline rush I can barely contain. With tears threatening to pour from my own eyes.

Because I want to believe her. I want so badly to love my mom again.

*   *   *

Wendy arrives that afternoon with a blank spiral notebook.

"A present," she says. In addition to the notebook, she dumps a dizzying assortment of writing implements onto my lap. Colored markers, felt-tipped pens, iridescent purple pencils . . . I gasp in delight. I love funky writing stuff.

"This," she explains, pointing to the notebook, "is going to be a journal. But not just any old journal. It's a counter journal."

"A what?" I ask.

"A first-strike weapon in the War on Ed," she says, grinning. "In shrink terms: a counter journal." She perches herself on the edge of my bed and opens the notebook. On every page, someone has drawn a straight line down the middle, forming two wide columns. On the left column, penciled in at the top, the word "Irrational." On the right side: "Rational."

"Ed is a clever liar," she says. "He disguises himself as your inner voice and tells you horrible things that you suspect might be true. They're never completely outrageous. Outrageous lies would be easy to dismiss. For example, you wouldn't believe it if Ed told you that Elvis lives. On Mars."

"He doesn't?" I say. Wendy smiles.

"Okay, maybe not a great example. However, you get my drift," she replies. "But if Ed said mean things about how you

 310

dance? How you look? How your friends feel about you? You might be willing to listen, because those things get at our insecurities. Those are the very things we worry about. And if Ed's voice sounds remarkably like your own, after a while it's almost impossible to distinguish his mean, negative voice from your own positive, balanced thoughts. No matter how crazy, or wrong, or"—she points to the left-hand column of the journal—"*irrational* Ed can be."

I stare down at the page. The neat lines dividing the pure white sheets into manageable, organized sections. Linear.

"So here's how it works," Wendy continues. "On the left, in the 'irrational' column, you write down what Ed says. All the mean, scary stuff. Then, on the right, in the 'rational' column, you write what Eva knows is true. You 'counter' Ed's lies."

She makes it sound so simple. As if irrational and rational thoughts are twin highways crossing my brain, with clearly marked speed limits and signage. What she doesn't realize is that my thoughts are more like a tangle of spaghetti. Or a Gordian knot. Try to pull one thread free and the whole mess tightens. Around your neck. Making it difficult to breathe.

"I don't know if I can do that," I say honestly. She smiles encouragingly.

"You can," she says, "but I won't lie to you. It's hard. It may be some of the hardest work you'll ever do. It'll make *pointe* class look like a walk in the park."

"Great," I grumble. She plucks a thin-tipped Sharpie from the heap and holds it out to me. I shake my head and go for the purple pencil instead.

 311

"Start simple," Wendy suggests. "Start with the biggest lie Ed tells you every day."

I clutch the pencil tightly, the tip poised over the first line of the first column of the first page. I am loath to put a mark on it, to sully the clean white sheets. But I know exactly what I have to write here.

"Eva is fat."

It hurts to see the words on the page. Making myself write it is hard, but reading it back is like getting slapped. I am so ashamed of being fat. I am such a weakling, so embarrassed that I can't control what I eat, that I've turned myself into this gross, waddling . . .

"Okay. Now counter it. What do you know is true?" Wendy's voice tugs at me.

"It is true," I whisper.

"Eva. If that were true, would you be in a hospital drinking Boost?" I shrug.

"C'mon. What *is* the truth?" Wendy prompts gently.

"Tell me," I plead with her. She shakes her head.

"You have to tell yourself," she says. "That's the only way this works." She waits.

What is the truth? Shouldn't that be easy to answer? Up, down. Left, right. North, south. When did I lose the ability to distinguish? When did my inner compass lose its bearings? I press the pencil against the paper. Maybe if I just move it, the words will magically appear.

"Eva is not fat. Eva is so skinny that she had a heart attack and has to stay in the hospital."

Oh, good for you! Goody-goody Eva! Doing exactly what Wendy-girl tells you. Since when do you let women with fat ankles tell you what to do? What to think? You are such a weakling. Anyone can boss you around.

"I am so proud of you," Wendy says emphatically. "I know that was really, really hard." My eyes swim.

"Can we stop now?" I ask her. I don't feel better. I feel worse. He's shouting at me. He, it, Ed, whatever. I just want him to stop. I just want it all to go away.

Maybe later, at lunchtime, if they're not watching too closely, I can dump a little, just a little, of the Boost into that plant. He'll shut up then. I'll show him that Wendy doesn't boss me around.

Okay then. Lunchtime. Catch you later.

Chapter Thirty-Seven

HENRY

Ray Giordano sits across a table from me in the Chadwick Academy conference room. He's a little less tan than I remember, and not quite as lean. His green eyes smile along tiny creases at the corners, road maps left by a thousand sunny afternoons spent on tennis courts. He'd flown in today from Chicago, a few hours before my own flight into Fort Lauderdale touched down.

I'm dressed to drill. I've got the pro court reserved in thirty minutes, which gives Ray and me just that much time to talk. He'd requested this one-on-one with me, no Chadwick people present. They think my sponsor has flown down here to ream me out for leaving campus. I know better.

"I was pretty surprised to get your letter," he begins after our awkward handshake and hey-it's-great-to-see-yous.

"Yeah, I guess that makes two of us," I reply. "Being surprised, that is." Ray looks a little sheepish when I say that.

"I hope you understand why I felt . . . anonymity . . . was important."

I study my fingers, the tops of my hands, so brown against the white of my tennis skirt. There are calluses between my thumb and index finger, where the racket rubs.

"I'm not a big fan of secrets these days," I finally say, looking up at him. "I know why you did what you did. If my father had known you were involved, he never would have let me come here. And as I said in my note, I'm really grateful to have this opportunity. But we're . . . beyond that now." He raises his eyebrows.

"Why do I suspect telling your parents about me and Philmont was hard?" he says.

"It wasn't pretty," I admit. "But once the three of us got started, we just couldn't stop."

"Couldn't stop what?" he asks.

"Telling the truth," I say firmly. "The good, the bad and the ugly. And that brings me to something I needed to say to you in person: I'm sorry." Ray looks surprised.

"It was my fault Dad fired you. I mean, it wasn't my fault he went berserk. But it was my fault that the whole thing happened. You see, I thought . . . ." I can't go on.

Ray helps me out.

"You thought something inappropriate was going on between your mom and me," he says gently. I nod, grateful that he said it.

"Marian and I figured it out a few days after the big blowout," he explains. "She realized that you had come home from school early and seen us talking on the patio." I nod again.

"Your mother and I had become friends, Henry. Over you,

315

initially. Discussing your talent, figuring out what was best for you. But then it moved into talking about your father and what a potentially damaging influence he was. That's dangerous ground: a man outside the family talking to a woman about her husband? Especially when that husband is . . ."

"Paranoid," I mutter. Ray grins ruefully.

"I overstepped," he says simply. "I started giving her advice about things that were none of my business. That was a mistake. But it was my only mistake. And you shouldn't blame your mother for anything."

"I know that now," I tell him.

So does Dad, I neglect to add. It wasn't easy, dredging up all those bad feelings. Especially when you've got years of resentment and suspicion clinging to them like barnacles. But somehow we Lloyds had done it, and everyone was still standing when it was over.

I look at Ray. I see him, maybe for the first time, for what he really is. No hero, no devil, just an adult like any adult, who sometimes makes mistakes and sometimes gets things right. Like my parents. Like me.

"So, since we're telling the truth, explain the overnight-mail letter bomb you sent me," Ray continues. "Why are you quitting tennis?"

This startles me.

"That's *not* what I wrote."

"Henry, you are asking if Philmont would transfer your sponsorship from Chadwick to the Greenlake Academy. That's as good as quitting."

"Seventy percent of Greenlake grads go on to play college tennis, some even Division One—" I begin. He cuts me off.

"I've read the Greenlake brochures, too," he says. "But Henry, in the tennis community it's considered second-rate. And you're a first-rate player."

"And a third-rate everything else," I say quietly.

"What?" he asks. I sigh. There's not enough time to explain, and I'm not sure he'd get it anyway. But I have to try.

"I love tennis, Ray," I tell him. "But I don't own it here. It owns *me*. It owns me with all the expectations, the glamour, the hype. It owns me by telling me that what makes me special is my ability to smack a tennis ball. Nothing else. Friendship, family, loyalty . . . behavior . . . they are way less important than winning. I've experienced that here, up close and personal. And you know what? It's sick. And scary. Because where does that leave me if I lose? Or get injured?"

This look comes over his face, as if someone's just turned a light on for him.

"This is about your dancer friend, isn't it? The one who got sick," he says. "Missy told me you were upset about that. . . ." I shake my head.

"That's *not* it," I say. "I mean, sure, Eva's illness has made me take a hard look at things. But it hasn't changed the way I feel, or who I am. It's helped me . . . sort out what I really want."

I can tell he's listening. He wants to understand.

"And what do you really want, Henry?" he asks.

"I want to play serious tennis, but I need to take it down a

 317

notch," I explain. "I want to be sane about it. Listen, Green-lake is a real school. Chadwick is where the kids pretend to do homework between workouts and drills. Greenlake is trying to develop players, not just spit out future sports celebrities. And I gotta tell you: if Philmont is looking for the new fresh face of Tag Heuer or Nike, I'm not your girl." He laughs softly.

"You could be, you know," he says. I shrug.

"I've had my picture taken a few times lately. I'm not into it."

He considers me as he thinks, those green eyes boring, unblinking, into mine.

"Your parents are on board with this?" he asks.

"Both of them, one hundred percent," I tell him.

"And you're sure Greenlake would be different?" I shrug.

"I hope so. 'Cause I'm not staying at Chadwick," I say firmly.

Ray's heard all he needs to hear.

"I tell you what," he says. "I'll tour Greenlake and meet with the staff. If I like what I see, we can *try*. No guarantees. Philmont has never withdrawn support from one school and transferred it to another. But if I tell them it's the difference between you staying in tennis or quitting?" He pauses. "Well, nobody wants you to quit, Henry."

I stand up. It's almost my court time.

"Thank you, Ray," I tell him. He stands and extends his hand.

"You're an impressive young lady, Henry Lloyd," he says. "And not just on the tennis court."

 318

We say good-bye, and I grab my gear and head out. People are drifting out of the dining hall; dinner has just ended. A few call out to me, "Welcome back!" As if I'm some returning hero. I need to get behind those privacy windbreaks and pound a basket of balls, for sure.

As I cross campus, I think about Ray's words. Impressive off the court. If he believes it, maybe I should, too.

* * *

Someone on staff has set out an iced pitcher of water for me with lemon slices floating in it. Plus fresh towels stacked on the teak bench. You'd never know I'd just broken every rule imaginable, short of drinking and smashing the windows.

I don't hear him come in. My back is to the entrance, and of course, the pro-court gate swings open without squealing. I've just hit a sweet second serve into my imaginary opponent's backhand, and I'm about to toss up another one.

"Nice kick," he says.

He looks like he's just come off the court himself. The roots of his hair are dark with sweat.

"Oh. Hi. I didn't see you there." We look at each other awkwardly.

"D'you just finish practicing?" I say. He nods.

"Yeah, nothing much. Scotty hit ground strokes with me for an hour while Harvey commented." His eyes scan the court. "You serving?" I reach into the basket and pluck out another ball.

"Yup," I say. I toss it high. The trajectory is off; I catch it. I try a calming breath and focus on the toss. I hurl the racket face

 319

forward. A resounding *pock!* echoes through the enclosed sanctuary of the court.

Yes! Grace under pressure. If you can serve now, you can serve through anything, girl. You Jersey Tomato.

"Why didn't you answer my phone calls?" he says. I turn my back to him. I fire another serve over the net. Not quite as good this time.

"I didn't have anything to say, David," I reply. I pull out another ball.

"I was worried about you," he says angrily.

One, two, three bounces. Toss, palm open to the sky. This one goes a little long.

"Yeah. Right," I say. His enormous bag hits the ground. I hear a zipper. I look to see him pulling out one of his rackets and walking quickly to the opposite side of the court from me. There are a few balls in his way and he kicks them viciously to the side.

When he reaches the baseline, he bounces the strings of his racket a few times on the heel of his hand.

"Go on," he calls, almost savagely, to me. "You wanna practice instead of talk? Fine. Let's hit some balls." I blink. I stare at him in amazement for about two seconds, then I reach into the basket, grab two, then shove it, hard. It rolls swiftly away and bangs against the fence.

I float a rally ball to his forehand. He attacks it brutally. He smashes it crosscourt, both feet in the air when he makes contact. It's behind me before I can whiff at it.

I drop my racket and clap.

"Awesome. Just awesome, David. You know, I can wail on easy feeds, too." He glares.

"Another," he calls back.

This time, I pound it. I hit it low, flat and deep into his backhand. It skitters on the baseline, but he manages to return it high crosscourt. I take it in the air, and come in. He smashes it back. Kindly enough, not at my face. But so hard, I practically hear a *whoosh*ing sound as it clears the net and flies past me, unanswered.

"Tell you what, Tarzan," I say angrily. "How about three *reasonable* rally balls beyond the service line, then anything goes?" He nods.

"Fine," he says. His feet shift restlessly. I return to my baseline.

Somewhere along the way the grunting starts. "YUH!" David shouts as he fires one down the line. Miraculously, I get my racket on it and lob it defensively to his backhand corner, a desperate "EH!" escaping from my lips when I make contact. "A-YUH!" he yells back, a screaming shot I can't return. We start again . . . one, two, three unfriendly smacks . . . then "YAH!" I finish it with a sharply angled forehand.

"Shit!" I hear him say.

"No swearing," I bark at him.

"Says who?" he snipes. He fires a rally ball over the net.

"Says me. We're on *my* reserved court time." I slice it back to him.

"Well, f-you, Henry. I'll swear all I want." He smacks one at me.

321

"Oh yeah? Well, happy f-you to you, too!" I yell. I lay on the ball with everything I've got, straight down the middle. David returns it hard up my middle and races in. I lob. He anticipates, and spikes an overhead into my backhand.

"Shit!" I exclaim. He aims a wolfish grin at me.

"No swearing," he says.

"Jerk," I say. He takes two steps forward.

"Baseline grinder," he retorts. I move in as well.

"Prep-stroker," I say. He's still closing.

"Typical," he replies. Quietly. He's about a racket's length from the net. For a split second I don't know what he means. Then I remember. That night in the Overlook. That first night we ever actually spoke, when he rescued me from the evil Dundas. Right before he insulted my game. Once upon a time, before he made me fall, head over heels, so hard for him . . . I reach the net, resting my racket on top of it.

"Traitor," I whisper. I'm spent. I've exercised the anger clear out of me. I think I'm going to cry. His face falls.

"What the hell are you talking about, Henry?" he says. "How am *I* a traitor?"

"I needed you," I say to him. A wail, caught in my throat, threatens to rise. I gesture, with my free hand, around me. The court. The teak table. The beautiful grounds and buildings beyond. "But all this? And these people? They're more important to you than I am." He shakes his head vehemently.

"You asked me to make an impossible choice!" he says angrily. "It was like, 'Hey, David. Breathing or eating? Pick one.' What was I supposed to do? I've got my girlfriend telling me I have to drive to freakin' Jersey or else, and my coach telling me to get my ass back to Florida or else!"

"Don't diss Jersey!" I fume at him. This random response startles both of us for a moment.

"I'll diss Jersey all I want," he says.

"Don't," I say threateningly.

"Why are New Yorkers so depressed?" he snaps.

"What?"

"Because the light at the end of the tunnel is New Jersey!" he exclaims.

Jersey jokes. Unbelievable.

"Oh, that's so weak!" I sneer at him. "I heard that in fifth grade."

"Why do seagulls fly upside down in New Jersey?" he continues. "Because they can't find anything worth crapping on." The corners of his mouth turn up slightly. He likes that one.

"This is ridiculous, David," I say. "Stop it."

"What do you call a smart guy in Bayonne?" he says.

I've heard this one, too.

"Lost," I reply quickly. This draws a genuine smile from him.

"Very good," he says. "How do you know you're from New . . ."

There's a Wilson in my pocket. I pull it out and attempt to stuff it in David's mouth. He lets out a yelp of laughter, drops his racket and grabs both my wrists. My racket clatters as well, and the two of us stand there with the net between us. I look into his eyes. They remind me of the caramel center of a Cadbury chocolate bar. I sigh. A long exhale. A long letting go.

"David, you called Missy, and made a plan to dump me at a train station in North Carolina. How do you think I felt?"

"You forget: I asked you to come with me. They wanted us *both*."

"It felt like a plan made behind my back."

"Henry, no offense, but . . . you sound like your father. All paranoid."

This stings. A ready comeback flies to my lips. But I don't want to confirm what he just said and act like Mark. I count to ten before I reply.

"It's not just that. She's too into you. They all are, and it creeps me out. You know, sometimes I got the feeling that our relationship was just one big Chadwick photo op." He looks a little embarrassed when I say this.

"Okay, when you started winning at the invitational? Missy did take me aside and tell me to pull you into a few photos. But I don't see why that's bad. When we win, they win. You know? Win-win?" I shake my head. It's so easy to think clearly about all this when I'm alone. But now, with him again? With those warm, melting chocolate eyes pleading with me?

I could get so lost in all this. In him.

He's still grasping my wrists, and I pull them free. I pull them free so I can think beyond the electric current that travels from his fingertips to mine.

 324

"I'm going to ask you a question and I don't want *you* to take offense, but if we'd done it? That night in the motel? Would you still have left me at the train station?"

He looks like I've just slapped him.

"Is that what you think of me?" he says, incredulous.

"It's not what I thought until it happened, David."

Hurt and confusion play out across his face. It would be so much easier for him if I were yelling and unreasonable right now. You don't have to take responsibility for your own actions, or admit where you went wrong, if the other person conveniently acts like a lunatic. Something else I've learned from Mark Lloyd.

"I'm not Dundas, Henry."

"I didn't say you were."

"Yeah, you just did. C'mon! Don't you know me better than that?"

"No, I don't. That's the point. I'm just getting to know you, and I'm . . . not ready . . . for a whole lot of stuff."

"I respect that," he says quickly.

"Yeah, I know," I say patiently. "That's what a nice guy would say. And let's face it: you're a nice guy. But you're a *guy*. And I want to know. Did my saying no influence your decision to head back to Boca?"

An eternity passes as David thinks about this one. A light breeze blows across the court, ruffling his hair, which is drying into stiff, salty curls at his neck. When he finally answers me, his eyes are clear.

"Probably," he says. "If things had gone the other way that

night, I probably wouldn't have checked my cell phone messages in the morning. Instead, I woke up thinking, *Damn! What the hell am I doing here?* Then, once I started talking to Harvey and Missy, I got completely reoriented. Nothing seemed more important than getting back to Florida." I nod.

"Thank you," I say. "For being honest." There's a buzzing sound as lights from the surrounding courts flicker on. Dusk. We've been out here for a long time. David frowns. He takes one step closer to me.

"I was also being honest about what I said after the *quinces*," he continues. I nod again.

"I know that. And David, for the record? Never in a million years would I compare you to Jon Dundas. He's not in your league."

The hands, the fingers, are lacing themselves through mine now. He's moved so close I can feel his breath on my cheeks as he breathes.

"But it's not enough, is it?" he says quietly. Sadly. My eyes fill, and everything I've held back through sheer will and anger spills out now.

"See, that's what I don't get," I say tearfully. "The way 'I love you' doesn't go with what happened in Smithfield. You lose me there."

"Sure it does! Absolutely it does! 'I love you' means I want what's best for you. I don't want you to make stupid choices that will hurt you."

"Putting my best childhood friend before tennis is not a stupid choice!" He sighs, shaking his head.

"There's no comparison," he says wearily. "Why are you comparing the two?"

"Because I had to. David, I knew I wasn't going to make Eva better. But if my best friend in the whole world died while I was practicing forehands in Florida, I'd have never forgiven myself. I *had* to be there, and let her see me."

He wants, so badly, to see things my way. But we're not there. We stand on opposite shores of a great, rushing river. A huge canyon. Or maybe just a thin, invisible line that separates the ways we see the world. He thinks I'm careless. I think he's so caught up in this crazy life that he doesn't realize what he's given up to be here.

He pulls me against his chest and holds me, tightly, as my tears soak into the front of his shirt. When I finally lift my head, my face feels puffy.

"You know the one thing, the only thing, that makes sense right now?" I ask him. He shakes his head.

"Hitting a tennis ball. Before you came out here, I was really getting into it. It's just . . . pure."

This flash of recognition crosses his eyes. This he understands. He smiles and gently, softly, brushes his lips against mine.

"So let's do it," he says. He releases me, then picks up his racket. For a moment, he reminds me of a little boy. An eager little boy who's just been told he can stay up past bedtime to play his favorite game. Something in my chest fills, and I'm there, too. This familiar place, once upon a time, back when I was a little girl playing *my* favorite game. . . .

 327

"Okay, but no more death shots."

"I promise," he says. He's already backpedaling to the base-line.

I drop-feed him a deep forehand. He returns a crisp cross-court shot, great topspin.

Mental note, Henry: you've got to get him to show you how he does that.

It's a perfect Florida evening. As the sun sets, the court lights burn brighter. The sky glows pale blue, then pink, then deepening gray. A light breeze fans our sweat-soaked bodies, carries a hint of flowers. The only sound is the steady, solid *pock!* of our rackets hitting the ball. My feet have springs. My legs are tireless. I could do this forever.

But, of course, we can't. Eventually, it's time to pack it in and head back to the dorms. The showers. Dry clothes and the reality of sweat-soaked laundry.

Chapter Thirty-Eight

EVA

"So what's the weather like?" I ask her. "Not that I'll be getting out much."

Henry and I are making the most of her unlimited minutes, riding the cell phone airwaves between Florida and New Jersey. She's called to wish me good luck. I'm getting transferred tomorrow.

"Let's just say you will definitely lose your aversion to air-conditioning," she replies. "There's nothing like an August day in Florida to make you appreciate one of the greatest inventions ever."

"Right. Air-conditioning. I forgot about that," I mutter.

"What?" she says.

"Nothing. Just having random thoughts about global warming and wondering if it might not be such a bad thing after all." Understandably, she doesn't know how to respond.

"So . . . how're you feeling about all this?" she asks.

"It's like I landed on Chance and picked up the card that

 329

reads 'Go to jail. Go directly to jail. Do not pass Go. Do not collect two hundred dollars,'" I say. Henry laughs.

"You always hated Monopoly," she says.

"Yeah, and you always wanted to play!" I remind her. "I hate competitive games, especially Monopoly. I always end up with my properties mortgaged."

"That's because whenever I started losing, you'd lend me money," she says.

"I know. I'm a real sucker, aren't I?" I sigh.

"You're a softie. And the best person I know," she says emphatically.

We're quiet for a while, then she speaks again.

"But really, Eva. How are you feeling?"

"I'm a rainbow of emotions. Resigned. Terrified. Angry. Depressed. All of them crashing down on me simultaneously. Wendy says that's why I don't eat. So I can feel in control of *something*." I hear a familiar sound from her end.

"You're snorting," I say. Henry laughs.

"Sorry," she says.

"Don't apologize. It's your only flaw, and I love it."

"Oh, I have many flaws, Eva. You're just too nice to notice."

"Hmmm," I say in response. More silence between us. Again, broken by Henry.

"Wendy told me you hear a voice that runs you down and tells you not to eat," she says.

"That's my boyfriend, Ed. Remind me to introduce you to him. He's joining me in Florida. We're living together, you know."

"Eva. Seriously."

"What makes you think I'm not serious?" More silence from Henry's end.

"Well, at least in Florida you'll be a thousand miles away from that Wendy. Jeez, Eva, where'd Rhonda dig *her* up?"

"Actually, Wendy starts to grow on you after a while," I say.

"Really?" Skepticism in Henry's voice.

"Yeah," I say. "I think I might even miss her."

No snort that time. I can practically hear the gears turning in Henry's brain as she tries to process that new revelation.

"You know, you can visit me," I tell her.

"You're allowed visitors?"

"Sure," I say. "Even prisoners are allowed visitors. You can get that Little David to bring you in his sweet ride."

"Yeah," Henry replies, hesitantly. With about as much enthusiasm as wilted lettuce.

Why would she want her new boyfriend to meet you, stupid? Her weird, sick loser friend in psycho rehab? Gimme a break.

"I mean, if you can get away. I know you're really busy."

"Eva, I will come to see you at the very first possible moment. It's just . . . more complicated than I want to get into right now. Trust me: I will be there."

The conversation ends shortly after that. I get her off the phone, make something up about the nurse coming in to check my vitals. I feel tired. Just a little shuffling around this room, the exertion of pulling on shorts and a T-shirt, has winded me. Was it really only four weeks ago that I was spinning, on my toes, across gleaming wood floors?

331

Yeah, you're pretty out of shape, blub butt.

"Shut up." I say it. I actually say it out loud.

Ate your whole breakfast this morning, didn't you? Just wait. You'll be the big pig in rehab now. Oink! Oink! Here comes Eva!

My hands shake as I reach for my canvas bag of writing supplies. I paw through it until I feel what I want. I pull them out: counter journal, pencil.

I flip quickly to a clean, blank page. Left side. I take a deep breath, grip hard and write:

"You are out of shape. You are a fat pig. Henry would only visit you because she feels sorry for you."

I read it back. Tears slide down my cheeks and fall in round, soft plops onto the paper.

"Even my tears are fat," I say. This sentence, spoken aloud, strikes me as completely idiotic. Somewhere in the back of my throat, a familiar sensation stirs. It emerges.

I laugh.

Now the other side. I can do this. I write:

"I'm not out of shape. I'm tired because I've been sick. I'm not fat. I'm so thin that I'm going to a rehabilitation center for women with eating disorders to gain weight and get healthy. Henry is sad for me because I've been sick. She'll visit me because we are best friends. Jersey Tomatoes. No, Hothouse Tomatoes. Forever."

I read my words back, once, then close the book. I wait.

Nothing. For right now, at least: silence.

Chapter Thirty-Nine

HENRY

She pulls up in this . . . boat. This purring wide body, color of old gold, and it's got *fins*. It's buffed to mirrorlike perfection, especially the Cadillac emblem on the hood.

As she rounds the circular drive of the Greenlake Academy entrance, I see a magnetic sign adhered to the back passenger door: "Enrique's Classic Car Restoration." Phone number in bold just beneath the words. He was willing to lend her the Caddie . . . the latest result to roll out of his newly created weekend garage business . . . as long as she agreed to the sign. No problem for Yoly, who'd agree to anything if it meant trying out her new license.

She's got the passenger-side window rolled down, and as I saunter toward her, backpack slung over one shoulder, I see her smile in my direction.

"*Hola, chica,*" she says. I poke my head through the opening and check out the leather interior.

"When you said 'classic,' I didn't know you meant 'antique,'" I say. "How old *is* this thing?"

"It's a 1957," she says. "You don't want to know what Enrique will do to me if we get a single scratch on it." I get in, heaving the stuffed pack into the backseat.

"Ay, Henry, what did you bring?" she says as it lands with a thud.

"Blank books and art supplies, mostly. Eva says half the markers are dry and all the crayons are broken in the art room. She also says her bathroom is sad, so I got her these amazing aromatherapy products. Even if it looks like a hospital, it'll *feel* like a spa."

"You are such a good friend," she says.

"I'm pathetic, actually," I reply. "I don't visit her nearly enough. You, on the other hand? Friendship Hall of Fame. Thank you so much for doing this!"

"Are you kidding me?" she says. "This is going to be so much fun! First, we are driving in an awesome car. Second, we are going to see David play in a *professional* tournament. Third, we are all going to party at my parents' restaurant tonight. Fourth, I get to finally meet Eva . . . which, okay, *does* make me a little nervous. Fifth, and best of all, I get to actually *see* you, instead of just talking to you on the phone! How's it goin'?"

"Good. Really good, as a matter of fact."

"Still no regrets?" she prods.

"Absolutely no regrets," I say firmly. "The coaching staff is great, the academic staff is legit, and I'm really happy with the tennis. They've got me entered in a couple of Super Series tournaments next month, and that's cool. Not too over-the-top, you know?" Yoly bursts out laughing.

334

"You are the only person I know who describes Super Series as 'not too over-the-top'!"

"You obviously don't know enough super-intense tennis people," I tell her.

"*Speaking* of super intense," she says, "does he know we're all coming today?"

"He knows. He's psyched. Especially for *cerdo asado* tonight," I say. "Otherwise . . . he sounds like he's doing okay, even though he got his ass kicked and didn't earn any prize money playing Futures tournaments in California this fall. He plans to hang out in Florida for the next few months. Work with Harvey. Practice at that club near Chadwick. I don't know. I still think he should have gone to college, but hey, no one asked me. . . ." Yoly clears her throat.

"Uh, I was actually asking about *you* and David. Not *tennis* and David." She smiles suggestively at me. I shrug.

"Oh, don't give me that!" she exclaims. "Hanging out in Florida for the next few months? Like, there's nowhere else in the country he could train?"

Okay, so even I laugh. There's really no point being coy with Yoly.

"I guess we're 'on again.' In a long-distance-let's-take-things-slowly sort of way. In a you're-a-pro-and-I'm-a-high-school-student sort of way. So, yeah. It's all good. At least for the next couple of months." She takes her hand off the wheel to punch me playfully on the arm.

"He's *so* cute," she says.

"Tell me about it," I sigh.

It's a twenty-five-minute drive from Greenlake to the rehab center, but Yoly crawls at ten miles per hour below the speed limit (Enrique's threats clearly on her mind), drawing more than a few long horn blasts from impatient motorists. Still, this is a treat. Over the past few months I've relied on expensive cab rides to visit Eva. The Greenlake people say as soon as I've got my permanent license, I can borrow one of the academy's Zipcars. But I'm hoping Eva will be long gone from Florida before I ever get around to taking my driving test.

Because she's getting better. Two and a half months of treatment have pushed the protruding bones back into her body, forced the teeth back into her face, and restored the light in her eyes. Her hair, she tells me, has finally stopped disappearing down the shower drain. Her pulse has climbed back to normal. And her weight . . .

"I'm trying not to think about that," she said. It was sometime during the first month, and I had arrived for Friday-night visiting hours. The evening air was damp, and she was dressed in sweatpants and a big, loose hoodie. We sat outside in molded plastic chairs, on the patio of the residence hall. Patients and their guests kept passing through the glass double doors, as visitors signed in with the aides on duty and handed over their bags for inspection.

"No contraband," Eva explained. "No magazines. No drugs. No diuretics. No gum or mints. No sharps . . ."

"Sharps?" I asked her.

"Tweezers. Nail scissors. Anything you might use to injure yourself." I gasped.

"Yeah," Eva sighed, "at least I only have one problem: I don't eat. For some of these gals? That's only the *half* of it." She shook her head sadly, no irony in her voice. She was one of the few, she told me, who *wasn't* on an antidepressant or sleeping pill or some psychopharmacological brew.

"Just a fiber pill and laxative for me," she said, almost smugly. "I didn't poop for the first ten days. That's how screwed up my system was."

It's taken me a while to get used to those sorts of comments. The new expression on her face. It comes over when she's deep in her own thoughts, staring into some inner reality that pinches her lips into a hard line, pulls her forehead into a determined frown. She's heard a lot at this place, and tends to make these surprising, soul-baring observations, sometimes with a hard little edge in her voice. Gone is the relentlessly bright girl who told me you could patch any hole in your heart with a little Pink Decadence.

Of course, she never really believed that. Not for one minute. And maybe, I'm thinking, it's actually a huge relief to her that she doesn't have to *pretend* to believe it anymore.

As we enter the rehab center parking lot, yellow-green iguanas race-step-slither between low, shell-pink buildings. There's a cleared central space on the campus, with an assortment of plants, benches and colorful totems. A "healing garden," Eva calls it. She and I will hang out there while Yoly runs some errands. Then we three will drive to this club just north of Miami, where David is playing in one of those minor pro tournaments that never makes it onto network television.

 337

Win or lose, the four of us will meet Enrique at La Cubana for dinner tonight.

As I walk toward the garden, I see her sitting by herself on a wooden bench. She's cross-legged, her back poker-straight, and her hands rest on her knees. If she had her eyes closed, you'd swear she was in deep meditation, but she's watching me approach and smiles widely as my feet crunch over the stones of the garden path.

"Did anybody ever tell you that you walk like a jock?" she says, grinning. I flop beside her on the bench, dropping the pack at my feet.

"How does a jock walk?" I say. She jumps up. She tries to lift the backpack.

"What'd you stuff in here, rocks?" she exclaims. She manages to heft it onto one shoulder. She takes a few steps back, then begins this swaggering, head-bobbing lurch toward me. She swings her free arm and scuffs a few stones for effect.

"I do *not* walk like a thug!" I laugh. She exaggerates the motion until it borders on gorillalike, then, giggling, drops the pack and returns lightly to the bench beside me. She drapes her arms around my shoulders and gives me a soft squeeze. I squeeze back.

"How are ya?" I ask.

She smiles, but does this pseudotremble, as if she's cold.

"Good, but nervous, you know? I mean, I haven't been off campus for more than a couple of hours in . . . well, ever!" I nod, but say nothing. Today is big for her: she'll be off grounds for almost ten straight hours, a privilege earned only by the patients at the top end of the recovery ladder. Patients who can be counted on to make healthy choices. Like eating.

I know that the menu at La Cubana, with all its oily fried food, is scary to her. Even scarier than meeting Yoly and David for the first time. But she says she's ready. She tells me she *has* to do this. And I'm so proud of her, I could bust.

"You'll do great," I tell her emphatically. Her eyes slip from mine and land on the pack.

"Did you bring me . . . things?" she asks mischievously. I zip it open. She squeals in glee over the rosemary mint shampoo I bought her at this Aveda salon near Greenlake.

"You are the *best*, Henry! Thank you so much!" she exclaims. We stuff everything back in the bag after she's seen it; the aides at the front desk have to okay each item. Then she sits back with this look of anticipation on her face.

"So . . . did I tell you what Mom sent in the mail last week?" I shake my head. I'm still not used to hearing Eva refer to her mother as anything besides "Rhonda." But part of her therapy has been to knock that off. "Too distancing. Objectifying," Eva explained to me. "And we have some serious healing to do." No kidding.

"Three guesses," she prompts me.

"A case of Dinty Moore stew?" I suggest. Eva shrieks and slaps my arm.

"Jeez, Eva, I don't know . . . Body lotion? A good book? Free weights?"

"My *pointe* shoes," she says. My mind stutter-stops.

"For dancing?" I say, stupidly. Eva nods. She beams.

"They've been letting me dance again. One hour a day, in the exercise room. There's no *barre*, so I use the window ledge. Mom sent the shoes so I can do some center work as well."

I don't know what to say. Ballet, and what it has meant to, *done* to, Eva, has been such a huge part of the discussion here. Even when her body returned to health, would she return to dance? On the one hand, she was dying to *move* again. On the other hand . . . she was so afraid of where it might take her.

"Is this . . . good?" I manage to ask. She nods, vigorously.

"Better than good. Amazing. I feel like a gift has been returned to me. You know why?" I shake my head.

"No mirror," she says. "At some point I had stopped feeling my body when I danced and just kept looking at my body. I became obsessed with the reflection, with relying on the mirror to tell me whether I was doing it perfectly. And you know what? There's no mirror on the stage. There's no mirror during a performance. If you want to dance, *really* dance, you have to just cut loose and feel it. So the fact that there's no *barre* here? No mirror? No Madame DuPres? Just me and the music coming from some crummy CD player? It's been . . . pure."

I reach over and squeeze her hand.

"Kind of like dancing in your basement playroom? With your best friend, the Mouse King?" I say. Eva smiles broadly.

"It's exactly like dancing in my basement playroom!" she says excitedly. "Henry, I want to get well. I want to get out of here, so I can dance again."

"You will," I tell her quietly. She smiles at me, squeezes my hand back.

From the corner of my eye, I see a girl walking toward us from the parking lot. Long, determined steps. Yoly's heels bite the sidewalk with every stride.

"Here comes Yoly," I say. Eva follows my gaze and breaks into this bright laugh.

"Oh my god. It must be a tennis thing. She walks like you!" Eva jumps up and goes out to meet her halfway. I watch *her* walk: splay-footed, a bit ducklike. Years of working on her turnout have permanently twisted her limbs in a direction unimaginable to most humans. But it's normal for her. Desirable. Joyful, even. Because it's who she is: a dancer.

I stay put and treat myself to the sight of my two awesome friends meeting for the first time. It's amazing. It's a miracle, really. And I'm probably in for some really intense teasing today, as they combine forces. But I don't care. Bring it on. Because if there's one thing I know for sure, about the three of us?

We *own* this day.

Acknowledgments

Although I am an avid tennis player as well as a great lover of ballet, I could not have brought Henry's and Eva's worlds to life without generous advice from: Cece Carey-Snow, who patiently answered the most mundane questions about ballet and told me things I never knew about dance; tennis pro Kevin Vincent of Maine Pines Racquet & Fitness in Brunswick, Maine; and Loretto Vella of the Evert Tennis Academy in Boca Raton, Florida, who gave me a firsthand look at a world-class tennis academy and also shared valuable insights about training young players.

My husband, Conrad Schneider, and daughter, Madsy Schneider, were encouraging, honest readers throughout the process of writing this book. My wonderful agent, Edite Kroll, who in another life must have been a lumberjack or a hair-dresser, because she's *that* fond of cutting, delivered tough but always spot-on criticism of my manuscript, and for that I heartily thank her. I am especially indebted to Edite for introducing me to my editor at Knopf, Nancy Hinkel. I cannot imagine a more intelligent, insightful reader, and my books are always better because of her. Associate editor Allison Wortche and copy editor Janet Frick also offered excellent suggestions.

There are angels in this world, and we meet them unexpectedly. I believe one answers the phone at the Renfrew Center for eating disorders in Coconut Creek, Florida, where every day women's and girls' lives are saved by caring professionals. I am grateful for my chance encounter with her.